THE LORD'S DESPERATE PLEDGE

The Dukes' Pact Series
Book Three

By Kate Archer

DRAGONBLADE PUBLISHING, INC.

ARE YOU SIGNED UP FOR DRAGONBLADE'S BLOG?

You'll get the latest news and information on exclusive giveaways, exclusive excerpts, coming releases, sales, free books, cover reveals and more.

Check out our complete list of authors, too!

No spam, no junk. That's a promise!

Sign Up Here

www.dragonbladepublishing.com

Dearest Reader;

Thank you for your support of a small press. At Dragonblade Publishing, we strive to bring you the highest quality Historical Romance from the some of the best authors in the business. Without your support, there is no 'us', so we sincerely hope you adore these stories and find some new favorite authors along the way.

Happy Reading!

CEO, Dragonblade Publishing

Additional Dragonblade books
by Author Kate Archer

The Dukes' Pact Series
The Viscount's Sinful Bargain (Book 1)
The Marquess' Daring Wager (Book 2)
The Lord's Desperate Pledge (Book 3)

PROLOGUE

White's, London 1817

THE SIX OLD dukes had settled themselves into their own snug corner at White's. Young bucks might swan around the bow window, pretending supreme disinterest in who might note their expertly tied neckcloths, but these seasoned old gentlemen had more sense. Soft chairs, good claret, and a cheery fire to take off the chill were in order.

At this moment in their history, it was the Duke of Gravesley's time to crow, and that particular duke was no stranger to the attitude.

"He's done it," the duke said. "My boy has married Lady Sybil Hayworth—there is finally a Marchioness of Lockwood and she is charming. Of course, I cannot claim to like the girl's father, he's as prickly as he ever was, but that's a small price."

"Lord Blanding? Prickly?" the Duke of Bainbridge said. "That's putting it delicately."

The Duke of Gravesley was in too high spirits to reminisce about Lord Blanding's confoundedness at the wedding breakfast. He said, "I understand the dear girl has already taken steps to whip Kendall Hall into shape. My son had the thing done up as some sort of hunting lodge. Now he writes that she takes them all in hand, various carpets roll out of the house, wallpaper flies from the walls, and everybody awaits her instructions. He's remarkably cheerful over it— precisely what that young rogue has always needed. I expect we'll soon hear of a grandchild on the way and praise God it be a boy."

The Duke of Wentworth winced as a servant gently placed his gouty foot on a cushioned stool. "I say, though, this effort to drive our sons into marriage and children seems to lead to the most confounded circumstances. There is no end of talk about what went on at Lord Hugh's house party. Sabotage on the water, wagers of every sort, even a house fire?"

"Do you say we give it up?" the Duke of Dembly asked. "I'd be happy to see the end of so many questions from my duchess." The Duke sighed, long and deep. "She always has so many questions. And comments. And then more questions."

"Gentlemen," the Duke of Bainbridge said, "we have made a pact between us. We do not throw up our hands in surrender at the smallest difficulty. They will all marry and we *will* see grandsons."

"Hear, hear," the Duke of Glastonburg said. "Chin up, Dembly."

The Duke of Dembly shifted in his chair. "That's what my duchess always says."

CHAPTER ONE

HAYES SUMMERSBY, VISCOUNT Ashworth and eldest son of the Duke of Dembly, trotted his horse through the early dawn streets of London. Horus occasionally reared his head, the lord's favored mount being fond of an early morning jaunt and having been cooped in a stable all evening. Hayes held the reins in one hand and patted his inside coat pocket with the other. It had been a profitable evening and he was becoming more and more convinced that establishments like Lady Carradine's club were where he should spend his time and efforts.

He'd spent the past year investigating every gambling opportunity that might be had in London. It was necessary that he do so—his father had, through bad management and one failing investment after the next, put his inheritance in a precarious position. By the time Hayes had grasped the enormity of the situation, they had skated dangerously close to a mortgage or a sell-off. It still made his heart pound to think of it. If he had not chanced to discover the situation through some dark hints dropped by the family solicitor, they would have lost everything by now.

His father was a distracted and haphazard sort of gentleman. The management of multiple estates had been quite beyond him. For years, while the duke had admired his collection of dead butterflies, or spent hours rearranging his books, or even days at a time hiding from his duchess, he'd allowed lazy and corrupt stewards to run things into the ground. Worse, whatever money there was coming out of the farms was invariably invested in a losing opportunity. The duke's hopes were always raised high and his scrutiny and skepticism kept low. The estates had paid a heavy price for it.

Hayes had exchanged some strong words with his father, the first of a hard nature that had been spoken between them. The duke had finally relented and turned the management of the estates over to his son. There had been the caveat that nobody was to know it, especially his duchess, and so the duke routinely took himself off to his library and shuffled various papers this way and that to create the illusion of remaining at the helm of the family ship. The newly-hired stewards knew the truth of it though, and communicated all serious business to Hayes by letter. Nobody else was the wiser, so the duke held onto his dignity while Hayes took the steps needed to rescue the family legacy.

Hayes had put good men in place, increased efficiencies, straightened out lax tenants, and trimmed expenses where he could, but it was not enough. His mother could not live without two carriages, his sister could not survive without her expensive fripperies, his younger brother appeared to require three horses at Oxford, and his father could not carry on without a cellar full of champagne and port. The estates were on their way back to firm footing, but he'd required an infusion of money to fund his family's bare necessities lest they undo all of his good work. More money could only be had one of two ways—marriage to an heiress or gambling. It had not taken a moment to decide which direction he would go; he had no wish to marry so soon and he would never marry only for money. That sort of thing was a distasteful business that smacked of the marketplace. Whoever his lady turned out to be, he would bring her into a situation that stood on stable ground and did not need rescue from a dowry. His self-respect demanded that much.

Once making his decision, he'd holed up in a rented house and studied. When he was satisfied that nobody, with the exception of Hoyle, understood odds and strategies better than he did, he ventured to sample all London had to offer, from White's to low hells and everything in between. He found the gentlemen's clubs too fixated on chance bets and had no wish to risk even a pound over which direction a bird might fly, or which lord would produce a son sooner, or which color cat would first appear on the sidewalk. In truth, he was wholly uninterested in games of chance and thought only fools approached a hazard table without foreseeing what was to be the end of it.

He was only interested in games of skill—it was in those games that one had the best odds of trouncing a man who had overestimated his own abilities. He was particularly skilled at piquet. There were times he had difficulty finding somebody who would challenge him at it, and other times gentlemen sought him out in droves, it appearing to be some sort of badge of honor to play against him. He did not take much joy in relieving gentlemen of their funds, but it was a necessary occupation. When he thought of what might have happened if he had not taken the reins—his younger brother forced from Oxford, his sister's dowry gone—he felt a surge of energy that propelled him forward.

He had been to Lady Carradine's club often and it had a number of advantages. Lady

Carradine herself was the primary recommendation. The air of the place was more a private house of a genteel lady than a gambling establishment. There was none of the opulence found at some other places he frequented—all shabby façade when one looked closely enough. There were no copious glasses of wine always at one's elbow, meant to muddle the mind and judgment and invariably declining in quality as the night wore on. There was not even a hazard table, as Lady Carradine often said she would not be responsible for some young fool losing an estate over a roll of a dice and then doing a violence to himself. She charged a monthly fee, as any club might do, and fair interest on loans from the house bank. The emphasis was on serious attention to skilled gambling, and that was what he preferred. That she called it "Lady Carradine's Club for Ladies and Gentlemen" and had the odd musical evening was a touch absurd, but if the lady wanted to pretend it was anything other than a gambling house, that was fine with him.

One might go to Lady Carradine's to play at any number of card games, confident the house was on the up and up. A gentleman could be assured that the cards were not marked, and if one needed to borrow, the daily rate was reasonable. The betting sometimes did not go as high as some more famous clubs, but Hayes preferred it that way. The bets went high enough and fortunes were not made by one lucky night, though they could certainly be lost in one *un-*lucky night.

Lady Carradine's was a fair set-up, and as he knew all too well, *fair* was not often encountered in the world of gambling. There were no sharpers or shills and nobody was a pigeon unless they were determined to make themselves one.

That the club allowed females was the one point he did not find in Lady Carradine's favor. She had set up the place to cater to them and kept a sharp eye on the proceedings. There were never ending rounds of tea and dry cake—the sort of dull refreshment one might find at Almack's. There were middle-aged matrons whose sole employment seemed to be assuring Lady Carradine that everything went on proper—their hawk eyes perennially scanning the room. Gentlemen turning up the worse for drink did not get through the door. The air of the place was of a private house party where a lady might be free to sit down to cards.

He supposed the likes of Mrs. Jameson and Lady Edith, both notorious for gambling away their husband's money, must play somewhere. And then there was that peculiar older lady who was forever chattering about something. He was wholly uninterested in playing against any of them and wholly irritated by their overwrought emotions when the play did not go their way. It was not to be his problem to explain to those husbands what had happened to their four hundred pounds, and he very much wished *not* to have his name mentioned during the tearful explanations. Females did not have the steady nerves required for laying down substantial sums over a hand of cards.

Still, he supposed the general atmosphere of the place, tea-soaked as it might be, was useful to him. There would be no young and drunken fools inconveniencing him by loudly challenging him before vomiting on their own shoes in Lady Carradine's establishment.

Hayes leapt down from Horus in front of his house on Berkeley Square. He'd rented it at a dear price, but his winnings helped him afford it. A groom, ever ready for his arrival, raced out of the early morning shadows to lead his horse to the stables.

His penchant for gaming had produced a remarkable surplus. He'd been able to fund his family in the way they'd become accustomed. He'd thought one other particular benefit would be that it would stymie the old dukes in their ridiculous pact to force him and his friends to marry. He'd come near to threatening his own father to give it up, but the Duke of Dembly claimed he'd no choice in the matter, his friends were that determined, and that he was more of an onlooker than anything else. Hayes had pointed out that his father could hardly cut him off, as it was himself that held the purse strings. Ominously, the duke had claimed he'd take the purse strings back if necessary. That, of all things, could not be allowed to happen. His father would run the estates back into the ground, and they both knew it. They had reached an uncomfortable impasse on the subject.

Hayes reminded himself that he had one thing his father did not—an iron will to restore the family's estates. He would not be pushed into marriage. He would marry at some point, of course he would. But he would decide when and to who and he would bring that lady into a comfortable situation. The very idea of counseling a wife that she must curtail her purchases or some other small-minded directive filled him with disgust.

In any case, he had not yet encountered any female he could contemplate joining with forevermore. There were no end of pleasant ladies one might dance with, converse with, match wits with and tip one's hat to. *Pleasant* was not enough.

It was true that he and his friends had lost Hampton, and now Lockwood despite their best efforts, to the state of matrimony. But that still left himself, Dalton, Cabot and Grayson. They would hold the line and when their funds were cut off, his winnings coupled with Dalton's house would keep them afloat. If it came to it, his mother could live with only one carriage, his sister could make do with what she had in her wardrobe, his brother could survive with only one horse, and his father could drink his last bottle of champagne before Hayes Summersby would be pushed into a marriage he did not seek. When the estates were on solid ground, and when it was the right lady, he would not need to be pushed. He would chain himself happily enough.

But not until then.

LILY FARNSWORTH MUSED over the array of dresses strewn about her bedchamber. Never had this particular room been so graced with all manner of fine things. More usually, she might find herself examining a year-old garment and contemplating how she might spruce it up to look like new. Or, at least not horribly old.

The fine clothes almost inspired a sort of nervousness, an idea that they could not be afforded, though she did not owe a bill. All her life had been a series of calculations, what could be had and what could not, and it felt very foreign to find herself in the midst of such abundance.

The clothes had begun arriving after she'd sent a letter to her childhood friend Cassandra Knightsbridge, now to be known as Lady Hampton. She'd written Cassandra that she'd scraped together enough money for a season and would come in a month. Her father had no need of renting a house, Lily would stay with her aunt, Mrs. Amelia Hemming. Though the lady did not live at a particularly fashionable address, it was respectable enough. Lily had marshalled together the funds for theater tickets, a rented carriage to carry her about, a sum to compensate her aunt for the increased expenses of a houseguest, and perhaps even the means to host one dinner party, though not an elaborate affair. She'd used all her wits and skills to create a barely credible wardrobe, comprised of her old dresses re-worked, reclaimed fabric from the attics, and a judiciously small amount of new material. Nobody, she cheerfully assured herself, would guess that the blue velvet spencer had once been curtains. The end result of all her labor was the bare minimum, but it was just enough as long as nobody was looking too closely.

Lily had hoped, by telling Cassandra of her arrival, that her friend might provide some few introductions. She did not aim for the moon, but she doubted her aunt knew the sort of people who might throw a fashionable ball. She suspected Mrs. Hemming of maintaining a small circle of friends her own age who preferred tea and whist to dancing or routs.

Dear Cassandra had done more than vow to take Lily in hand and introduce her round the town. Lady Hampton had sent a dressmaker with instructions to fit her out with ten splendid gowns made of the finest materials. There were silks and velvets and satins, and a particularly fine muslin intricately embroidered with gold thread. There had also been an order for several day dresses and a lovely traveling cloak of ruby merino wool trimmed in fox.

Unbeknownst to Lily, Cassandra had gathered her measurements from the returning modiste and set about writing of her situation to the Marchioness of Lockwood, known to Lily through Cassandra's letters as the former Lady Sybil Hayworth. The Marchioness had taken those measurements and had made more day dresses, spencers, and a velvet riding habit. Then, somehow, Lady Lockwood told a certain Miss Penny Darlington, a lady entirely unknown to Lily, who had sent a carriage-full of accoutrements. There were nine pairs of kid gloves, a basketful of ribbons, silk stockings, five wraps of various materials, an elegant fur tippet, three parasols of different patterns, and four charming bonnets.

Another sort of lady might have worried that she'd somehow become a cause, a charity case pitied by those in more comfortable situations. Lily did not see it that way. In her view, a network of amiable ladies in possession of an ever-flowing fountain of pin money had seen another lady in need and ridden to the rescue. They had determined that one of their own would not arrive in London unprepared. In doing so, they had rid Lily of one of her worst fears— that great personages might raise their quizzing glasses and note the shabbiness of her refurbished wardrobe. That those elites might guess the truth of her family's circumstances.

Her dear father had spent a lifetime dragging their estate from the brink of ruin. He'd made sure her dowry was suitable, but just. No fortune hunter would eye Miss Farnsworth with any sort of satisfaction. Other than a respectable dowry, there was little money for new clothes of any sort.

Still, Lily had been determined to go to London for a season. She had looked around her little corner of Surrey and found the gentlemen wanting, ranging from gangly to insipid to irritating. Further, she would be able to do little for her sisters if she married some local gentry. Marigold and Rose did not yet even have dowries and though it had never been said, Lily felt her father depended upon her to marry well and somehow provide. She must not let them down.

Lily bit her lip as she examined the finery

given to her. None of those generous ladies could be in the least aware of how she'd scraped together the money to install herself in London for the season. She wondered if they would condemn her over it. While her father had no means to fund her, it turned out Lily herself *did* have the means. She had a particular skill at cards.

She'd spent the past year practicing that skill at a tidy profit. It had taken some doing, not the least of which had been convincing her mama and papa that it was the only practical solution. After she'd realized the potential value of her unique skill, she need only devise opportunities to use it.

Lily had, during this time, claimed an injury to her leg that made dancing impossible. She would arrive to an assembly with a slight limp, look helplessly about, and then make her way to the card room. She would not wear any of these new dresses to those outings, it would not be well to appear too prosperous. She donned one of her old, refurbished dresses and sat herself down of an evening. Most of local Surrey society appeared to pity her condition and find some solace in the idea that she was at least able to enjoy cards, while they graciously handed over their money.

Oh, she did enjoy cards! While she had struggled through her studies in the schoolroom, it seemed not the least trouble to remember which cards had been played and which had not. They arranged themselves in her mind like so many paintings, with gaps for those cards still in a pile or in another player's hands. She might have found it impossible to explain to her old tutor which English King took the throne at what date, but it was the simplest of matters to calculate the likely location of the king of hearts.

One was text and the other was picture—pictures formed in her mind like some kind of magic, while memorizing text was impossible, her mind a veritable sieve. Cards seemed as old friends that she'd known all her life. The cards spoke to her, and sometimes the backs even told her things. There might be the tiniest of variations in the design—a minute drop of ink or the smallest smudge. There might be a slight bend of a corner and she would know it was the nine of clubs. Over the course of an evening, it would prove handy to recall that the back of the ten of hearts had the smallest deviation.

Piquet was her particular game of choice. The thirty-two cards arrayed themselves in her thoughts, very helpfully providing their various locations—in her own hand, played, on the table, or in her opponent's hand. Once she and her opponent had declared, she was able to make reasonable guesses at what her foe held. Piquet had the further benefit of being a game with only two players. Aside from her skill at cards, Lily also claimed a skill at faces and more importantly—

hands. A skilled player might become adept at concealing various expressions, but they always forgot about their hands. A person holding strong cards moved smoothly and confidently. A person unsure of their hand moved ever so slightly less so and would often re-check their cards. The signals came to her as clear as daylight—she had a knack for detecting patterns.

Further, she could not bear to play with a partner. There was nothing worse than being saddled with an incompetent at a whist table. Unfortunately, there were far too many people sitting themselves down for whist who *were* sadly incompetent.

The money had been slowly collected, pound by pound and guinea by guinea. Now, all of this finery sent from three generous ladies must be packed and readied. She would leave for London in the morning. Thanks to Cassandra and her friends, Lily Farnsworth would arrive for her season appearing just as prosperous as any other young lady.

BELLAMY POURED BRANDY for the gentlemen gathered round Lord Dalton's table in the library. Since the *Lockwood Affair*, as the butler had taken to thinking of it, his master had been in high dudgeon. Fortunately, that high dudgeon had not in the least affected how the house was run. He and his footmen remained free with the lord's wine and must only be careful not to appear too cheerful in the face of their lord's wrath. At this moment, Bellamy adopted an expression that was suitably grave.

"I still cannot fathom how we lost Lockwood," Lord Cabot said, throwing back his brandy.

"We were hours from victory, then old Lord Blanding decides to start a fire and nearly get himself killed," Hayes said.

"I wish the old devil had found the decency to perish," Lord Grayson said. "If Lady Sybil was to wear the black bombazine, it would have bought us a good six months to knock some sense into Lockwood."

Lord Dalton, appearing to see no use in going over old ground said, "Blanding did not have the decency to kick off and Lockwood was the hero of the hour, launching himself into the flames to pull the old boy out. What's done is done."

Lord Grayson used his forefinger to move his glass, a signal that Bellamy ought to refill it. As the butler did so, the lord said, "I suppose Lockwood appeared a regular knight in shining armor. Rescuing the lady's father could hardly have been more providential, surprise though it was to us."

Lord Dalton looked suspiciously round at his friends. "As we were all surprised to lose Lockwood, is there anybody here who might deliver a similar surprise? Any flirtation that might grow out of hand?"

"Certainly not," Hayes said. "I've not encountered a single female I could countenance for a fortnight of close quarters, much less a lifetime."

"Nor I," Lord Grayson said. "My flirtations are many, but they never go too far. I am very particular to say nothing that might be construed as a declaration."

"As careful not to declare yourself as you may be," Lord Cabot said, "various mamas are beginning to complain. It is said that you led on Miss Mayfield most unmercifully last season and Mrs. Mayfield has declared you a rogue."

"Miss Mayfield was a delightful diversion, I was quite taken by her," Lord Grayson said.

"Until you weren't," Hayes said.

"Just so," Lord Grayson said. "I fear I should never encounter a lady who can hold my feelings in the palm of her hand for more than a few months. A curse, but there you have it. Anyway, what about you, Cabot? Precisely how many times did you dance with Miss Darlington last season?"

"Bah," Lord Cabot said dismissively, "we all danced with Miss Darlington, she is a pleasant lady."

"See that she stays only pleasant," Lord Dalton said darkly.

Hayes folded his arms. "And you Dalton? Are you in any danger?"

There was a long pause before the gentlemen round the table erupted in laughter. Even Bellamy was hard pressed to keep his expression somber. The last man on earth who would be in any danger from female wiles was the scarred Charles Battersea, Earl of Dalton.

LILY'S AUNT, MRS. Amelia Hemming, lived in a tidy house on Cork Street. The residence had the advantage of being so nearby more elegant addresses that it often prompted the lady to refer to it as *just off* Berkeley Square. The house was not overlarge by anybody's standards, but everything needed was neatly done. There was a suitable drawing room where one might receive callers, a dining room where twenty might be seated, a cheery though rather compact breakfast room, and even a snug library, though it contained more furnishings than books.

Above stairs, the bedchambers were on the small side of things, though Lily's aunt had been clever in avoiding oversized furnishings that might overwhelm the space they were given. Lily did not care two figs for a room any larger than the one she found herself in—it had a charming bedstead of wrought iron, a small fireplace enameled in a lively yellow and green diamond pattern, an overstuffed chintz chair, a slender and elegant writing desk, a large wardrobe, and a lovely view of the tidy rows of the kitchen garden.

Her aunt's lady's maid, Pips, had unpacked her trunks and helped her out of her traveling clothes. Lily had told the maid she was perfectly able to dress herself, as she had been in the habit of it all her life. Pips had not been daunted or put off and had muttered something about backward country ways. Lily had no choice but to let the maid carry on with it in all good humor.

Now, Lily hurried down the stairs to the drawing room to join her aunt.

Mrs. Hemming's butler, Ranier, was just bringing in the tea. He was one of those individuals that Lily thought of as "grumpy-faced." His jowls hung over his starched neckcloth, pulling his mouth down into a decided frown. She knew better than to think his depressing visage was any kind of representation of his spirit, as she had known him since she was a little girl. Beneath that grim exterior was a kindly man who highly approved of everything she did, even if it would not have struck anybody else as noteworthy. She fondly remembered being six or seven and favoring him with drawings of her puppy which she was now certain had verged on unrecognizable. Lily had been enormously pleased when he'd exclaimed that Holbein himself could not have done better. That Ranier had been the only person who had ever said anything nice about her rather mediocre drawing skills had further cemented him in her affections.

Now, he gave her the slightest of nods to indicate his approval of her current circumstances.

Her aunt sat on the sofa in front of a charming pink marble table. Mrs. Hemming was on the short and stout side, her cheerful round face and pink cheeks crowned with an elaborate pile of graying hair held in place with jeweled combs. She said, "There you are, Lily, come and sit by me and refresh yourself after your journey. Though, I suppose it was not a particularly long journey, and here I am speaking of it as if you had just arrived from the Americas. In any event, coming from near or far, you must wish for tea. Everybody does, I suppose."

Lily smiled. It was one of Mrs. Hemming's idiosyncrasies that the lady spoke all her thoughts as they arrived, no matter how willy-nilly they composed themselves. She sat by her aunt and clasped her hands. "It was so kind of you to allow me to come, Aunt. I could not be more grateful."

"Bah," Mrs. Hemming said. "Why should I not? Of course, there is always money to think of and I do not have all that much to think about as a general thing, though sometimes I have more. But here you are and somehow your father has come up with the sum. How *did* he do it, I wonder?"

Lily could feel her cheeks tinge pink. She had debated what she should tell her aunt about how the trip was afforded. In the end, she'd decided honesty was called for. Though, perhaps vague honesty would be best.

"We were fortunate to come into some funds that were not anticipated," Lily said.

"Did you?" her Aunt said, pouring the tea. "Funds not anticipated sounds delightful. I should like to know about that! What a pleasant idea—one is just going along as usual and then suddenly somebody gives them some money. Who was it, dear?"

Lily had somehow forgotten how inquisitive her aunt could be. While others might take the answer at its face and comprehend that the speaker wished to say no more about it, Amelia Hemming would take in no such hint.

Lily took her teacup and set it down on the marble tabletop. "Aunt," she said slowly, "as you know, my father has had a time of it bringing the estate back to what it once was."

Amelia waved her hands, "No need to be nice about it, your grandfather was a reprobate and nearly ruined us all. It was a blessing he got on his horse that day, drunk as a sailor, and returned in a wood box. I know I should have been very sorry to have seen him returned to us thus, but in fact I was delighted. We all were. He was a beast to our mother, cruel to his children, and careless of the estate—we did not miss him for a moment."

Lily pressed her lips together. Of course she was aware that her grandfather had ridden out rather the worse for wear and it had ended with a broken neck, but she had never heard it described in such terms. "Indeed," she said. "And so you know that my dear father could not have spared—"

"Yes! And now we come to the unanticipated funds. Do go on, dear."

"Well, it seems I'm rather good, as it happens, I find I have a penchant for—"

"Yes?"

"Cards, Aunt. I'm rather good at cards. I won the money. I've been gambling for the past year."

CHAPTER TWO

LILY HAD SUPPOSED the idea that she had gambled for the money to afford a season would shock, but Mrs. Hemming only clapped her hands. "Gambling! Now that is something to think of. Of course, I should only consider taking you to whatever little parties I can wrangle an invitation to. Of course I should. After all, one never knows who one shall meet here and there, which causes an invitation elsewhere and so on. That is precisely the sort of thing I should do. On the other hand, is it likely that we should be engaged every evening of the week? That, I cannot say with any certainty, but I rather think not."

Lily had tried her best to follow her aunt's mode of expression, but she could not be sure what the lady was debating with herself.

"And then," Amelia went on, "the place is so very respectable. Everybody says so. Nothing untoward could go on under the watchful eye of those matrons that mill about the place. The membership is everything one might wish for. Even those awful cakes advertise it as respectable—only last week, Lady Edith claimed they were drier even than Almack's."

Seeming to have come to a conclusion, Mrs. Hemming turned and faced her niece. "I suppose your father knows of your gambling?"

Lily nodded. "He was not enthusiastic about it, but I was able to convince him that coming to London was the best chance for all of us and the only way to get here was through a card table."

Amelia nodded. "Yes, of course, George is levelheaded like that. If one can present an argument logically, he's likely to be won over. He ever was practical as a boy."

"Aunt," Lily said, "do tell me what you think of. What place? What matrons? What dry cakes?"

Amelia set her cup down and said, "I think of my friend Lady Carradine. She is a charming woman who happens to preside over a charming club. There are musical evenings and sometimes the ladies form a reading circle. Those of us that stayed in town even knitted for the poor one Christmas season."

"Oh," Lily said, rather nonplussed. Her aunt's mind seemed to be more wandering than usual.

Mrs. Hemming pointed to a handsome secre-taire at the far end of the room. "See that? I purchased it with winnings, it is a Hepplewhite. Very fine."

"Winnings?" Lily asked. "From the musical evenings or the reading club?"

"Oh, neither," Mrs. Hemming said. "The musical evenings and reading circles are all well and good, but the real fun is the gambling. In truth, I cannot think that anybody has joined for any other reason."

The last thing Lily had expected her aunt to do was own to gambling. She'd been under the impression that the lady's funds were not unlimited.

"Ah, I see you wonder at it. Well, it is like this—years ago your father and I both inherited some money from a cousin. Unexpected funds, just as you were saying. It was three hundred pounds each and I am certain your father plowed his share back into the estate. As for myself, I thought, well I might spend it in drips on butter and flour and meat, or I might hold it back in a special fund. That's what I've done, I've used it to gamble and once it's gone, that's the end of it. But wouldn't you know, after all these years, it's not gone. It was only slowly creeping up until Lady Carradine opened her club five years ago. Now, I currently have four hundred and eighty pounds. Goodness, half the furniture in this house has come from that little pile. The *bon ton* all crow about their four percents, but I believe I've done rather better. If one were to add up all the furnishings."

Lily sat back, both surprised and amused. She would not have guessed for the world that her aunt had a gambler's spirit. "So, it is a gambling club that admits ladies?" she asked, having no inkling that such a thing existed.

Mrs. Hemming nodded. "Lady Carradine has been very clever in setting the whole thing up. Rather than it being a gambling establishment, it is a social club that also happens to have gambling. Though, only the type one might find at a ball—no dice games. The atmosphere could not be more genteel and, of course, you know how it is with the *ton*—once Lady Edith gave her stamp of approval it became perfectly accepta-ble."

Lily was fascinated and wondered if she had ever known her aunt as well as she had thought. Further, the idea that she, herself, might increase what she held, was interesting. It was very interesting. The bets would be higher in London. Surely, the bets must be higher in Lady Carra-dine's club than they were at a ball. In Surrey, she could only get so far at a local ball or dinner. Nobody played for particularly high stakes. And then, she could not *always* win, people would have begun to notice and comment on it. It had been a painstaking process of gathering pound after pound. She had not thought she would play in London at all. At a ball, she would dance. At a dinner, she would likely be asked to play the pianoforte. She had worked hard to come with everything she needed as she had never imagined there would be an opportunity to win more.

Lily had allocated to reimburse her aunt for the added expense of having her, for a few books, perhaps theater tickets, possibly a dinner, and some left to jangle in her purse as pin money. Her most significant expense had been a carriage, as her aunt did not keep one. It would set her back thirty pounds for the season. She had debated with herself on the practical merits of spending so much in that direction. Especially when a carriage could easily be hired when one needed one. She had finally decided to pay—a carriage rented in such a fashion would be well-maintained and look every bit the private conveyance. Were she to arrive to the sort of fashionable ball she aspired to in a hired carriage, it would be noticed. Her circumstances would advertise themselves loud and clear and no fine wardrobe would overcome it. It had been difficult to let go of so much money, but now her aunt spoke of gambling. Perhaps the pin money she still had might be increased?

"So you think," Lily said, "that we might visit Lady Carradine?"

"I do not see why not," Amelia said in a satisfied tone. "It is all very respectable, Lady Carradine sees to that. Mrs. Jameson is my regular whist partner there and brought her own daughter to the musical evening just last week. Lady Edith Fairfax is quite the regular. They are both well regarded."

"But did Mrs. Jameson's daughter play cards?" Lily asked, unsure of whether it would be permitted.

"Goodness, no," Mrs. Hemming said. "It was a musical evening, you see. In any case, I do not think the girl would have much luck. As far as I could make out, she is as dumb as a post. A shame, but there you have it. Now you, my dear, are a deal more clever and as you said, already quite experienced at it."

Lily felt a shiver run down her back. Though she dreamed of attending a fashionable ball, the idea of playing for stakes also appealed.

"Oh, heavens," Amelia said, "I nearly forgot. There is a note for you from Cassandra, or Lady Hampton as I suppose she is called now. She's sent me one too, she intends to call on us on the morrow."

HAYES HAD NOT seen his friend Hampton since

he'd left on his wedding trip. Now, he was to meet him at White's. They had both agreed to meet in a private room, lest Hayes's father or the other dukes of the pact were lurking about somewhere. Hampton had not the least cause to avoid his own father, having married suitably, but was sympathetic to his friend's plight.

Now, he sat in a rather cramped and dark room, its only window facing an alley. It at least had the benefit of comfortable chairs, well-padded and covered in fine leather, and an ample-sized table of intricately carved maple. A servant had brought him a bottle of claret and two glasses. The man was just leaving as Hampton came through the door.

The friends greeted each other with enthusiasm.

"I see you have not paled in the face of marital bliss," Hayes said, shaking his friend's hand.

"God no," Lord Hampton said. "Best thing I ever did."

"I presume your father will say the best thing you ever did is yet to come," Hayes said, as he poured the wine.

"Yes, you are right. He is like a falcon waiting to spy a mouse on the subject. His letters are filled with broad hints," Hampton said. "In fact, I believe he might not have to wait overlong. Lady Hampton has told me nothing, but I have my suspicions. I assume she waits until the danger has passed."

Hayes drained half his glass. "Good Lord, Hampton is to be a father. The world has gone mad."

"You may think so," Lord Hampton said, stretching out his long legs, "though it feels remarkably rational to me. In any case, I'd much rather, at this moment, be on my estate, but the Viscountess has insisted we come to town."

"Why ever would she wish it," Hayes asked, "if she is, well you know."

"My wife has some idea of helping to launch a childhood friend. A Miss Farnsworth, if I've got the name right. I imagine she wishes to do what she can before she must declare a confinement. It sounds like one of those typical situations—fine girl, but with little money or London connections."

"All too typical," Hayes said. "The girl will be out hunting and we bachelors must duck the arrows whizzing through the woods."

Hampton laughed. "I see you are still determined to avoid the church, then? You, Dalton, Cabot and Grayson will work to outfox your fathers?"

"We will. Though how we lost Lockwood, I still cannot understand. Lockwood, to that spitfire of a girl!"

Hampton raised his hand. "Now, I cannot allow you to disparage the new Marchioness.

Lady Lockwood is my wife's dear friend, despite her rather frightening disposition. When we meet, it is as if somebody had poured ice down the back of my coat. I am continually reminded of Shakespeare's *though she be but little she is fierce*. Still, the lady has forgiven Lockwood for our misstep those many months ago and I am assured she will at some point forgive *me*, so it must be past debate."

"I suppose so," Hayes admitted. "But for her penchant for insults, I suppose she *is* a pleasant lady. In any case, you may have fallen, Lockwood may have fallen, but I will not."

Hampton leaned back in his chair and contemplated his friend. "The problem with a vow to avoid marrying is that all of us have made it and two of us have already thrown it over. *Happily* thrown it over, I might add. Though, if it is your intention to avoid the state, then as a friend I wish you luck."

"Luck is usually on my side, as so many unfortunate gamblers have discovered. In any case, I am not against the institution of marriage, none of us are. Well, perhaps Dalton is. The rest of us simply have our own reasons for being against it *right now*."

"As was I," Lord Hampton said, laughing. "And yet, you must still frequent those places where a lady might conquer you. I suppose you have been invited to Lady Blakeley's dinner?"

Hampton asked.

Hayes nodded. "Yes, of course, and I am glad of it. She is one of the more amusing hostesses."

Lord Hampton smiled. "Then, bring all your resolve to avoid the vicar's noose, as I understand my wife's latest project will be there and she is said to be remarkably pretty."

LILY ROSE AND crossed her aunt's drawing room. "Lady Hampton," she said.

"Lily!" the lady cried. "How well you look. Though, I will scold you mercilessly if you insist on calling me Lady Hampton. We have known each other since we were children scrambling over fences."

Lily grasped her friend's hands. "Cassandra, then," she said. "I know you still sign your letters such, but I could not be at all sure of the rules of town and whether you might take it amiss for me to dispense with your title."

"Goodness, I am still the same girl you ever knew," Cassandra said laughing.

Lily was not certain that was altogether true. Yes, Cassandra appeared in her person very like she had when last they'd met in Surrey. She looked perhaps the slightest bit more substantial, but that was only an improvement—Cassandra had never been very slender. That was not the real change though. Her friend, her now *married* friend, had an air about her that was somehow different. More confident, more settled, more content. Though she did not look particularly older, she *seemed* older.

"Now," Cassandra said, "let us talk over everything."

They sat themselves down on the velvet settee in a cozy corner while Ranier brought in a tray. Ranier, as all good butlers were wont to do, had donned a particular grave air about him as he laid the tea things for a titled lady.

He closed the door behind him and Cassandra said, "He seems rather wonderful. He might go toe to toe with my own butler."

"He is the kindest fellow alive," Lily said, "despite his terrible scowl."

"Just like Dreyfus, then. A hard crust on the outside, housing an inside of jelly. My darling dog May and my lord's own mastiff, Havoc, barrel their way round the house as they please. You cannot imagine the delightful one-sided conversations I have overheard between my butler and those dogs. They sit very dutifully as he tells them where they've gone wrong. He invariably gives it up and gives them a biscuit when he cannot hold up against their doleful stares."

Lily poured the tea and said, "Dear May,

she's a lovely girl. Now, before anything, I must say that you cannot think how much I appreciate all you have done. And the Marchioness of Lockwood and Miss Darlington, too! You know well enough what sort of patched together wardrobe I should have arrived in had I not been so spoiled with presents. Imagine, I do not even know those two ladies!"

Cassandra smiled and patted her friend's hand. "I think we have all learned, through my own trial, that we ladies must have a care for one another. Someday, you will be in a position to lend your support to another lady and you will do so."

"Of course I will, it would be a pleasure," Lily said. She flushed and said, "Though it seems fantastical to imagine that *I* would ever have the means of helping another."

"You shall, I am sure of it. You must only meet the gentleman who takes your breath away, as I have met mine."

"I wonder who that will be," Lily said softly. It was an idea she had wondered on quite a lot in recent weeks.

"That, I cannot know, though I hope the thing is done with far less trouble than I encountered." Cassandra straightened her skirt, suddenly appearing thoughtful. "Speaking of trouble, I would caution you about some rather highflyers that you will wish to avoid. You already know about the Dukes' Pact from my own difficulties."

"And you would warn me against those gentlemen?" Lily said.

Cassandra smiled and said, "I know, it seems exceedingly strange, as I have married one and dear Sybil has married another. Nevertheless, I warn you against them as I think the four gentlemen who are left can each be dangerous in their own way. I would not wish to see you hurt, Lily."

"I shall avoid them, then. I do not suppose it will be difficult, as I am unlikely to travel in the same circles as those high-flying gentlemen."

"Indeed, you *will* travel in those circles. I have seen to that," Cassandra said merrily. "I have visited all my friends and they will call on you and you will call on them and the invitations will begin to arrive. As a matter of fact, I believe you and your dear aunt will be invited to Lady Blakeley's dinner on Tuesday. She was exceedingly kind to me last season and I have since learned there is little the lady likes more than to sponsor some worthy young person. I have got her quite enthusiastic over you."

"Goodness," Lily said, "Lady Blakeley! Even in Surrey she is known to be the first in fashion."

"Indeed, though do not attempt to imitate her style, only she can carry off a kimono." Cassandra said, laughing. "Though I am afraid

Lady Blakeley does favor a few of those highflyers I mentioned and so we may encounter them at the dinner. Particularly Lord Ashworth and Lord Cabot."

"I will not be daunted over it," Lily said, chin up. "You do remember Mr. Mignon and his dogged advances? I stepped lightly round them until he finally gave it up. If one of those gentlemen attempted to play with my affections, he should find himself quite unsuccessful."

"I am glad to hear it. I will stay in town for another week, and then I am afraid I will be retiring to the country. I wish to see you well on your way to success before I depart."

Lily was rather taken aback. She had counted on Cassandra to be nearby throughout this new adventure. "You will not stay for the season? Has Lord Hampton pressing business on his estate?"

"He *will* do," Cassandra said, "though he does not yet know of it. For now, it is only my own pressing business." She gently laid her hand across her midsection and gave Lily a knowing look.

"Are you really?" Lily cried, all thought of her own discomfort flown from her. What a ninny she was to have noted Cassandra's more substantial middle and not have guessed it. "Oh, Cassandra, how wonderful!"

Before Cassandra could reply, Lily's aunt came into the room. "Ah, Cassandra, Ranier told me you were here. Oh, I suppose I should call you Lady Hampton but that does seem formal. After all, I have been in the habit of seeing you wail over a scraped knee or weep when you were denied cakes. Dear me, though, I suppose I ought to call you whatever it is you wish. You are quite the grown lady now and I suspect you do not care to be reminded of any wailings or weepings that may have taken place in your youth."

Cassandra suppressed her giggles, always vastly amused by Amelia Hemming's winding thoughts. "Cassandra will do perfectly well for me, my dear Mrs. Hemming. Now, I must be off, but rest assured I have Lily's season firmly in hand."

LILY HAD THOUGHT she'd need to muster her courage as she'd entered Lady Blakeley's house. After all, the lady and her husband were quite famous. Lord Blakeley was outspoken in the House of Lords, the couple held progressive ideas, and there seemed to be nothing the lady would not dare when it came to her mode of dress. How often had Lily seen a sketch of her in some newspaper or other as she sat by a sunny window at Farnsworth House? In those moments, Lady Blakeley had been tall, exotic and very far away from Lily's own little sphere. It seemed extraordinary that Lily Farnsworth should find herself in the company of such a woman and she had prepared herself to be overwhelmed.

And yet, the fine muslin gown she wore, embroidered with delicate gold thread, had instilled some little bit of confidence. Then, there had been Lady Blakeley herself. She was just as tall and graceful as Lily had imagined, and daringly dressed as an ancient Roman in elegant waterfalls of white silk. Her appearance was everything Lily expected—what Lily had *not* expected was to find the famed London hostess so cordial.

"Dear Mrs. Hemming," Lady Blakeley said, "I am honored to receive you. And this must be Miss Farnsworth."

Lily curtsied at the introduction.

"Goodness," Lady Blakeley said, "Lady Hampton told no tales, I see. Very pretty and even prettier manners."

"Oh, yes," Aunt Amelia said, "my brother's children are all very pretty. All daughters, you see, so I suppose it is well they are pretty. One never knows what to do with a plain girl. But then, one must eventually do something, otherwise they just hang about the house forever."

Lily had begun to become alarmed by her

aunt's speech. While many in her aunt's circle found Amelia Hemming's racing thoughts charming, she could not expect the great Lady Blakeley to think so.

Much to her surprise, the lady's soft laughter reached her ears. "I see you are a woman of good sense, Mrs. Hemming, with the delightful habit of saying a truth most pretend does not exist."

Lily was more than grateful for Lady Blakeley's kind treatment of her aunt and they had passed on to the drawing room.

Though she had supposed the house would be all luxury, Lily had not guessed it would be all eccentricity. She had never seen a room like it in all her life.

The wallpaper was red silk, the pattern of Chinese temples embroidered in gold. The carpet was not of a pattern, but rather the darkest indigo and made one feel as though one might fall through it and into a bottomless pit. The pianoforte was painted white, giving it the illusion of floating over the indigo bottomless pit, and stood next to a marvelous golden instrument that appeared to be a foreign harp of some sort. Perhaps most alarming, there was something standing in a corner that Lily thought might be an Egyptian sarcophagus.

Aunt Amelia looked in that direction and said, "My goodness, I hope there is not some old and dried up fellow lounging about inside. I should not like to think of him dropping out at an inopportune time. But then I suppose whoever put him in there knew what he was doing and we must trust to that workman's skill. At least, I would like to think so."

Before Lily could comment on whether they might view an Egyptian mummy tumbling out of his casket, Cassandra crossed the crowded drawing room.

"My dear Lily," Cassandra said, "you are lovely."

"As are you," Lily said. "I am convinced that marriage suits you."

"I thought the very same," Aunt Amelia said. "I imagine Lord Hampton has been plying you with sweetmeats. Of course, I could be mistaken, it might be tarts for all I know of it. People do have their own preferences."

Before Mrs. Hemming could expound further on Lady Hampton's slightly increased girth, she was blessedly called away by Mr. Jacobs, an old friend she had not seen in some time.

"I am sorry," Lily said, "you do know how my aunt says whatever little thing comes to mind."

"Indeed," Cassandra said with a smile, "I have always found it very informative to hear spoken what everyone else must be thinking. I fear I cannot hide my condition much longer."

"Does Lord Hampton know?" Lily asked.

Cassandra looked pensive. "It is hard to say, actually. Though I've said nothing, he has suddenly taken to inquiring into my comfort an extraordinary amount. I have barely sat somewhere before he is suggesting a pillow for my head or a throw for my lap—he has become an absolute captain of fire screens. Then, of course, he will have noticed that I have not taken out my horse these past weeks. No more wild rides for Cassandra for the foreseeable future."

"Goodness, please do not," Lily said. "I often trembled to see you flying over a fence when you had not anything to risk but your own neck."

Cassandra patted Lily's hand. "I have been very staid ever since I suspected, and I have resolved to tell him the news on the morrow. I am past the danger and would prefer to inform him of it before he positively guesses and wonders what I am waiting for. I am only afraid he will urge that we retreat to the countryside immediately."

"As you no doubt should," Lily said. "Do not press yourself to stay on my account. You've done quite enough, and my aunt and I will get along very well."

"I believe you shall," Cassandra said. "If I am not here to supervise, I am certain Lady Blakeley will lend a hand, then Penny Darlington is to arrive next week. Lady Sedway, you remember her as Anne Hamilton, may come down from

Scotland, though I have yet to hear from her. I would count on Sybil too, but I understand the marchioness is busy redoing everything in her new house that Lord Lockwood ever did. She says his wallpapers are so ghastly that they cannot spare a moment for London, but I rather think they only have eyes for each other and cannot be bothered to come."

As Lily took in the news of who would be where, Lord Hampton came by his wife's side, accompanied by another gentleman.

"Lady Hampton," the other gentleman said, bowing low.

Lily looked at this unknown gentleman with no small interest. He was tall and lean, even a hair taller than Hampton, with dusky fair hair and striking green eyes. He had an air about him that she had not noted in the gentlemen of her Surrey neighborhood—he seemed at once at his ease and alert, rather like a leopard casually surveying his territory from the vantage point of a high branch.

"Lord Ashworth," Cassandra said in greeting. "May I present Miss Farnsworth."

Lily curtsied. So here was a gentleman of the Dukes' Pact—one of the gentlemen highflyers Cassandra had counseled her to avoid. It was a shame, he was handsome. *Very* handsome.

Cassandra and her lord's attention were suddenly sought out by Lady Mainteneau. The lady and her lord had hotly debated if the rumors were true that Lord Byron just now resided at the Mocenigo Palace with a pair of monkeys and a fox. Her lord said it could not be so, no right-minded Englishman made friends with a fox. Lady Mainteneau thought it all too likely—Lord Byron was nothing if not an eccentric. They were determined to confirm the truth of it from two who had so recently been on the scene in Venice.

Lady Mainteneau took both Lord Hampton and Cassandra by the arms and steered them toward her eagerly awaiting husband.

Lily felt awkward, left behind to converse with Lord Ashworth on her own.

"Lord Hampton tells me you have been long acquainted with Lady Hampton," Lord Ashworth said pleasantly.

"Yes, indeed," Lily said, grateful that the lord had not allowed a silence to hang between them overlong. "We are childhood friends; her father's estate is not five miles from my own."

A solemn footman who had appeared at the door to the drawing room caught Lily's eye. With great ceremony, he held up an enormous bronze gong and rang it with a mallet. Lily looked at him with interest.

"I understand it is from China," Lord Ashworth said, "and meant to say that dinner is served."

Lady Blakeley swept in, appearing as if from nowhere. "Ashworth, do take in Miss Farnsworth."

Lily suppressed any hint of her feelings about the suggestion. She found she was not entirely certain what those feelings were. She had no wish to put herself in front of a gentleman involved in the Dukes' Pact, though she could not entirely claim she minded having this particular handsome gentleman in view.

She could not discern Lord Ashworth's opinion on the matter—he maintained a neutral expression that she found vaguely disconcerting. He merely put out his arm.

LADY BLAKELEY'S DINING room was nearly overwhelming in riotous color. A vibrant yellow silk covered the walls, embroidered with eccentric scenes of Indian maharajahs. The gold-leafed chairs were padded in ruby red silk, the tablecloth a bold orange satin, and the chandeliers were draped with ropes of semi-precious stones that cast a dizzying array of colors. The totality of the room's impression was that of a circus and Lily would not have been surprised to see the footmen turn themselves into acrobats.

Lord Ashworth noted Lily's wonder. He said, "Lady Blakeley's dining room tends to have a startling effect on one newly introduced to it."

"It is most original," Lily said, hardly knowing how to describe the room's impact on her senses.

Her aunt was handed to her chair across the table by Mr. Jacobs. Mrs. Hemming said loudly, "I'll be glad to sit down, I think. I feel quite overpowered. I am sure if I were younger I should like the brightness of it all. I suppose I am rather dull these days. I venture I should go on quite well as long as the food does not arrive in so many shades."

Lily stole a look at their hostess. Lady Blakeley had most assuredly overheard her aunt's comments. The lady pressed her lips together as if she would stop herself from laughing.

Mrs. Hemming's attention was captured by her niece seated so nearby, and then Lord Ashworth by her side. "Is that one of those Pact fellows? Yes, I suppose it is, though he does not resemble his father. I see him at Lady Carradine's on occasion though I don't get to talking to him. I wonder how old Dembly gets on these days, always a pleasant fellow. Though rather on the short side, if I recall rightly."

Lily's cheeks, she knew without needing to peer into a glass, had darkened to match the ruby red chairs. Lord Ashworth stared at Mrs. Hemming.

Quietly, Lily said, "Do forgive my aunt, my lord, she is prone to speaking all her thoughts."

"Apparently so," Lord Ashworth said.

His expression was impossible to fathom. Lily

could not at all determine if he were irritated or amused.

Fearing he might be annoyed and feeling a great urge to defend her aunt, Lily said, "She is kind, for all that. She has very graciously opened her house to me."

"You do not stay with your father?" Lord Ashworth asked.

"I do not," Lily admitted, knowing that she was also likely admitting that her father could not afford to rent a London house for the season. "My father had too much pressing business to attend to."

"Business? Cannot his steward manage during the season?" Lord Ashworth asked, the surprised tone impossible to ignore.

"Apparently not," Lily said hurriedly.

Lord Ashworth considered this and said, "It seems hard luck to have to forgo a season because one's steward cannot go forward on his own. Your father might perhaps do well to employ a more skilled man. He would not find himself so harried if he had a competent fellow at the reins."

"I'll not seek to advise my father on any matter, my lord," Lily said with some asperity. The truth was, she was not particularly offended by the comment, but could not admit to the real circumstances. Her father did not employ a steward. He was his own steward. In fact, their collection of servants in general had always been on the thin side. Lily had never had a lady's maid, and she had only sometimes got help from her mother's maid, Clara. Even her aunt's maid, Pips, found the notion bizarre.

"No, of course you must not advise him, I only think of my own experience," Lord Ashworth said, appearing to perceive that he had stepped too far. As if he would change the subject, he said, "What amusements are to be found in that neighborhood in Surrey?"

Glad he had taken himself off the examination of her father's estate, Lily said, "All the usual sorts, I suppose. The riding is picturesque, we have various routs and balls. There is an assembly in Guildford that is pleasant."

"You are fond of dancing?" Lord Ashworth asked.

"Oh yes! Though, it is sometimes a less welcome diversion, for I might prefer to play cards. I am very fond of cards."

"Indeed?" the lord asked, and Lily was certain he suppressed a smile. "I do not believe I have ever heard of a young lady preferring cards to dancing."

In all seriousness, Lily said, "That would surprise me, my lord. After all, one knows how a dance will unfold. Beyond whatever idle chatter that might be had, the outcome is known. The outcome of a game of cards is not known and therefore more interesting. And then of course, there are stakes."

Lord Ashworth nodded. "Do you consider yourself skilled in any particular game? I suppose whist must be your preference?"

"Whist?" Lily said, a shade more derisively than she'd meant to. "I prefer to play without a partner. Piquet is far more to my taste."

Now Lily could see that the lord was vastly amused. She supposed he thought himself the far greater master of the game. She had noticed that same attitude among some of the gentlemen in Surrey. She was a female, and so could not possibly best them at anything. That particular attitude had assisted her in winning tidy profits from those mistaken gentlemen.

"I presume you have won great sums in Surrey," Lord Ashworth asked, with a small and patronizing smile.

"Enough to teach those who may doubt my capability," Lily said.

"I wonder," Lord Ashworth said softly.

"I do not see why you should," Lily said.

The lord laughed. It was not a loud or long laugh, but that hardly mattered. It was a supremely condescending laugh.

"You must realize, Miss Farnsworth," he said, "that the play in London is at a more advanced skill level than what one might find in England's more bucolic locations. I only mention it to caution you."

He thought she was ridiculous. He thought she'd gloried in winning at piquet against another country bumpkin who played as badly as she. He thought she could not measure up to London standards.

Though Lily had always prided herself over her mastery of her own feelings, she was very much aware that when she perceived an insult she was somewhat less of a paragon.

"If we were to play against one another," she said boldly, "I imagine you would cease your disdain of England's more bucolic locations."

Lord Ashworth bristled at her declaration. "Indeed," he said. "Then let us hope Lady Blakeley affords us the opportunity."

Lily's chin went up in utmost defiance. "Let us hope," she said.

CHAPTER THREE

NOW THAT THE challenge of a game of piquet had been issued, Lily turned to her other neighbor, Mr. Simmons. He was an agreeable sort of gentleman who did not make too many inquiries into her circumstances. In truth, Mr. Simmons' conversation was dull and she need only half attend him. It seemed he was a great reader—books of every sort, newspapers, broadsheets, old family letters, scientific treatises—no written word was to escape his notice. It also seemed that he was intent on communicating *all* that he had read.

As she listened to him drone on about the collapse in grain prices, Lily found herself conjecturing over her conversation with Lord Ashworth.

After her temper had settled, she began to see

the foolishness of having thrown the piquet gauntlet at Lord Ashworth's feet.

What had she been thinking? Of course, he was very wrong in his opinions. It hardly mattered where one learned the game of piquet—the rules were the rules. One either had a head for it, or one did not. It did not matter a whit if that head belonged to a lady or a gentleman. Further, there were those in Surrey who had been rather sharp and not that easy to prevail over. For all that, though, she began to very much wish she and Lord Ashworth had never landed on the subject of cards.

Throughout the dinner, she found she must turn to Lord Ashworth on occasion, else she look a fool by staring at the back of Mr. Simmons' head. She found the lord stiff. She found herself stiff. It seemed neither of them wished to talk to the other and so they landed on such subjects as the weather and the soup. Lily had been vastly relieved when Lady Blakeley rose.

The ladies had retired to the drawing room and Lily held great hopes that the gentlemen would stay long over their port. After all, she knew perfectly well from dinners in Surrey, the gentlemen might land on a subject with varying opinions and air those opinions long into the night to the chagrin of their hostess. Politics was always a handy distraction, there had even been the dinner at Mr. Cahill's that had devolved into a shouting match that could be heard throughout the house. Mr. Randolph and Mr. Braker had not spoken since and every hostess took pains to see they were never together again.

Before the gentlemen arrived, Cassandra had pulled Lily to the far side of the drawing room where they might pretend to examine a row of books on a shelf.

"I saw that Lord Ashworth took you in," Cassandra said. "Of course, it could not be helped. I will only remind you that they have all vowed they will not marry."

Lily had pulled some book or other from the shelf and pretended to flip through it. She laughed despite herself. "My dearest Cassandra, you have no cause to fear that my interest is in any way engaged. If anything, I believe Lord Ashworth finds me a bit silly and I find *him* a very much larger bit condescending."

"Is that so?" Cassandra said in some surprise. "I would not have expected Lord Ashworth to be rude, but if he has, I should like to inform my husband of it."

"Please do no such thing," Lily said hurriedly. "The fault is half my own. We engaged in the most ridiculous conversation about cards." Lily paused, not certain how to explain what must come next. "I believe," she said slowly, "that he may challenge me to a game of piquet, as he is certain my skill will be found wanting."

Cassandra was silent for some moments. "This is very strange, Lily. Why should Lord Ashworth wish to humiliate you in such a manner?"

"I expect because he thinks he will teach this country bumpkin a lesson," Lily said. "I hinted at my skill and I do not suppose he believed it."

"This is outrageous," Cassandra said. "You are not to fear a scene, my friend. I will not allow such a thing to occur. Goodness, I would not have imagined Ashworth to be so petty, regardless of any words said between you." She patted Lily's hand. "I shall manage it."

Lily did not answer one way or the other. On the one hand, she had no wish to make a spectacle of herself in any way. It had occurred to her that she might do so, in playing against Lord Ashworth. Would it not be more appropriate for her to take a turn on the pianoforte and leave the elders to their cards? Or, if she should play cards, would not whist seem more suitable? A wager between a lord of the pact and a girl just out might be talked of. She particularly feared it as Cassandra had just mentioned it as *a scene*.

On the other hand, she was fairly certain she could trounce the gentleman. After all, she had yet to meet with a person she could not triumph over, as long as the hands she was dealt were reasonable. Would it not be satisfying to put a stop to the lord's condescension?

Before she could settle on a firm opinion, the gentlemen came in. It had been the shortest of delays. Lily quietly sighed. She had been foolish to think that Lord Blakeley would keep the gentlemen long over the cloth. Mr. Cahill might dare to displease his wife, but Lily doubted anybody would dare displease Lady Blakeley.

Lily pretended to scrutinize the book in her hand as she surreptitiously watched Cassandra in conversation with her husband. Lord Hampton seemed to laugh, and then be brought back to seriousness. He nodded to his wife and joined Lord Ashworth at the far side of the room.

Lily turned to Mr. Simmons who had promptly seated himself on her right. She realized he'd seen she held a book and had made his way over with alacrity, eager to discuss it. She felt rather foolish over it, as she had not even looked at the title when she picked it up and the subject of it was wartime commerce. She could not think of anything she would be less interested in understanding.

As Mr. Simmons waxed on about supply chains, Lily was certain that Lord Hampton was delivering his wife's advice to Lord Ashworth— he was to give up any notion of a card game with Miss Farnsworth. It was just as well, it was her first evening out in town and she had no wish to put herself forward as anything unusual. She was fairly certain that *unusual* in a lady was not a quality celebrated by the *ton*. At least, her mother had often pointed out that if one wished to be eccentric, one had better be very old, have a lot of money, and hopefully a lofty title.

She glanced back to the other side of the room. Lily had expected that Lord Ashworth would heed Cassandra's advice and only look condescendingly satisfied that his opinion had been right all along. She had not expected that he would make his way toward her to make comment on it, which appeared to be what he was doing.

"So you see, Miss Farnsworth," Mr. Simmons went on gamely, "it is not only in battle that the game is won. If a force can successfully blockade another's supplies, it can be ruinous. I've always said so, you know. We that understand such things can be vital contributors to any war effort."

Lord Ashworth had arrived and waited for Mr. Simmons to complete his assessment. The lord did not look as impressed or interested as that gentleman might have hoped and Mr. Simmons trailed off on his lecture.

Lord Ashworth said, "I was devastated to understand that our looked-for card game has found disapproval with Lady Hampton."

Lily did not answer. She did not trust herself to answer. The man was infuriating. Why could he not leave well enough alone? Rather, he must come to her with such condescension! Devastated, indeed.

"Though I expect Hampton was right after all," the lord went on smoothly. "I do not like to be unkind and have made it a habit of foregoing taking advantage of naiveté."

Naiveté? Is that what he thought of her? The last thing Lily Farnsworth would consider herself was naive to the ways of the world. She had not grown up in a sheltered hothouse. She had grown up with creditors at the doors and a footman failing spectacularly to pretend he was the butler in an effort to fend off those circling wolves. She still remembered the very early years when her mother's face was pinched, her father was consumed with worry, and the dinners were scant on meat and filled with vegetables from their garden. She remembered a conversation overheard as her parents debated whether they could hold on to the estate and what they were to do if they could not.

Good Lord, even America had been spoken of. Her childhood had been one long night of uncertainty and fear.

Lily looked coldly at Lord Ashworth. "I see you remain confident you would end victorious, though I assure you that you would be wrong. Further, I see nothing amiss in a lady relieving a very mistaken gentleman of his pounds and pence."

"I say," Mr. Simmons said with enthusiasm, "this is rather famous. The young lady ventures to wager against the most notorious gentleman gambler in town."

Lily glanced at Mr. Simmons. What did the fellow mean, the most notorious gambler in town?

"I make no claims at notoriety," Lord Ashworth said. "The word conjures a flamboyance I do not aspire to. I merely seek to challenge anyone worthy of it."

"You have very decided opinions of yourself, my lord," Lily said in as curt a manner as she could muster.

Of all the words that had been exchanged between them, that particular salvo seemed to be the most affecting. There had been the slightest bloom of pink on the lord's cheeks.

"To speak the truth is to speak a fact, not an opinion, Miss Farnsworth," Lord Ashworth said abruptly.

"What's the use in talking?" Mr. Simmons said. "What shall you bet? Ten pounds seems right for a drawing room. I will secure a pack of cards and then we shall see how the drama unfolds! Goodness, this is the most interesting thing that's happened in months."

Mr. Simmons had hopped up from his seat and was away before Lily could stop him. She had no idea how she would have stopped him, had she the time, though she would have dearly liked to try.

"You are free to renege," Lord Ashworth said. "In fact, I urge you to do so. I will tell Mr. Simmons it is I who refuse to play, and I'll throw some flattering folderol into it for good measure."

Lily fumed. Never was there such a highhanded fellow. How dare he speak to her as if she were some flighty empty-head who must be rescued from an ill-considered scheme.

Lord Ashworth glanced behind him. He turned back to her and said, "You ought to make your decision, Mr. Simmons returns in unbecoming haste."

Lily smiled. "Oh, I have made my decision, my lord," Lily said sweetly. "You are to leave this house poorer than when you came into it."

MR. SIMMONS HAD apparently alerted all and sundry to the unusual wager proposed between Miss Farnsworth and Lord Ashworth. Those who had not been informed had noticed the crowd convening around a table at the far end of the drawing room and soon made their way to the scene. Even Lily's aunt had given up on the tea tray and joined the gathering.

Lily did her best to resist becoming unnerved by the attention, or to speculate if it would lead to talk on the morrow. Lady Blakeley appeared amused, but then it seemed to Lily that the lady was generally amused. Cassandra, on the other hand, looked exceedingly worried. Aunt Hemming seemed more perplexed than anything else. What struck Lily more, though, was Lord Ashworth. He was disdainful, if he was anything at all.

Mr. Simmons had removed the lowest cards from the pack. The lord had offered to deal, but Lily claimed the right. Everybody knew that the dealer began at a disadvantage and she had no intention of allowing anyone to suppose she was victorious as a result of having an advantage.

She was satisfied with her hand. It was not the most auspicious she had ever looked upon, but she was certain she knew how to play it. It had one particular advantage that would serve her well. She only discarded one. Lord Ashworth exchanged only one card as well, and looked at the next four. So, the lord thought himself skilled at memorizing which cards were where. He thought he held the advantage of memorizing them in order to make better guesses at what she held in her hand. Lily suppressed a smile. Nobody was more skilled at those strategies than herself.

The declarations would begin.

"Three," Lord Ashworth said.

"How much?"

"Thirty," Lord Ashworth answered.

"Good," Lily said. Were she not playing

cards, she would smile. As it was, she must hide her glee. The truth was his run was *no good*, though she was not obligated to declare it. She had a triplet of aces and she would keep that information to herself until the time was right.

The declarations went on, Lord Ashworth unaware that Lily had sunk the triplet of aces. It was a tactic often talked of but rarely actually used. Most players were too faint of heart to delay taking points that were right in front of them. She was already in a solid enough position regarding her declarations and she wished Lord Ashworth to remain in the dark regarding the extent of her hand until it was time to lay down those cards. She had a mind to take most of the tricks, especially the last.

Making their way through point, sequence, and triplets or fours, the declarations concluded and the play could now begin. As they laid down card after card, it slowly became apparent to Lord Ashworth that he might have underestimated his opponent. For Lily, herself, it was as if she entered a dreamlike state. The cards played arranged themselves in one area of her mind, the cards in her hand in another. The variations that Lord Ashworth might hold, based on his declarations and what had been laid down, in still another corner. The individual cards laid down by Lord Ashworth hinted at his strategy and state of mind, suggesting what other cards might remain in his hand and how he would play them.

He *had* underestimated her ability, though he did not yet know how much. Lily glanced down at her last three cards—they were her triplet of aces, and the lord did not know it.

It had been a daring gambit, one she had used before. Her opponents never seemed to consider the idea that a woman could keep her nerves steady enough to try a sink. Certainly, Lord Ashworth would never consider the idea. Now, it was about to pay off handsomely.

Lily did her best to ignore the whispers around her but could not help to overhear some of them.

"She plays like a sharp."

"I never did see the like of it."

As she laid down her second ace and took the trick, Lily watched Lord Ashworth's expression with interest. This would be the moment he might guess that she'd sunk a triplet of aces.

The idea did clearly dawn on him and he looked up sharply at her. Lily smiled graciously. He would know now that her final card was likely an ace. She would win the last trick.

She slowly laid down her ace.

Lord Ashworth laid down the queen of hearts. He had saved a high card to take the last trick, and he had failed.

And so the play went on with new hands. Lily had varied her strategy so that he might not detect a pattern and had not sunk anything since the first play. The lord was equally dodging, she had to use all her concentration to divine his likely strategies. However arrogant Lord Ashworth might be, he was the most skilled player she had yet encountered. Skilled though he might be, he would not overcome her.

At the final play she'd sunk three kings, knowing full well the aces and the other king were already played. She handily won the last three tricks.

The scores told the story, she had won the game, and handily.

The crowd surrounding the table stamped feet and there were various "bravas" called out.

Lord Ashworth having had a moment to collect himself, said, "I congratulate you, Miss Farnsworth."

"It was nothing, my lord," Lily said. She was in the habit of expressing that very sentiment every time she took an opponent's money. It was so vague it might be construed that she thought herself only lucky, or that it had only taken the slightest of efforts to succeed.

"Hear that?" Mr. Simmons cried. "The lady trounces a renowned gambler and it was nothing!"

"I presume you will not be alarmed to wait until the morrow to settle the debt," Lord Ashworth said. "Though I am happy to sign for it if you like."

"I assume you may be trusted, Lord Ashworth," Lily said graciously.

The party round the table dispersed after some few minutes, Lord Ashworth dispersing himself perhaps faster than most. Mrs. Hemming was lured away for a game of whist and left her niece with Cassandra.

"Well," Cassandra said, sitting down next to Lily, "I suppose we can at least be grateful that you won."

"I know I should not have done it," Lily said, "but he really was provoking beyond anything."

Cassandra patted her hand. "I learned for myself that it's no use pretending you are anything other than who you are. And you, Lily Farnsworth, are quite the card player."

"Yes, I know it," Lily said, with no hint of false modesty.

"Does it have to do with your memory?" Cassandra asked. "It's always been rather good. I remember in my own house, when something was misplaced, my father would say, *If only Lily were here, she'd remember what became of it.*"

"Indeed, I can see where I saw something last and it has come in very handy with cards. But for all that, I do not wish to be talked of."

"I am afraid that is a rather empty wish," Cassandra said. "A lady new to the town defeats the famed Lord Ashworth at a card table? It will be talked of everywhere. However, there is nothing disreputable in it and so you can expect only idle chatter. Simply hold your head up and face the talkers down."

LILY AND HER aunt had finally taken leave of Lady Blakeley. Lily wondered if, by playing Lord Ashworth, she had caused her hostess any discomfort, but Lady Blakeley had whispered, "Well done, my dear, I do so like a girl with spirit," as they had donned their cloaks.

Now, their carriage rattled through the dark and damp roads toward Cork Street.

"I'm not sure it was at all the thing, though," Mrs. Hemming said.

Her aunt had not said she spoke of the card game, but Lily was certain that she did.

"Ashworth, goodness," Mrs. Hemming went on. "He makes the most frightening bets at Lady Carradine's. Frightening to me, anyway. Now that I think of it, you might be better served only making bets at her club. I fancy it's more discreet, though I'd be hard-pressed to say exactly why. It just seems so… well, in any case, what a talent for piquet! I never saw the like of it. You seemed positively clairvoyant, my dear."

"Cassandra says the wager will be talked of,"

Lily said, wishing to get that piece of unpleasant business out of the way.

"Everything is talked of," her aunt said with complacency. "After all, what is the *ton* to do but talk? None of us have any real employment. Oh, we fancy that embroidering a seat cushion or painting a screen is the most vital thing in the world. The gentlemen run around pretending at politics but accomplishing little. It's all nonsense. Gossip is our real lifeblood."

Though her aunt's thoughts could sometimes be inexplicably winding, they also just as often hit upon some truth that nobody was willing to give voice to. In any case, it was encouraging that Mrs. Hemming, for one, was not overwrought by what she had viewed this night, nor what might be said about it on the morrow.

Lily was gratified that she'd won, though not particularly surprised by it. She'd taught that arrogant gentleman a lesson that she imagined must sting.

It was a shame he was so filled with arrogance, for there could not be a more handsome man in London. Those eyes! They were the color of dark emeralds. She had never seen anything like them.

Lily suppressed a smile. What a ninny she was to swoon over the first pair of fine eyes she encountered in town. Especially since those eyes were placed in the head of one who was so irritating. And, even if he were the most pleasant man alive, he was a gentleman of the pact. He'd sworn he would not marry, and so every lady of sense would be well advised to give him a wide berth.

In any case, Lily reminded herself that for all the diversions of the season to come, she was here for a serious purpose. She must get herself settled creditably, if not for herself, then for her sisters. There was no room in any of that for pondering a pair of fine eyes.

HAYES SAT ALONE in the breakfast room of his house in Berkeley Square, glaring at the sideboard. He had consented to a cup of strong coffee but had not an appetite for anything more substantial. He was dimly aware that one of the footmen was staring at him fairly agog, as the boy was used to watching his master fill his plate with as much as it could hold.

Finally, he heard his butler clear his throat. "Is something amiss, my lord?" Cobb asked. "Might I fetch something else?"

"No, nothing," Hayes said.

What an evening! What a blasted evening. It had begun with Hampton thinking it amusing to drag him in front of Miss Farnsworth's notice.

Now that Hampton was married, he seemed to find it a great game to tempt his friends who would avoid the state.

He would admit to Hampton presuming that Miss Farnsworth might tempt. At least, in looks. She was tall and slim, with a marvelous amount of dark hair. Then, there was that face, the chin with the slightest dimple, the lips so perfectly proportioned, and her eyes, those dark eyes…

Had she been an actress, he would have pursued her relentlessly.

However, looks alone did not make a lady. There was her temperament to consider, and that was where Miss Farnsworth fell far short of ideal.

She had none of the feminine graces! What lady would challenge him in such a manner? Her confidence was, well, it was *irritating* to say the least.

Hayes felt himself flush as he recalled the card game. It was his own fault that it had even occurred. Lady Hampton had wished to put a stop to it, but he found he could not resist putting the bold Miss Farnsworth in her place.

How was he to guess she would be so skilled? There had been something almost supernatural in her play. She seemed to always know what he held, and worse, what he would do. If he'd been in a gaming hell, he'd have looked for a strategically placed set of mirrors. He could not unravel how she'd been so good. She'd sunk a triplet of aces like a hardened card sharp! Worse, he'd fallen for it and lost some high cards for his trouble. He'd been all confidence that he'd take the last three tricks during that first game, never imagining she'd sunk her aces.

And then, so many people standing around to witness his defeat. He assumed it would be mere hours before the story was told in one drawing room after the next and likely embellished to boot.

After he'd left Lady Blakeley's house, he'd gone to Lady Carradine's club to gamble the night away. He knew perfectly well that he'd been drawn there to recover some of his dignity by ending the night as a winner, rather than loser. He had won, though not in a spectacular fashion. It had been a middling sort of evening, though he'd come out ahead.

While he *had* been in the frame of mind for cards, he'd not been in the right temperament to put up with Lady Carradine's recently arrived relative. Mr. Shine was come from America, Hayes was to understand. Mr. Shine had sold off something or other, a farm perhaps, and was now relocated to London.

Why the man kept talking to him, and why he had the temerity to relay so much information and ask so many questions, Hayes could not fathom. He liked Lady Carradine, but if her cousin insisted on making himself a pest, Hayes would go elsewhere.

Lady Carradine really ought to know better. Nobody came to her house for the conversation, and if they did, nobody would be much interested in conversing with Mr. Shine. Perhaps the proprietress ought to confine her cousin to attending the musical evenings nobody but a few of the ladies ever attended.

Hayes's thoughts drifted out of Lady Carradine's club and back to Miss Farnsworth and her miraculous amount of dark waves of hair. It was a shame she was not as a lady should be. Or perhaps it was a blessing. Who knows how far down a road he might travel if she'd made herself pleasant.

A footman came in and announced Lord Cabot.

"Cabot?" Hayes asked. "What does he do here so early?"

Cabot himself strode in and answered. "I decided I'd avail myself of your board," he said, glancing at it. "I thought it might be amusing to attack a plate of sausage and eggs while you tell me how you possibly lost at cards to some chit of a girl named Famesworth."

"Farnsworth," Hayes said. "Good God, how has the story made the rounds this early?"

"It was rather late, actually," Cabot said, piling his plate high. Though he'd only mentioned sausage and eggs, it seemed the lord would not look askance at absolutely everything else the house had on offer. When he'd filled one plate and looked about, Cobb handed him another, which was promptly stacked with rolls.

Sitting down with the two plates ranged in front of him, Lord Cabot said, "A fellow named Mr. Simmons arrived to Lady Galliton's house while we were all settled into cards and told the story. I said he must be mistaken, but he claims he was on the scene at Lady Blakeley's dinner."

"So he was. I found him annoying."

"He is, rather," Lord Cabot said. "But, out with it—how did it happen?"

"I hardly know," Hayes said.

"Luck," Cabot said, shaking his head. "One never knows who she will favor. Except to know she usually turns her back on *me* at a table. I've only luck with my horses."

Hayes would very much like to imagine it was luck that was on Miss Farnsworth's side, he would very much like it if everybody else thought so too. He did not, however, believe it.

"I am afraid it was something more than luck," he said.

"Well, even *you* might have a bad night I suppose. Simmons says she's a pretty thing, I reckon you were distracted."

"I do not get distracted while playing cards," Hayes said.

Lord Cabot shrugged. "Jolly good story,

though. The young lady launches her season by burying the great and terrible Lord Ashworth at cards."

"Wonderful," Hayes said softly.

CHAPTER FOUR

Lady Judith Carradine was doing her level best to enjoy the bright sun just now coming through the windows of her breakfast room. It had often been an enjoyment, though everything had seemed to lose its luster upon Mr. Shine's arrival to the house.

She had thought it impossible that anybody would have discovered her secret—ten years prior, an obscure family with a title but no money emigrates to America. Five years prior, the lot of them die of yellow fever. The sole survivor, the lady's maid, takes on the identity of her mistress and uses the families' funds to come back to England as an unfortunate widow.

The family she'd served had lived on a lonely farm and knew so few people. How was anybody to discover that she was in fact Nancy Manton, the lady's maid who had traveled with the family, and that the real Lady Judith Carradine had perished alongside her husband and children? Further, what was so wrong with it, really?

She *had* nursed the entire family at great risk to her person, though none of them could be saved. When the fever hit, the servants and the hands on the farm all disappeared into the night shadows to get away from it. She'd been left on her own and worn herself thin digging the graves. Then, she'd contracted the disease herself and suffered alone with nobody to care for her.

Slowly recovering, she had developed her plan. The servants began to drift back, finding only she had survived. When she was well enough, she dismissed them all, claiming she'd been directed to do so by Lord Carradine's heir. She was bold enough to say it as she knew from Lady Carradine herself that the real heir was some fellow in Yorkshire who was entirely unknown to them. As far as the family knew, the connection was so remote that fellow did not even know he was the heir. In any case, there was no English estate to inherit. Further, she and Lady Carradine were not that far off in looks— both blessed with nondescript brown hair, brown eyes and of a medium height.

Once the old hands were got rid of, she promptly hired new staff. Those recently arrived hands knew her only as Lady Carradine. Why should they not? She'd installed herself into the lady's bedchamber, taken over her wardrobe, and donned the best black gown. It had been easy enough to explain that all the prior servants were dead of the fever. It was a circumstance happening everywhere.

Once she had firmly established herself, she made a trip to the nearest large town, far enough that the real Lady Carradine would be unknown to its residents. She had once cursed the very remoteness of the Carradine's property, but now it became a blessing. Nobody in these parts had the first idea of what Lady Carradine had ever looked like. She'd ordered headstones made for the graves, Lady Carradine's own bearing the name Nancy Manton. She'd presented the master's will and herself as the master's widow, made arrangements for the livestock and the land to be sold, and booked passage home.

The Carradine's homestead had filled her pockets somewhat, but not enough that she might retire to a life of leisure. It was on the ship home that she'd come upon the idea of a gambling establishment. To her surprise, it had been the ladies who were the most vociferous, sitting at table long into the night. One particular lady explained their enthusiasm when she mentioned that it was unfair that, save for a ball, there were precious little chances for women to test their skill. Ever ready to spot an opportunity,

Nancy became determined to open a club that would welcome men *and* women.

The club would cater to a genteel crowd, as those gentle souls tended to walk the earth with deep pockets. It would be a welcoming atmosphere for ladies, at least, ladies who dared—she had seen on the ship how much money they had at their disposal. She would personally provide the aura of respectability needed to lure in well-born ladies. Tea would be served and men not acting the gentleman would be ejected speedily. She would employ the sorts of women who might otherwise work as a governess or companion—middle-aged spinsters who would act as chaperones if a single lady wished to play a gentleman. She would run it as if it were her own house and she merely entertained guests.

Word would get around, it always did, and those ladies interested in more than a few shillings wager would make their way to her. It would be the Almack's of gambling. She would charge a membership fee of a pound a month. It had all gone smoothly and now her current members were providing her with nearly fifteen hundred pounds income yearly.

That she was a titled lady had cloaked the club in respectability. Nancy had been fairly certain she could succeed in her impersonation. She'd spent years closely watching and then imitating her lady's every manner and phrasing.

On the occasion that she stumbled on something, she blamed it on her years in America. She resembled her old mistress enough that should she encounter a person who had known her before she left for America, she thought she might carry it off. Though, she did not fear the prospect overmuch—the lady was raised in some backwater in Cornwall and had never had a season. Over the course of five years, Nancy Manton had in fact become Lady Judith Carradine and her club had become known for its staid and respectable atmosphere.

How Mr. Shine, recently of Baltimore, had discovered that she was the maid and not the lady, she knew not. The difficulty was, he did know it. And now he was insistent on posing as her cousin and becoming her business partner. Either that, he'd said, or he'd expose her.

She did not know what was to be the end of it. How could she carry on with such a partner? He did not even seem at all acquainted with the rules of the *ton*. She did not know how she would proceed out of this mess, but she must at least stop him from destroying her list of loyal customers.

Mr. Shine, himself, came jauntily into the breakfast room, having had the audacity of commandeering a bedchamber for himself and installing his person in her house.

"Madam," he said by way of a greeting.

"Mr. Shine," Lady Carradine said, in a tone that was more reminiscent of condemnation than welcome.

"Blast it all, on your high horse so early in the morning?" he asked, laughing and taking a roll from the sideboard.

"Sir," she said, "I must insist you cease harassing my customers. Lord Ashworth was highly irritated last evening, with your pushing into conversation with him. I am only surprised you did not note it."

"Oh, I noted it," Mr. Shine said, buttering his roll.

"Then why did you go on with it?" Lady Carradine asked, as always perplexed by the workings of the odious man's mind.

"Because I have a plan for the great Lord Ashworth and his ilk," Mr. Shine said.

His tone sent a shiver down the spine of his breakfast companion. "I'm sure I do not understand—"

"Never mind what you understand," Mr. Shine said darkly. "Nancy."

THE KNOCKS ON the door seemed to come one after the other as Lily worked on a bit of sewing. First, there was the folded up ten-pound bank note. It was enclosed in fine paper bearing Lord Ashworth's seal and accompanied by a polite and formal note congratulating her on her victory. She had stared long at his signature, as she thought how one wrote their own name must reveal something about their nature. His hand was direct and lacked any fancy flourishes, just as a man's should be. That led to her contemplating his eyes. That led to her crumpling the note and throwing it toward the fire. That led to rescuing it from the fire, folding it up, and putting it in a book.

Next came a note from Cassandra. She would leave for the country on the morrow and wished to see her friend before she went.

Following, were a number of invitations. Lady Blakeley's famed half-mask was among them, and Lily felt a wave of trepidation over it. She knew from Cassandra that the mask she would wear would come from Lady Blakeley herself, and be a comment upon her. The lady had been most kind to Cassandra last season and cast her as a fawn, Lily could only hope for the same sympathetic treatment.

There were also invitations to various routs and dinners—Ranier brought them in as they arrived, wearing a look of pride and approval.

To her surprise, there were invitations to both the Bergrams' and the Hathaways' balls. Lily was certain that was Cassandra's doing—both of those balls would be a delightful first-rate crush. The Bergrams invited hundreds and the Hathaways always hosted a themed ball—she remembered reading somewhere that last year had been Russia.

"Well, my dear," her aunt said, examining the pile of invitations, "it seems we will be very much out and about. Though, we have nothing this evening and you do have that ten pounds from Lord Ashworth. Perhaps we might go to Lady Carradine's. You might get the feel for the club if we just pop in for an hour and place very small bets. There are those who bet too high for the likes of us, but there are always a few who don't mind keeping things comfortable."

"That sounds like a fine idea, Aunt," Lily said. The thought of a gambling club filled her with a tingling sort of excitement.

"Though I wonder if we might see Lord Ashworth there," Mrs. Hemming murmured.

Lily wondered the same thing, though she would not for the world say so. "I hardly think we should factor the lord's whereabouts into where *we* choose to go," Lily said.

"Yes, I suppose that is right. Goodness, if I was always thinking of who I do not wish to see I should never go anywhere. Well then, we'll go if you like, dear."

"I'd like it very much," Lily said. "There will be other nights for balls and such. We surely should take advantage of an evening in which we are not engaged."

"Yes, my thoughts too. Now, about balls. You won't mind if I make my way to a card table almost as soon as we enter the house? I like to have some choice of partner and if one wanders in too late, one runs the risk of spending the evening attempting to keep Lady Saffey's attention on her cards. She is a dear creature, but her memory…she's as old as Methuselah, so you can imagine."

Lily could not be certain of Lady Saffey's memory, having not met the lady, but was sympathetic to her aunt's wish to obtain a better partner for whist.

"Perhaps Lady Saffey will not make an appearance so very often," Lily said hopefully.

"Oh, she will," Mrs. Hemming said, nodding vigorously. "It's her son, you see. He takes her everywhere. Mind, he does not have much choice. She lives with him and if he leaves her behind, she's likely to slip out and go wandering. They say she once turned up at Brook's in a nightdress, asking for a cup of brandy and berating the poor footman at the door for gambling away her dowry."

Before Lily could inquire what had been the result of Lady Saffey's nocturnal adventure to a gentleman's club, Ranier came in and announced Lady Hampton.

"Ah, Cassandra, there you are," Mrs. Hemming said. "I suppose you'll want cakes or something sweet. I can see that you've grown fond of those sorts of things. Though, one might find that one had grown perhaps *too* fond of them."

Lily blushed for her aunt and said to Ranier, "If we might have tea?"

Cassandra suppressed her laughter until the butler had closed the door behind him. "Dear Mrs. Hemming, my recent expansion is due to quite another cause. I am with child."

Mrs. Hemming laid down her sewing. "Are you? That is exceedingly welcome news. I had grown afraid you were running to fat. I did hint at it, you know."

"Yes, I do know," Cassandra said, laughing.

Mrs. Hemming rose and said, "I will leave you two friends to talk on your own. Very nice to see you, Cassandra, and I am exceedingly relieved that you haven't gone wild with fairy cakes."

With that interesting pronouncement, Lily's aunt bustled from the room.

"Oh, Cassandra…"

"Do not *oh Cassandra*," her friend said. "You know I find your aunt the most delightful lady."

"I must confess, I do too," Lily said. "Though I sometimes wonder if everybody does."

Cassandra patted her hand. "I expect so. At least, the good humored of us do. Lady Blakeley was delighted with you both."

"She is very kind," Lily said. "We received an invitation to her half-mask."

"I will be very sorry to miss it," Cassandra said, "but I am off to the country on the morrow."

"So you have told Lord Hampton?"

"I have, and the dear man is over the moon," Cassandra said, "though he claims he guessed weeks ago. He barely consented to my making calls this morning and I overheard him telling Dreyfus to instruct the servants that everything is to be done quietly, lest the mistress be disturbed. I will be cossetted to distraction."

"How fortunate that he is so considerate!" Lily said.

"He is a darling of a man," Cassandra said, nodding. "Now, to you. I have not the slightest fear for you. I have only heard very complimentary notions about the idea that you defeated Lord Ashworth at cards. I suspect most people do not mind hearing that Lord Ashworth has been taken down a peg. He *can* be a touch arrogant on occasion."

"He most certainly can," Lily said.

"All that's come of that silly wager is the gossips say you are pretty *and* clever."

"Well," Lily said, "I cannot say if that is true, but I am grateful the talk is no worse."

"Never mind," Cassandra said. "It was only a

card game and it is not as if you plan on making a career of it."

Lily felt the slightest flush, as she had so recently conferred with her aunt about visiting Lady Carradine's club. Though she did not think there was anything wrong about such a visit, she also did not feel inclined to mention it to Cassandra. She wondered if that meant it might not be perfectly right. After all, she should not be ashamed of anything she chose to do. And certainly, her aunt would not encourage her in anything to be ashamed about.

Ranier brought in the tea and Lily ceased her wonderings about it. At least, for the time being.

As Lily poured, Cassandra said, "Penny Darlington has arrived to town. She will call on you as soon as she is settled. You will find the lady fairly horse-mad, but a dear all the same. She's already offered to drive me in her phaeton. My poor lord was prepared to rail against it, until I pointed out we need not decide, as we will be off on the morrow."

"She drives a phaeton!" Lily said.

"Indeed, she does. It does not sit as tall as what one might see with a gentleman at the reins, though I've yet to see a fiercer tiger than one of Lord Mendbridge's hanging off the back of it. Nobody really comments on it—her father is rather renowned as an expert on horses and so if he condones it, it must be right."

Lily was rather cheered by the notion. She did not suppose anybody would stay talking about her wager with Lord Ashworth while a lady driving a phaeton sailed by.

"I shall be sorry to miss watching your season unfold, Lily," Cassandra said, "though I shall also be happy to return to Derbyshire. You must write often and tell me everything."

"Of course, I will," Lily said. "You never did tell me how you found Weston Hall. It must be a great change to be the mistress of your own house."

"Not so very much, as I always acted as such for my father and as it turned out my lord and I had quite a lot of help," Cassandra said. "Edwin had not paid much attention to the estate and there were not many servants employed. While we were in Italy, the dear dowager and my aunt fell upon the place, hired servants, and marshalled them into order. It was quite arranged when we came home. Both will be there when we arrive, neither Lady Marksworth nor the dowager have any intention of missing the first grandchild to come on the scene. We shall be quite the party, as the dowager will have brought her dog and I am certain that fierce little Pomeranian will spare no effort to rule over our own Mayhem and Havoc."

"You will be surrounded by those that love you," Lily said, wistfulness creeping into her voice.

"So I shall," Cassandra said, rising. "I ought to be off, the house is likely to be at sixes and sevens getting ready for our departure and I suspect my dear husband of hiding in his library to avoid the chaos. He is all energy when it comes to my own comfort, but Dreyfus will be left to struggle on alone."

Cassandra kissed Lily on the cheek. "Do enjoy yourself and write me every detail." She shook a playful finger at her friend and said, "And no more gambling, if you please."

After Cassandra had taken her leave, Lily sat for some time considering her friend's words. Perhaps, in light of the talk of her wagering against Lord Ashworth at Lady Blakeley's dinner, it would not be wise to be seen in a club that was known for its gambling. At least, not so soon.

Before she could come to any real conclusion on the matter, her aunt bustled into the drawing room, waving a card in her hand.

"I'm afraid our little excursion to Lady Carradine's is quite off, at least for this evening. I received a summons we dare not ignore."

"Goodness," Lily said, "we are not ordered to Carlton House?"

"That might be a deal more pleasant than where we *are* summoned," her aunt said mysteriously.

Lily waited with some trepidation. She was not accustomed to see her aunt ruffled, and ruffled she certainly was.

Mrs. Hemming sat down with a huff. "Harriet Montague, of all people."

Lily started. That was not a name she would ever be likely to forget. "Is that… Lady Montague? The lady who caused Cassandra so much trouble?"

"The very one," Mrs. Hemming said nodding.

"But why should she—"

"I haven't the faintest idea. Further, why does an invitation for a party come so late? It is for this evening! It does not even specify the nature of the entertainment. And, I hardly dare call it an invitation. We are expected, is what she says. Well, I suppose we'd better eat before we go, I rather think if it were a dinner she might have said so."

"But surely, we need not attend," Lily said, the idea of entering Lady Montague's house feeling rather like contemplating entering a lion's den. The woman had ruined Cassandra's ball and drove her out of town with her scheming. "We might invent any sort of excuse."

"Now that's a pleasant thought, not at all true, however. Lady Montague has never brooked excuses. Goodness, I remember seeing Mrs. Killion at a rout and I am quite certain she had come down with the measles. She tried to cover the rash with paint, but with very little success. It was a crowded business, but people gave her a very wide berth."

Lily was unwilling to allow her aunt to travel down a long path regarding Mrs. Killion's measles. To bring her back to the subject at hand, she said, "I did understand, though, that Lady Montague had been forced to retreat to Yorkshire last season."

"Oh, yes," Mrs. Hemming said. "We were all delighted, I can tell you. Nobody said so, of course, but there were vague little things mentioned about forgetting to answer her letters and so forth. I have never been a part of her personal correspondence and so did not need to consider what to do on that front."

"Then how is it," Lily asked, her trepidation growing, "that she is come back and seems to be able to order everybody about as she did before?"

Mrs. Hemming squinted her eyes, as if she attempted to peer into the past for the answer. "I am not in possession of all the facts," she said, "but somehow, Lord Dalton decided to back her return. He's another nobody dares cross—he's an earl, but he'll step into a dukedom one of these days."

"He's one of the gentlemen of the pact," Lily said softly. "How extraordinary that one of those gentlemen, with their connection to Cassandra's husband, should choose Lady Montague's side."

"I do not claim to understand half of it, I

assure you," Mrs. Hemming said. "What I do understand is that it appears the lady is back and none the worse for wear. The best we can do is comply and not attract her ire. You see, dear, she's quite harmless until you attract her ire. I've known Harriet these past twenty years and have been enormously successful by simply agreeing with everything she says. She knows me, but she does not think about me. She invites me to routs and such, but not to anything cozy. *That* is how one needs to get on with the dragon of Mayfair."

"Perhaps this evening is only a rout," Lily said hopefully. "We might turn up, make ourselves known to the lady, and then be off. It would be a crush and our departure would not be noticed."

"Hmm," Mrs. Hemming said. "I do not think it is a rout. She always has those invitations printed and sends them well in advance. This is a handwritten note. Really, I do not know what we are in for this evening, but we will go and find out. Perhaps it is a musical evening and she has decided very suddenly that she did not invite enough people, or somebody has bowed out at the last moment. Whatever it is, if it is awkward or unpleasant, we can content ourselves in the knowledge that it cannot last forever—there are only so many hours in a night."

THE LORDS DALTON and Ashworth sat in a corner of Destin's, drinking the owner's remarkably strong coffee. They had belonged to the club for some years, but ever since their fathers' pact to force them to marry, they had found it a more and more convenient spot. White's came with the chance of running into the old fellows; Destin's did not. It was a young man's club and there did not seem to be a member over thirty.

"Why don't we just beg off," Hayes said. "There is not much Lady Montague could do about it."

"You forget," Dalton said, "we gave our word that we would back her. The lady drove a hard bargain in exchange for her assistance."

"In exchange for her scheming, you mean. God, we did not even succeed."

"We failed spectacularly. I cannot even stomach the letters Lockwood writes of his darling wife and how she's managing his house. I cannot imagine why he thinks I wish to know how adorable she is when she is condemning a carpet."

"One of these days, he'll realize he should have held off, that there were still a few years left of doing as one pleases."

"Meanwhile," Lord Dalton said, "Cabot and Grayson have gone off to Somerset. Cabot wants to look at a baron's horse. I suspect Grayson only wants to look at the baron's daughter. It is just us currently in town and so we must attend Lady Montague's card party."

"It will be a colossal bore," Hayes said. "I expect the wagers won't exceed five pounds."

"Cheer up, Ashworth. You know the sort of people Lady Montague is bound to invite. It might only be five pounds at a time, but they will all be easy marks."

"No doubt," Hayes said.

"Perhaps Miss Farnsworth will make an appearance and you might try to win back your ten pounds," Lord Dalton said, with one of his rare smiles.

Hayes hid his discomfiture. He was really very tired of hearing of that blasted game. "Miss Farnsworth is a particular friend of Lady Hampton. I imagine she would be the last person Lady Montague would invite."

Hayes thought that must please him, though he had noticed, twice now, that when he entered a house for a dinner, he looked about to see if Miss Farnsworth was in attendance. He supposed he was only eager to get their inevitable second meeting out of the way. There would be some sort of lingering embarrassment hanging over him until he could show the world that he was not in the least affected by the lady and her cards.

CHAPTER FIVE

HARRIET MONTAGUE SURVEYED the drawing room. The usual furniture that adorned the room had been moved out and square card tables moved in. Fresh packs of cards were liberally spread throughout. On a table by the door, a small tray of expensive graphite pencils sat alongside a stack of fine paper cut into small squares for keeping scores. A sideboard had been set up that would hold all manner of cold meats, cheeses, jellies, rolls, pastries, and fruits. A tall rectangular table would be manned by a footman, ever ready to dispense Madeira, tea, orgeat, and her own special recipe cordial—"Lady M's Restorative," depending heavily on cinnamon and coriander.

Lady Montague smiled. She had only thought to hold the card party as an exclusive evening that might be talked about everywhere—the young lords destined to be dukes had graced the lady's drawing room, it would be said. Those powerful gentlemen would indicate their backing by their attendance. The world need not know she'd bargained for it while they'd all been in Yorkshire. The gentlemen's public acknowledgement would be one more step in her campaign to regain the influence she had lost over that debacle with Cassandra Knightsbridge.

She had, just the day before, been in a fury upon hearing that Lord Cabot and Lord Grayson would not attend. Lord Cabot had sent an excuse that there was a horse to be seen somewhere in the countryside. It had felt a slap in the face. That would leave her with two would-be dukes, which was not nearly as good as four.

And then, as if the Gods smiled down upon her, everything began to fall into place.

Miss Knightsbridge, now Lady Hampton, though Harriet could hardly bear to call her so, had chosen to sponsor some little chit from Surrey, a Miss Farnsworth. Harriet had not seen anything to do about that, unfortunately. She would have liked to take any opportunity to punish Lady Hampton by somehow making Miss Farnsworth uncomfortable, and yet, she had not quite dared. Her standing was still tenuous, and Lady Hampton would eventually become a duchess.

That was, she had not quite dared until two pieces of gossip came to her attention.

One—Lady Hampton was retiring to the country; it was said she was with child. The lady would not be on the scene to provide cover for her newly launched dove.

Two—Miss Farnsworth had made a fool of herself by wagering Lord Ashworth over a game of piquet. Oh, it was said she beat him handily, but that could only have been luck.

The plan to invite both Lord Ashworth and Miss Farnsworth to a card party was delicious. It would be talked about in hushed whispers. News of it would travel to Hampton's estate and Lady Hampton would come to know that Harriet Montague had a very long memory and might even involve one's friends. Most importantly, it was exactly the sort of thing she wished people to remember about her. She was clever, and not afraid to design a scheme when she had a mind.

One should not cross Lady Montague.

It would elicit a subtle fear, the sort that made people wonder what she might do next. That wonderment would fix her firmly as the arbiter she had once been. And *that* was the purpose of her life.

All the way back to town, Lord Montague had warned her off meddling and scheming. Fortunately, she had not taken any of his advice since the first week of their marriage. She did sometimes wonder why he went on with it.

This evening, she would promote another card game between Lord Ashworth and Miss Farnsworth, and no matter the outcome it would set the town ablaze with gossip. Lord Montague could think what he liked about it.

Harriet Montague was securely on the steps back up to her throne and she would not stumble.

As LILY DID not have the faintest idea what sort of evening was to be held by Lady Montague, she'd chosen a dusky rose silk dress. She thought the coloring did something well for her dark hair and rather pale complexion, but most importantly it was a very simple cut with no undue adornment. She supposed it would be suitable for any sort of evening party. As well, she had taken in her aunt's advice about Lady Montague and even if it had been a ball, she would not have chosen a dress that would be a standout. Aunt Amelia said the trick was to remain unnoticed by the lady and that was exactly what she proposed to do.

"Goodness," Mrs. Hemming said, as their carriage barreled ever nearer to the lady's house, "you look terrified. I ought not have said Lady Montague was the dragon of Mayfair, I think it has put visions in your head. Really, she is just an unhappy creature. She never had children and I suppose that's led her to put all of her attention on her power in society. One should never put all one's eggs in one basket as she has."

Lily put her chin up and became determined to at least have the appearance of ease. After all, to appear unduly nervous might attract the lady's attention.

She smiled to herself. Her aunt had been right, she'd invented visions of the dragon and had begun to think of herself tiptoeing past the lady's lair.

"I have been silly, I know," Lily said. "I don't expect a great personage like Lady Montague will take the least notice of a simple girl from Surrey."

"Well, here we are," Mrs. Hemming said. "It is certainly not a rout, I see no carriages but the one just trotting away. Very strange, it appears it will be a small party and I have never been invited to one of those. In any case, it will not pay to sit here and wonder. We shall go in and discover it for ourselves."

A STERN-LOOKING BUTLER directed footmen to take their cloaks and led Lily and Mrs. Hemming to the drawing room.

Lady Montague rushed to greet them, the ostrich feathers planted in her hair waving in all directions as she crossed the room.

Lily felt momentarily speechless. Not only was the great lady before her, but she could see over the hostesses' shoulder that this was to be a card party. There were people already arrived, but based on the number of tables it would indeed be an intimate evening. Worse, Lord Ashworth stood at the far end of the room. He stood next to a man with a long scar running down his cheek—Lord Dalton, she presumed. Everybody had heard of the scarred earl.

That scarred gentleman regarded her with some amusement. Lord Ashworth stared at Lily with an expression she could not unravel.

What was the meaning of it? Why had she and her aunt been invited to such a small gathering? Why had they been invited to a *card* party?

Lily began to wonder if Lord Ashworth had some hand in it. He had been less than pleased to lose to her at piquet and she guessed he would have been even more displeased to become aware of the talk that had gone round about it.

Was it possible that he sought to trounce her at cards and had prompted Lady Montague to arrange it?

It seemed an elaborate scheme, but Lily did not forget what Lady Montague was capable of. Further, if the lady sought the lord's backing to reclaim her place in society, she might well agree to anything.

"Dear Mrs. Hemming," Lady Montague said, sweeping up to them. "And this must be Miss Farnsworth."

Lily curtsied low enough for a queen, her intention being to flatter the lady.

"Gracious, Lady Montague," Mrs. Hemming said, "that headdress sets off your features *very* finely."

Lily pressed her lips together. Apparently, her aunt had the same notion to flatter. Lily knew perfectly well that Mrs. Hemming thought ostrich feathers ridiculous outside of a court presentation. Further, Lady Montague's features were of a heavy and broad sort and no feather could set them off to be anything other than what they were.

"Let me take you round, my dears," Lady Montague said, grasping Lily rather firmly by the elbow.

Lily had no choice but to allow herself to be led, though she had a great urge to throw off Lady Montague and run from the house. Whatever scheme was at work here, it could not be to her benefit.

In somewhat of a daze, she was introduced to various people. They all seemed to find her of interest, in particular Mrs. Layton, who had to be persuaded to give her up. With every introduction she came closer to the far side of the drawing room. And Lord Ashworth.

Lord Montague had very civilly greeted her. Though most seemed to understand she was the lady who had challenged Lord Ashworth, he'd not seemed to know anything about her recent wager over piquet. He'd wondered if a young girl such as herself might not be bored with an evening of cards and he was under the impression that the young ladies preferred to find themselves on a ballroom floor.

Lily had not answered these opinions, though she might have responded in the affirmative. She would much prefer to find herself in a ballroom at this very moment.

She'd at least had her aunt by her side, but even that was not to last. Lady Montague very determinedly directed Mrs. Hemming to speak to Mr. Dresher. It seemed the gentleman had a number of questions about cultivating roses and Mrs. Hemming must share her expertise.

Lily was certain it was the flimsiest of excuses to get her aunt away. If one wished to speak to a person with expertise in roses, one ought to speak to one's own gardener. Further, she was sure her aunt was one of the last people to claim special knowledge. Her garden, small in dimensions, was a most decidedly practical kitchen garden.

She felt some trepidation in the knowledge that Lady Montague wanted her separated from her aunt.

"Ah, Lord Ashworth, Lord Dalton," Lady Montague said. "Here is Miss Farnsworth. Ashworth, I understand you are already acquainted?"

"Yes," Lord Ashworth said.

Lily could not help but note the curtness of the reply. One would expect a gentleman to answer such a query in the manner of, *Indeed, we met at so-and-so's dinner last week,* or some other pleasantry.

"Of course you have met," Lady Montague said smoothly. "One could not avoid hearing of the wager over piquet in Lady Blakeley's drawing room."

"One could always *try* to avoid hearing of it," Lord Dalton said quietly.

This momentarily paused the lady's stride, but she speedily regained her footing.

"We are to be a small party this evening," Lady Montague went on, "but that does not mean we shall be dull. After all, a rematch between our Miss Farnsworth and Lord Ashworth? Too diverting."

"But I—" Lily stuttered.

"Do oblige me, dear," Lady Montague said. She turned on her heel and set off to greet her other guests.

Lord Ashworth looked to Lord Dalton, who only shrugged. Lily felt rooted to the spot, mortified. This was why she and her aunt had been invited. To become some sort of entertaining spectacle for Lady Montague's friends. Of course, there was no thought to how it might affect Miss Farnsworth.

She could see now how Lady Montague managed people and got her way. The lady did not stand still to hear an argument or opinion. She simply said what she wanted and walked away, confident she would not be defied in her wishes.

"I am afraid I will not be able to oblige Lady Montague," Lily said. After all, the lady could not force her to a card table. At least, she did not think so.

"You're a brave lass, to cross the dragon," Lord Dalton said.

"I do not mean to cross anybody," Lily said, beginning to wonder what the precise consequences of crossing Lady Montague might be. As her aunt had explained to her, the trick to the lady was not inviting her notice, much less her ire.

"You need not cross her, I will do it," Lord Ashworth said. "She is fully aware of my opinions about ladies and gambling. She may be made unhappy by my lack of cooperation, but she will not be surprised by it."

Lily felt a great sense of relief wash over her. The difficulty had been effortlessly lifted from her shoulders. She would not have expected Lord

Ashworth to be so helpful, but then she supposed he did not wish for another opportunity to be found wanting.

Though, what did he mean, his *opinions about ladies and gambling?*

"Lady Montague," Lord Ashworth said, loud enough to get her attention. "A word."

The lady left the party she had been speaking to and walked toward them, ostrich feathers swaying over her head. Lily thought she looked like nothing so much as a peacock strolling a lawn. A determined peacock, as it happened.

She reached them and Lord Ashworth said, "I am afraid I will have to decline your amusing scheme to once more play against Miss Farnsworth. You are aware of my opinions on females doing any serious gambling."

"Pshaw," Lady Montague said dismissively. "I'm sure I do not know where you get such ideas, Ashworth. Ladies do not swoon over a few pounds."

"That is never what I said," Lord Ashworth said.

"You said, I believe," Lady Montague went on, "that females do not have the steady nerves necessary to be successful and they do not lose with any sort of composure."

Lily stared at Lord Ashworth. She very much doubted he would deny it, as it was just the sort of ridiculous opinion he would hold. Steady nerves and composure indeed. Clinging to such ideas as those, he must have been especially mortified to lose to her.

"What I expressed as my opinion is true," Lord Ashworth said, "and come upon through careful observation."

"Do not go on with this, Ashworth," Lord Dalton said quietly.

Lord Ashworth glanced irritated at his friend. "Why should I not? The fairer sex is blessed with many other fine attributes."

"Though not the steady nerves for a serious wager," Lily said softly.

"That is correct," Lord Ashworth said.

"I do not think Miss Farnsworth agrees with you," Lady Montague said with some delight.

"I do not," Lily said.

"Well, diverse opinions make the world go round," Lord Dalton said. "Perhaps we might make the leap to another topic."

Lady Montague raised an eyebrow. "Do you try to rescue your friend, Lord Dalton?"

"I do not require rescue, Lady Montague," Lord Ashworth said curtly.

Lily fumed. How on earth could this man keep hold of his condescending opinions about females when the female in front of him had trounced him just days ago? Further, she'd employed the sort of tactics that only the steadiest of nerves could withstand and he well knew it.

"Lord Ashworth is right, he does not require rescue," Lily said. "What the gentleman requires is a proper amount of respect for the skill he has encountered so recently."

"One game does not prove anything," Lord Ashworth said.

"Would two?" Lily said, smiling.

"Ashworth!" Lord Dalton said under his breath.

"If you are insistent on a rematch," Lord Ashworth said stiffly.

"Oh, I think she is," Lady Montague said, her voice full of satisfaction.

"She is," Lily said.

"I suppose fifty pounds will not be too rich for either of you?" Lady Montague asked, before sailing away to her guests.

IT WAS NO wonder at all that the news of the proposed game between Miss Farnsworth and Lord Ashworth was swiftly communicated to all of the clusters of people in Lady Montague's drawing room. Like rabbits overrunning a garden, the idea hopped from here to there and back again.

Lily had moved away from Lord Ashworth and Lord Dalton and sought out her aunt.

As she watched Lord Dalton whisper furious-ly at Lord Ashworth, she listened to her aunt's opinion on the matter. Mrs. Hemming did not see anything good in it and Lily was forced to own that she'd been severely provoked. That had led her aunt on a winding path about young people and their prickly natures. According to Mrs. Hemming, with youth came a propensity to be offended. That uncomfortable attribute gently faded with time, until one hardly cared for anybody's opinion. Though the idea took some time to finally arrive at, Lily thought her aunt was likely right.

She did not tell her aunt that the wager was fifty pounds. She could hardly have even spoken such a thing. She'd never played for such a sum in her life!

As much as she had been intrigued by the idea that the bets would be higher in London, fifty pounds! An amount such as that had never occurred to her.

Now, she sat across from Lord Ashworth. The other card tables were empty, as everybody else had gathered round them to watch. The lord had claimed the deal, noting that she had been the dealer on the last. Lily thought him a fool for taking the disadvantage and assumed it was the pride in him that pressed him to do it. It was not very clever, as he would have had a time of it beating her if *she* had taken the disadvantage.

On the other hand, she was grateful he was

being so foolish. There was the fifty pounds to think about. Were she to lose, it would take everything she had, and some borrowing from her aunt besides, to pay the debt.

Her hand was a good one, very good. Her draw was even better, and she took careful note of the next few cards so she could remember them if Lord Ashworth picked them up. She'd had such hands before and knew precisely how to play it.

They moved through the points, sequences, triplets, and fours with alacrity. She sunk nothing, her hand was so strong that she need not feint and rather thought it would be pleasant to communicate that strength to her opponent. He was good enough at the game that she could see he did rapid calculations in his head. He knew he was in for a time of it.

She took the first trick, and then the majority after that.

Now that she played Lord Ashworth for a second time, she began to see more clearly some of his weaknesses.

He twice turned over his discards, so his memory was not as good as her own. She had no need to examine her pile or wonder about his. They conveniently ranged themselves in her mind. This put him at a serious disadvantage—he might peek at his own pile all he liked, but he could not look at hers.

His expression, while for the most part neutral, did give some hints. When he was disturbed, there was the slightest tightening of his mouth. When he thought he'd win the trick, there was the smallest narrowing of his eyes.

His hands showed his confidence, or lack thereof, in his cards. Smooth and quick, or slower and slightly uneven.

These subtle changes would go unremarked by most people, but not to Lily.

Lily handily won the first game. She noted Lord Dalton move away with a look of disgust while Lady Montague appeared a well-fed cat. Mrs. Hemming, despite having reservations about the game, could not help but be approving of Lily's win.

The match went on, point by point. Lily would give the lord some credit for being more skilled than most. She found she must use all of her concentration, all of her strategies, and all of her attention to her opponent's varying expressions, lest she allow him to overcome her.

That he did not overcome her was evidenced by the applause as she reached one-hundred points.

As she always did at the end of a hard-won game, Lily felt a sense of exhaustion. It was as if her mind had expended every ounce of energy in her body.

As the onlookers drifted away, talking among

themselves of this famous rematch, Lord Ashworth said quietly, "What trickery do you employ?"

Lily felt a burst of flame upon her cheeks. Trickery? Did he just have the audacity to accuse her of cheating?

"My lord, you have been soundly beaten, and fairly," she said.

Before Lord Ashworth could respond, he was unceremoniously hauled to his feet by Lord Dalton.

"My apologies, Lady Montague," Lord Dalton said, holding tight to his friend's arm. "You do recall we said we had another engagement? Otherwise, we would have been pleased to stay longer."

Lady Montague might have, in other circumstances, been irritated to see her two prize guests depart her evening early. In this circumstance, however, she appeared to view it in all good humor.

As well she should, Lily thought. The lady had maneuvered to produce enough gossip for a week.

LILY HAD SPENT the rest of the evening at Lady Montague's as an object of interest. There were those who sought out her advice on this strategy or that. There were those who congratulated her on prevailing over one of the most respected gamblers in town. There were many who pressed her to partner at whist, particularly Mrs. Layton, though none of them had never seen Lily play that particular game.

Lady Montague was all condescension, as if she had done Lily some great favor. The lady's friends congratulated her on an interesting evening and she took it in as if she were a feudal lord accepting her vassals' fealty.

Finally, she and her aunt had made their departure. Lily hoped to never see the inside of Lady Montague's drawing room again.

As exhausted as she was when she returned to her aunt's house, Lily had a deal of trouble falling asleep. Her thoughts were agitated as they could not settle in one direction.

She had won fifty pounds! It was such a marvelous idea that it did not seem real. What a sum! Of course, Lord Ashworth would not miss it, it would be nothing to him. But to Lily Farnsworth, it was an incredible amount. She would send half to her father and use the rest when she and her aunt went to visit Lady Carradine's club.

It was a happy thought, indeed.

And then, there were the unhappy thoughts. Lord Ashworth was everything contemptible in a man. His good looks and competency at cards had led him to believe he was superior in every way. As if his enraging condescension were not enough, he could not even lose graciously.

He'd asked her what trickery she employed, as if she were some sort of scoundrel who had devised a way to cheat.

She did not think many had overheard that particular comment, perhaps only Lord Dalton. Still, it infuriated her. Everybody who viewed that game would be well aware that skill had won the day, not trickery. How dare he imply such a thing?

He was intolerable and it would please her if he and his handsome face jumped off London Bridge. It would please her even more if he did so and suddenly recalled that he could not swim.

CHAPTER SIX

THE LORDS ASHWORTH and Dalton trotted through the dark streets after departing Lady Montague's card party.

"As you mean to be silent," Lord Dalton said, "I will carry on both sides of the conversation. You say to me, thank you for pulling me out of Lady Montague's house before I said anything else outrageous. Then, I say to you, you're very welcome friend, but you must watch your tongue. The girl has a father, and perhaps even brothers, it will not do well to accuse her of trickery, which is tantamount to an accusation of cheating."

"You saw it for yourself!" Hayes muttered.

"I did not, actually," Lord Dalton said. "I walked away after she trounced you on the first play. I occupied myself with a cold ham until it seemed the game was coming to an end."

"Nobody is that good," Hayes said. "Nobody."

"It appears *she* is that good," Lord Dalton said drily.

Hayes did not answer, but spurred his horse to a quicker pace. There was something about Miss Farnsworth's play that he did not understand. If it was not trickery, and now that he was reflecting on it he saw that it could not have been—she had not been in her own house and had not produced her own cards—there was some method involved.

How could it be that there was some method or strategy that he had not discovered for himself? He'd studied the game backward and forward. He'd spent endless hours playing out one scenario after the next. He understood Hoyle as he understood himself and he'd studied every treatise on probability and chance. Nobody knew the game better than he did.

Except, apparently, Miss Farnsworth.

He really hoped she would keep herself out of his way going forward. She might be exceedingly pleasant to look at, but their encounters always ended unpleasantly.

"I know you are in the habit of winning," Lord Dalton said, "but you must practice being a more gracious loser. Rather unsportsmanlike to talk of trickery."

"I have no intention of playing the lady again," Hayes said through gritted teeth. "Further, it was not a trick exactly, but there is some method to her play that is new."

Lord Dalton snorted. "Careful you do not begin to sound like a boy who needs his governess while you're at it." The lord turned his horse down a side street toward his house and left Hayes on the avenue.

As he watched his friend's dark figure pass under a lamplight, Hayes attempted to brush off the sting of his friend's remarks. The sting was deuced hard to brush off, as it had the ring of truth. Regardless of what he'd thought in the moment, he should not have actually said it. Especially now that he'd had time to reflect. It had not been trickery, but it had been *something*.

He silently vowed that he would do his utmost to avoid Miss Farnsworth in future. He had lost sixty pounds to the lady and he would not lose a pound more.

LILY SAT IN the drawing room, barely attending to a piece of embroidery.

"Infuriating!" she whispered, once more reviewing Lord Ashworth's comment on trickery.

"Miss?"

She glanced up to see Ranier standing before her.

"Goodness, Ranier, I did not even hear you enter. I was too far away in my own thoughts."

Ranier nodded and said, "Whatever or whoever has infuriated you, I stand firmly against them."

Lily smiled. It was comforting to know that whatever went on out in the world, as far as Ranier was concerned, she was always in the right. The dear man did not even need to inquire into the circumstances before staunchly siding with her.

"You have little idea how much that sentiment cheers me," she said, taking the card the butler held out on a silver tray.

"Miss Darlington is here," Ranier said. "She is aware that it is not your at-home day, but decided she might chance a visit." The butler gazed over Lily's head and said disapprovingly, "She has arrived driving a phaeton, with a rather fierce looking boy of a tiger hanging off the back."

"I have heard of her penchant for it," Lily said. "Do show her in, Ranier."

The butler bowed and said, "I will arrange for tea forthwith."

Ranier left the room and Lily rose to greet Miss Darlington. She was eager to make the acquaintance of one who had already been so kind to her.

Miss Darlington fairly danced into the room behind Ranier. "There you are, Miss Farnsworth!"

Lily had not been sure what to expect, but the lady who stood before her had been nowhere in her imagination. She was more petite than Lily and hardly seemed a lady who could control the sort of horses that pulled a phaeton. Her copper curls wound charming circles round her features and her expression was all cheerful friendliness.

"Miss Darlington," Lily said, guiding her to a sofa. "How kind of you to come and see me."

"Nonsense," Miss Darlington said. "Cassandra recommended you highly and so I must make myself known to you as soon as I could."

"And *I* must thank you for the lovely things you sent to me in Surrey. I presume Cassandra told you I did not have the means to outfit myself in such a fashion."

"Yes, of course she did," Miss Darlington said. "Though you need not thank me again, your letter was quite sufficient. In any case, I was delighted to throw myself into the scheme— my father is very generous and I never know what to do with the money he gives me. That is, unless it's about the purchase of a horse. By the by, is your aunt nearby? I wonder if she would allow you to go on a drive, it is a very fine day and the park will not be crowded at this hour."

"In your phaeton?" Lily asked in some wonder.

"Yes, indeed in the phaeton. You are not to worry over it, I'm a capital whip."

Before Lily could respond to that particular comment, Mrs. Hemming came into the room. "Ah, it is so," she said. "Rainier told me a lady was here. Miss Darlington, well! Look at you! Those curls are the color of a copper roof. Before it goes green, you understand."

Lily's eyes widened at this assessment of Miss Darlington's hair, and dearly hoped the lady was not easily offended.

Miss Darlington only laughed and hopped up in an energetic fashion to make her curtsy to Mrs. Hemming.

"I wonder, Mrs. Hemming," Miss Darlington said, "if you would allow Lily to go on a drive. I find it is so conducive to conversation and the day is particularly fine."

"It would be in a phaeton, Aunt," Lily added, to be certain her aunt understood the real circumstance.

"In that phaeton just outside?" Mrs. Hemming asked.

"The very one," Miss Darlington said.

"But there's only a boy holding the reins. Goodness, did you drive it? Do you mean to drive my Lily in that contraption?"

"Just so," Miss Darlington said.

While her aunt considered this unique proposal, Lily hid a smile. *She* might think it unusual, but it was clear as day that Miss Darlington viewed it the most commonplace thing in the world.

"I am her guardian while she is here," Mrs. Hemming said to herself. "I must be careful on that front. On the other hand, there is no use denying the fineness of the day, I was just out there myself. This is a bit of a muddle."

"I can assure you, Mrs. Hemming, I am a very experienced whip and exceedingly sensible. There will be no racing down streets or chasing coaches or all that nonsense the gentlemen get up to. Further, my tiger can be counted upon to be a *veritable* tiger if we run anywhere near trouble. He is my father's own and well-armed."

This, for reasons only known to Mrs. Hemming, seemed to sway her opinion.

"I will agree to the scheme, as long as a carriage with two grooms follows behind. Lily, send word to your stable that you have need of them. There, I think that is a fine solution. I do not like to say no to a pleasant scheme, but I do not like to say yes unless everything is comfortably arranged."

Miss Darlington appeared delighted. Ranier, barely containing both his disapproval and alarm, said, "I will take the liberty of sending one of the footmen to the stables. The carriage will arrive shortly."

LILY'S CARRIAGE TROTTED to the doors before a half hour was up. When she had arrived to London, she had taken Ranier's advice that she might depend upon Mr. Thurber when selecting a carriage house. His stables were nearby, he was a reliable sort, and he only hired the most competent and respectful grooms.

Lily stepped outside, tying her bonnet, and nearly staggered. She was certain Cassandra had said Miss Darlington drove a conservative little phaeton, but that was not what was before her.

It was an exceedingly tall vehicle, with enormous wheels on the back, painted a bright yellow with black trim. It was light-boned but towered above her to such a degree that she wondered how it did not tip over. It was pulled by two fancy greys who pawed the ground when they caught sight of their mistress. The whole set-up looked suitable for a member of the Four-in-Hand.

"She's new," Miss Darlington said, gazing lovingly at her vehicle. "A Hooper High-Flyer. Goodness, I had a time of it convincing my father to buy it."

Miss Darlington lifted her skirts with one hand and deftly pulled herself up to the driver's seat with the other. Lily walked round to the other side, not having the least idea how she would mount.

Fortunately, one of the grooms who had come with the carriage raced ahead of her with a box to step on. Miss Darlington reached down for her hand and in a trice she was up. Lily felt as if she had just ascended a dizzying height. The ground seemed very far away.

Both grooms had appeared amused to hear that their carriage was to proceed empty and follow behind a lady whip, but that amusement had speedily disappeared when they'd watched Miss Darlington mount with ease and with no help from them. Then of course, there was her fierce-looking tiger hanging off the back, who seemed to find nothing amusing.

They set off, Lily clutching at the side of the phaeton as they rolled down the street. She slowly began to relax as she watched Miss Darlington expertly weave around stopped carriages, men on horseback, hackneys, a street sweeper, and lumbering wagons hauling supplies to one place or another.

As they passed through the Stanhope Gate and into the park, Miss Darlington herself seemed to relax. "There now," she said, "I've got you into the park safely, just as I promised I would."

"It is rather wonderful how you do it," Lily said.

"Bah," Miss Darlington said dismissively, "it is no great trick to develop a knack for horseflesh and the vehicles they pull. In any case, everybody has their own skill at things. I understand you are rather a master at piquet."

Lily felt the faintest of flushes. "I will not be missish and deny it," she said. "Though I do wish it was not talked of."

Miss Darlington expertly guided them toward the Serpentine. "I am not very good myself, and rather abominable at whist as any poor partner of mine would tell you," she said. "But if I *were* very good at cards, I should not at all mind trouncing Lord Ashworth."

Lily smiled. "I cannot claim to have minded it," she said. "He was so certain of his superiority."

"As they ever are," Miss Darlington said, laughing. "I blame their governesses, most young men are spoiled terribly. How is one to be humble when one has always been hailed as a veritable prince?"

"It is a shame, I think, that one so handsome should be so disagreeable," Lily said daringly.

"I suppose he is thought handsome," Miss Darlington said, "though I prefer a dark-haired man myself. Goodness, speak of the devil. Both of the devils, as a matter of fact."

Lily followed Miss Darlington's gaze. Lord Ashworth and another gentleman rode toward them.

"Why must he be here," Lily said softly. "It is a very strange hour to be out riding."

"And yet here we are too," Miss Darlington said.

Lily could not help but note Lord Ashworth's expression when he spotted the phaeton. It was one of consternation. She did not know who the other gentleman was, but he seemed exceedingly pleased by the oncoming phaeton.

Despite Lord Ashworth's less than complimentary expression, Lily could not help but note, once again, his good looks. He sat upon a fine bay and carelessly held the reins in one hand. He was tall in the saddle, his coat close-cut, and his interesting eyes could be seen even at a distance.

The gentlemen reined in their horses. "Miss Darlington, Miss Farnsworth," Lord Ashworth said. Lily thought he very much sounded like a butler announcing visitors.

"So this is Miss Farnsworth?" the other gentleman said.

"Miss Farnsworth," Miss Darlington said, "That gentleman with the ever-casual manners is Lord Cabot."

Lily nodded at the introduction.

Lord Cabot looked admiringly at the phaeton. "You have prevailed over your father, Miss Darlington."

"As you see, Lord Cabot," Miss Darlington said.

"And Miss Farnsworth prevails at the card table," Lord Cabot continued. "I fear the women take over the world. What say you, Ashworth?"

"So it seems," Lord Ashworth said.

"I do not think we attempt to take over any-thing," Lily said. "But I also do not think we should pretend to be less than what we are."

Lord Cabot laughed. "Come, Miss Farns-worth," he said, "it makes us gentlemen very comfortable when we can delude ourselves that we are superior in anything. The fairer sex has always assisted us in it."

Lily did not answer. Miss Darlington glanced at her, then said merrily, "Carry on with your delusions, then." She smartly slapped the reins and they moved off, leaving the two gentlemen behind.

As they trotted along the Serpentine, they were silent for some moments. Finally, Miss Darlington said, "I would not have stopped if I had perceived how uncomfortable it would be for you to meet Lord Ashworth. I had thought he would take his losses at cards with all good humor."

"I have yet to see that particular lord display good humor over anything, Miss Darlington," Lily said.

Miss Darlington laughed and said, "You'd better call me Penny. I am firmly decided on being your staunch defender against Lord Ashworth's disagreeableness."

Lily smiled. "And you will call me Lily."

Though Lily was more than discomfited to have encountered Lord Ashworth in the park, and to experience his coolness, she was at least satisfied that she had made a friend in Penny Darlington.

THE LORDS CABOT and Ashworth had neared the gate out of Hyde Park as Lord Cabot nattered on about their recent encounter with Miss Darlington and Miss Farnsworth.

Though Cabot did not mention it, Hayes could not be entirely satisfied with himself. Dalton's caution not to appear as if he needed a governess still rang in his ears and he could not ignore his less than genial comportment upon encountering Miss Farnsworth.

He could not countenance displaying any sort of unsportsmanlike behavior and he was afraid that he had in his recent encounters with the lady. That he supposed she employed some method of play he did not yet understand was not an excuse for rudeness. It had slowly dawned on him that his aggravation with the lady was in large part caused by his aggravation with himself.

He'd never found himself in such a situation! To be beaten, handily and twice, by a lady.

"Miss Farnsworth, eh?" Lord Cabot said. "She's a pretty enough filly."

"No doubt," Hayes answered.

"I know her looks are the type you go for, so on behalf of all the gentlemen of the pact, I say I am glad she has invoked your ire at a card table. No danger of you falling for the lady now!"

"Certainly not," Hayes said.

"Shall you go to Lady Carradine's this evening?" Lord Cabot asked. "I've determined to give up hazard and so may make that house my preferred establishment. No hazard table, no fine wine, no chance to empty my purse. I am determined to carefully guard what's left of my funds in anticipation of Newmarket."

"It is unlikely I will be at Lady Carradine's," Hayes said. "Or if I go it will be late. Lady Catherine's dreadful ball is this evening. As you know, my mother would skin me if I did not attend."

"Good God," Lord Cabot said laughing, "is the old thing still alive and going on with it?"

Hayes nodded.

"Well, at least Grayson will be there to keep your spirits up. He never has any luck dodging the engagement either."

Hayes suspected Grayson would be one of the few people he was anxious to meet there. Every year he was forced to attend Lady Catherine's ball. His mother was a dear friend of the lady, having been steered through her first season by the dowager countess. That the lady must be in danger of departing her sixtieth decade by now had not appeared to slow her down.

The ball would be a small one, as it was always. The invitations would be carefully curated and apparently no consideration would be given to a lady's looks. Those invited would be families who were considered to be of the right type by Lady Catherine, and the year before he'd spent the evening dancing with one tiresome female after another.

Where did the lady even find such creatures? He dreaded encountering Miss Blaise again, as he had heard the lady was as yet unmarried—she had bulging eyes and was forever directing those orbs in his direction. When she was not staring, she embarked on something he supposed was flirtation—it consisted of blinking, high-pitched chortles, and fan waving. Occasionally, she would swat his arm with her fan and claim he was *"Very bad,"* though he'd not said anything.

He had wondered if the lady could read his thoughts, for they had been in truth *very* bad.

Then, of course, there would be the supper. A small table graced with old-fashioned, heavy dishes, and he forced to entertain some person he was certain he would not like.

He was only thankful such an evening came but once a year.

OF THE MANY invitations that had arrived to Mrs. Hemming's door, most could be attributed to Cassandra's efforts on Lily's behalf. One invitation, though, could only be ascribed to Mrs. Hemming herself. Lady Catherine Markham, Dowager Countess of Thornbridge, was a very old friend of Mrs. Hemming. They had met in the late 1790s and discovered in each other a keen interest in whist. They were often partners at this or that card party and knew each other's play so well they could practically read each other's thoughts. Mrs. Hemming had ever been in the habit of attending Lady Catherine's annual ball, as she could count on an interesting evening of cards and a good supper at the end of it.

Lily had been told of the peculiar nature of the ball, its small size and its interesting collection of people Lady Catherine favored. According to Mrs. Hemming, Lady Catherine felt it her duty to bring together those from suitably old families in the hopes that there might be some marriages made. Though Lady Catherine thought herself quite the matchmaker, Mrs. Hemming could not recall any particular match ever having been accomplished.

When Lily had looked over her dresses, she'd settled on the midnight blue satin. She was well aware that had her aunt not been Lady Catherine's favored whist partner, Lily Farnsworth from Surrey would not have received an invitation at all. The gown was simple in its cut and would not put her forward in any way. Lily did not wish for Lady Catherine to regret her decision.

CHAPTER SEVEN

Lady Catherine Markham, Dowager Countess of Thornbridge, had never been impressed by the *ton*. It was her estimation that far too much weight was thrown on the side of money, fashion, and glib manners. Lady Catherine was not impressed by any of those things. The only attribute that interested the lady was bloodlines.

Could a family's line be traced back to *at least* the fifteenth century? Or were they some sort of newcomer with pretensions?

She employed a gentleman who researched such things, as it was her wish to keep England's bloodlines unsullied. He was the second gentleman to hold the post, as she'd had to dismiss the first when he insisted that if close relations married too often down the generations, it could result in physical and mental deformities. What an old-fashioned notion—had not Henry Tudor decisively ruled on the subject with the Marriage Act of 1540? Deformities might arise in the lower classes. After all, who really knew what sort of muddled blood they carried round? The nobles, on the other hand, had rarified blood that could not be sullied. It only made sense that first cousins should marry.

When she sent out the invitations to her annual ball each year, it was with an eye toward uniting the young people of various old houses. Upon hearing that her friend Amelia Hemming currently had her niece staying with her, she'd set her man on a quest to document the girl's bloodline. There had not been anything to recommend it and Lady Catherine found herself torn—the girl should not be included in her illustrious company, but she did so prefer to partner with Amelia Hemming at whist. In the end, she'd issued the invitation despite some misgivings. Let nobody think Lady Catherine Markham was illiberal.

Lady Catherine could not say what she had expected of Miss Farnsworth, except to suppose she would be a small and retiring sort of person who would be awed to be in the presence of England's *real* nobility. She had, therefore, been surprised to find the girl pretty. Very pretty and elegantly dressed, if she were forced to swear to it in church.

As Lady Catherine scanned the ballroom room, she could not help but to wonder why so many girls with pristine and gloried descents should be so plain. Poor Miss Blaise—she could trace her family back to the twelfth century, but why must her eyes resemble that of a fish? Why must she dress in a silver silk, which only reminded one of a landed carp? Lady Catherine could only hope that some gentleman in attendance this evening would see the girl's true value and look past any outward charms that might fail to present themselves.

That hope was forced to waver somewhat, in noting that it was Miss Farnsworth who seemed to garner most of the attention.

Lady Catherine quietly sighed. At least she would have Amelia Hemming as her whist partner. That must serve as consolation.

HAYES WAS STUDIOUSLY avoiding the eye of Miss Blaise, who was just as determinedly trying to catch his own. In truth, he hardly knew where to look, there were so many directions to avoid.

Much to his surprise, he'd seen Miss Farnsworth enter the ballroom. He'd had no notion that she could be one of Lady Catherine's set. He'd thought she came from some middling family in Surrey, and in any case, she was a deal too pretty in a dark blue gown to be in attendance at *this* particular ball.

At least there would be no card game with Miss Farnsworth. While the older people in attendance would settle to whist, the paltry number of single gentlemen in attendance would be required to be on the ballroom floor.

"My God," Lord Grayson said, standing next to him. "What on earth is happening to Lady Catherine's ball? She has let in a pretty girl."

"That is Miss Farnsworth," Hayes said quietly.

"Indeed," Grayson said thoughtfully. "How interesting. Well, let us not allow the moss to grow on our boots, her card will be filled in a trice."

"I have no intention of entering my name on the lady's card," Hayes said.

"Do not be ridiculous," Grayson said dismissively. "If you do not apply to her, you will seem a poor sport. You might get away with it at a large ball, but she is clearly superior to every female here and your motives for passing her over will be mocked from here to Brighton. It will be said that Lord Ashworth experiences a temper tantrum upon losing at cards."

Hayes bristled at the idea, though he knew very well that Grayson was right. Further, he had been waiting for his opportunity to show the world he was not bothered by losing a few hands at piquet.

Grayson grasped his arm and pulled him forward. "Hurry now, or we shall be beaten to it."

LILY HAD GUESSED from her aunt's description that Lady Catherine's ball might be somewhat odd. Most glaring, there were not so many people as would be usual. Perhaps if it were to be a small party confined to the drawing room, with a dance struck up by somebody on the pianoforte, it might seem the thing. But this was to be a formal ball, with an orchestra, and there were not above sixteen couples.

Worse, of all people who should find their way in the door, there was Lord Ashworth.

He was impeccably dressed, as always. His coat perfectly tailored to his tall frame and his cravat tied elegantly simple, its only adornment a small emerald pin. He stood talking to a gentleman Lily did not know.

Though she could not help admiring Lord Ashworth's physical person, she had no particular wish to speak to him. She could not say the same for a lady in silver silk, who seemed to regard him as a quarry that must be silently stolen up on. The lady had been staring at him and edging ever closer for some minutes.

Lily turned away as she noted the lady in

silver silk was to be disappointed in her attempt to capture. Both Lord Ashworth and the unknown gentleman made their way toward her.

"Oh dear," Mrs. Hemming said to her softly. "No card game here, Lily. I must be firm on that idea, Lady Catherine would not like it. She abhors low gossip. So she says, in any case."

"You must not fear on that front, Aunt," Lily said. "He shall not goad me into it, though he will likely do his best."

The gentlemen had arrived and Lily curtsied.

"May I, Miss Farnsworth?" Lord Ashworth said, holding out his hand.

Lily handed over her card as she did not know what else to do. Why would he take a dance? It was most unaccountable.

As Lord Ashworth put his name down, he said, "Miss Farnsworth, Mrs. Hemming, may I present Lord Grayson?"

Lord Grayson executed a bow with rather more flourish than Lily was used to seeing.

"Mrs. Hemming, delighted," Lord Grayson said. "Miss Farnsworth, charmed. May I hope to be among your partners this evening?"

Lord Ashworth had done with her card and Lord Grayson took it from him. Lily noted the peculiar twinkle in his eye as he viewed it. "I see these callow youth who have gamed up the courage to take a dance with Miss Farnsworth did not go so far as to dare supper. But you,

Ashworth? I am surprised that I find myself so fortunate."

And with that, Lord Grayson marked his name down for the dance before supper.

THOUGH LILY HAD thought Lord Grayson had been unfair to deem the gentleman on her card as callow youth who had not dared supper, her opinion underwent a significant transformation after the ball had begun. It felt as if she were back in Surrey again—perspiring hands leaving a mark on her glove and a trodding of toes for good measure. Even more uncomfortable, the young gentlemen seemed to be not very experienced in polite conversation. She had been rather more lectured to than conversed with.

She was to know that Mr. Hackeray was the younger son of an earl whose family went back to the fourteenth century. He had come to London to marry an heiress and pour that lady's fortune into a crumbling estate he'd come into. He would bring the house back to its former glory. He had quietly mused that any lady would be eager to take on the esteemed Hackeray name. Lily had quickly assured him that, despite the scheme's obvious allure, she was no heiress. He seemed to take it very badly.

Lord Claymoore, on the other hand, spoke of his family seat, Granger Hall. Lily was to understand all of its glories, including drafty rooms, murder holes, and secret passageways. The family did not go in for modernization and they stuck to old habits as they had done for hundreds of years. She was to know that the family did not approve of excessive amounts of vegetables, though their table *could* be counted on to provide meat of every sort. If it was good enough for Henry Tudor's table, it was good enough for them.

Lily hinted that while Granger Hall sounded rather marvelous, she had a weak chest and would find herself dead inside of a year in such drafty accommodations. The Lord had briefly toyed with the idea of modernizing a bedchamber or sitting room, and even providing the occasional lettuce, but Lily had put an end to those ruminations by gently coughing.

All in all, Lily thought it fortunate that these fellows were born to families of some consideration, for had they been left to make their own way in the world they would surely have starved by the roadside.

She had not at all looked forward to finding herself Lord Ashworth's partner. Though over time, and with the help of her clumsy partners, her dread had faded to a remarkable degree. At least he would be counted on to leave her toes alone and she doubted he would lecture her on the charms of his estates or what was put on the table in those places.

Now, he led her to the floor. His hand appeared dry on her glove and exerted just the proper amount of pressure. She felt she was guided by a man who knew what he was about and it gave her a thrill after the tediousness that the evening had so far provided. His tall person moved with an elegance that Lord Claymoore and Mr. Hackeray could only aspire to.

As they waited their turn, Lord Ashworth said, "Miss Farnsworth, I dislike enmity with anybody and hope that we can be on friendly terms."

Lily was silent for a moment. It was precisely the sort of thing a gentleman highly placed would say. While another might feel pressed to apologize for rude behavior, the lord simply wished her to know he found discord disagreeable.

"My lord," she said carefully, "to be accused of trickery is not easy to dismiss."

The lord had the good grace to flush. He said, "I regret the use of that word. I did not mean to imply cheating of any sort; I know that was not the case. I should have been more careful in my speech."

Lily only nodded.

"What I meant was that there is some method you employ that I have never encountered. I was surprised by it."

"Apparently so," Lily said, wondering if he would ever get round to a proper apology.

"I was correct?" Lord Ashworth said. "There is a method?"

"Indeed," Lily said.

"I wonder if you—"

"No," Lily said firmly.

The lord was not able to proceed further with the inquiry, as it was their turn.

He led her through the changes with grace, which was a relief considering her other partners. Not worrying about her toes gave her time to think. The lord was convinced that she had developed some method in her play. She supposed she had, though it was not one that she could teach to another, even if she cared to, which she did not.

It had not escaped her that others did not have the same facility for remembering cards that she did. She had noted it with Lord Ashworth when last they played, and others in Surrey. In fact, she had always known her memory was better than most. Was she not the person everybody turned to when an item was lost? She could view in her mind where she'd last seen the item. If she had not seen it, she was as hopeless as everybody else in locating it, but if she *had* seen it and it had not been moved, she could recall it in a trice.

In fact, she had just received a letter from her

sister Rose, asking after a particular spool of yellow thread. She would write back that it sat on a windowsill in the schoolroom, just behind a curtain. She had noted it there months ago when she'd chanced to pull the curtain back to look out onto the park. Now, she could see it as well as if she were in Farnsworth House looking at it.

The skill was a blessing when it came to cards, and one Lord Ashworth would have to carry on without. Let him believe she'd studied heavy tomes on gambling and chance and had developed some new strategy. She hadn't, though she had tried. She had located an old book full of numbers and odds in her father's library and had stolen it away to her bedchamber. There, the words and numbers fairly swam in front of her eyes and she had given it up. Lily Farnsworth was not a learned scholar, but she had a *very* good memory for what she saw.

The rest of the dance with Lord Ashworth had carried on in a more regular fashion, he apparently understanding she had no wish to talk further on the subject of cards. They had some desultory conversation about Lord and Lady Hampton, as they were a mutual acquaintance, and then she was collected by Lord Grayson.

That lord, unlike Lord Ashworth, was all pleasantries. In truth, he was all flattery. While she enjoyed it, Lily found it made her a bit wary, too. She almost began to wonder if he thought she was an heiress of some sort.

Still, he took her into supper and entertained with amusing stories and did not once mention any card games she may have been involved in. He was all geniality and Lily wished she could say the same for Lord Ashworth.

He was across the table and had taken in Miss Fitch, though Miss Blaise was on his other side and each time he turned to her, he looked as if he'd bitten into a lemon. Miss Blaise did not seem to notice and spent a deal of time hitting his arm with her fan and telling him he was *very bad*.

THE LORDS ASHWORTH and Grayson trotted through the quiet streets of Mayfair. It was just past one in the morning, Lady Catherine's balls never going on too late from excessive enthusiasm.

"Well, my friend," Grayson said cheerily, "we have done it. We have survived another of Lady Catherine's dreadful soirees and you have dodged Miss Blaise for the third year running."

"I wish the lady would cease hitting me with her fan," Hayes said.

"She cannot!" Grayson cried with glee. "You are so very bad, she says."

"Perhaps she will marry some country squire

or other and trouble us no more," Hayes said.

"She does not trouble me in the least," Grayson said. "In fact, I had a remarkably fine evening, considering where we were. Miss Farnsworth is everything charming."

Hayes did not answer his friend. In truth, Miss Farnsworth *was* charming now that the sting of his losses to her had begun to fade. Somehow, dancing with her had softened his view.

He'd had more than one thought of unpinning her hair, never more than when he'd led the lady through the steps. He'd found himself unhappy when Grayson came to collect her and wondered if he ought not have taken the dance before supper. After all, what cared he for the loss of sixty pounds? What cared he for anything said about it? It had all begun to seem a bit of nonsense after he'd touched her hand and found himself in such close proximity.

Miss Farnsworth was a beauty and she was clever. He had never imagined that a lady might develop a method or strategy at cards, but she'd admitted as much. Though, she would not reveal her secret and he supposed he'd no right to ask.

It had dawned on him that he'd taken the whole thing so seriously because of his peculiar situation. While most gentlemen played for amusement, *he* played to keep his family afloat. It was a far more serious pastime. She was not to know that, though. And certainly, it was not right to condemn her over her remarkable skill at the game.

His condemnation had slowly transformed itself into admiration, though he could not claim the lady's own feelings had changed. He assumed she disliked him thoroughly and he knew he had earned it.

"Miss Farnsworth might be just the thing," Grayson said. "I think myself half in love with her already and one always requires a pleasant girl to while away the season with."

Hayes stared at his friend. "You do not mean to make Miss Farnsworth your latest flirtation?"

"Why ever not?" Grayson said. He reined his horse in from a trot.

Hayes reined in Horus.

"I turn here," Grayson said, "I promised old Crackwilder I'd stop in for a port. He was an excellent lieutenant, despite his rather bookish nature. He saved my skin more than once. I've vowed never to lose touch with him and he swears he never retires before three."

Grayson turned his horse and trotted down a side street. Hayes watched him disappear into the shadows and then turned his own horse home.

Until this moment, Grayson's flirtations had been amusing. Every season, the man homed in on some girl recently arrived to town. Flattery and flirtation were his calling cards, though he never let the thing go too far. The young lady would be overcome with his attentions and the idea that she might find herself a duchess someday. The girl's mama would be embarrassingly encouraging. Toward the end of the season there would be the inevitable cooling off. The lady would go home with a basket of disappointed hopes and a furious mother riding beside her, though most would say nothing of it to save themselves embarrassment.

Grayson always claimed he liked to be in love or to be challenged, but alas the love and the challenge never made it quite a full season. Therefore, he was scrupulous in his words. No lady he had trifled with could accuse him of declaring himself. No parent could demand that he honor a promise never given.

But Miss Farnsworth!

Hayes paused. Why *not* Miss Farnsworth? What was it to him if the lady was so foolish as to come under the sway of Grayson's rather shallow charms?

After all, it was not as if his friend would actually marry the lady.

But what if, by some miracle, Grayson *did* marry the lady? What was that to him? Aside from encouraging the old dukes in their ridiculous pact, why should he concern himself over whether Miss Farnsworth would end disappointed or the next marchioness? He might now find he admired the lady, and there was no use denying her looks, but that was all.

"It is nothing to me," Hayes said to the empty street. "I only think his friends ought to curtail Grayson's flirtations. He runs too much risk of being caught at the altar or dueling an enraged brother."

LILY AND HER aunt had finally departed Lady Catherine's house. Lily gazed out on the dark streets, thinking of Lord Ashworth.

She was well aware that he'd appeared in so favorable a light that evening because the other gentlemen on hand had not. Well, she supposed Lord Grayson could not be condemned, he'd been all amiability. Though, Lord Grayson did not have... he was not... what was it?

She could not say and, really, there was no use attempting to puzzle it out. Lord Ashworth had made as good an apology as she would ever get and that was the end of it. She very much doubted he would ever again put his name to her card at any of the balls on her calendar. They were all to be much larger and he would have his choice of ladies to squire.

"That was a very pleasant evening," Mrs. Hemming said. "Lady Catherine and I won handily at whist, as was to be expected. I cannot imagine how Lord and Lady Cavill have played cards these twenty years and yet remain so bad at it—it's as if they'd never met one another. I suppose you had a tolerable time? Though I admit myself surprised that Lord Ashworth was so eager to dance with you."

Lily smiled at the thought. "Dear Aunt," she said, "the very last descriptive I would use for Lord Ashworth is eager."

"I suppose not," Mrs. Hemming said. "But then, Lord Grayson seemed terribly genial."

"That he is," Lily said. "I suspect he makes a career out of it."

"You may be right," Mrs. Hemming said. "I am sure I heard something about a girl with disappointed hopes last season. On the other hand, I find people often are responsible for disappointing *themselves*, so one wonders. Are you tired, my dear?"

"Not especially, Aunt. I presume you are not either. Perhaps I could read to you for an hour or so?"

"I was thinking we might stop in at Lady Carradine's club. We are not far off."

CHAPTER EIGHT

L ILY OPENED HER eyes. From the brightness behind the curtains, she guessed she had slept very late. She was not surprised by it. She and her aunt had not returned from Lady Carradine's club until nearly dawn.

What an evening! It had all been so new to her.

They had arrived to a large stone house, whitewashed and sporting a large portico. Mrs. Hemming had shown her how the front door was left unlocked and how one was to let oneself in. There was a cloakroom and a man there to take their coats. Then, they proceeded down a long corridor with a drawing room on one side and a library on the other. Various servants milled about and Lily thought their eyes were more trained on her and Mrs. Hemming than on any task they had been sent to accomplish. They reached large double doors at the end of the corridor and a man seemed to appear from nowhere to let them in.

They entered a cavernous room, tastefully decorated. Its plastered walls were painted an elegant cream, its carpets thick under her feet. Lily suspected it had once been a ballroom, such was its size and dimensions, but now it contained tables of people playing at cards. In the center, was a larger table with a dealer.

Mrs. Hemming stared at the center table and said quietly, "That is new."

Before Lily could inquire about it, Lady Carradine bustled over to greet them. "Dear Mrs. Hemming," the lady said, "how good of you to come to my little club. And, you bring a guest!"

"This is my niece, Lady Carradine. Miss Lily Farnsworth. I thought she might be amused to come and look about. She is very good at piquet, by the by."

A man who had been standing to Lily's left sidled over to them. "Cousin, you must introduce me to these two lovely young ladies."

Mrs. Hemming, never one to be conquered by flattery and having no illusion about her looks or her age, ignored the idea that she and her niece must be equal in years. Instead, she said, "Did you say cousin, sir?"

"Indeed," the man said. "My dear cousin,

Lady Carradine, and I have gone into business together and so you shall see me here often."

"Mr. Shine," Lady Carradine said, her lips rather tight, "may I present Mrs. Hemming and Miss Farnsworth."

Mr. Shine bowed low.

Mrs. Hemming said, "May I ask, what is that large table? What are they doing?"

"Vingt-et-un," Mr. Shine said smoothly.

Lily's aunt seemed surprised by it. Lady Carradine said, "My cousin has convinced me that my patrons would find entertainment in the game."

"Oh, not for me," Mrs. Hemming said. "Those sorts of games rely too much from the heavens choosing to rain down luck upon one's head."

Mr. Shine seemed momentarily put out, but he recovered himself and said, "Did I hear rightly that somebody is skilled at piquet?"

"Oh, my niece is very good, Mr. Shine," Mrs. Hemming said. "I must warn you about that. Though really, I cannot say why I should warn you, now that I think of it. I do not suppose anybody has ever warned me that they were very good at whist. I should think it rather bad form if they did."

"I consider myself warned," Mr. Shine said, appearing eager to end Mrs. Hemming's debate with herself. "Now, Miss Farnsworth, perhaps we can get up a little game together to pass the time?"

Lily had looked hopefully at her aunt.

Lady Carradine had motioned to an older woman dressed in a somber attire. "Mrs. Melton would be happy to sit at the table with Miss Farnsworth."

Lily assumed Mrs. Melton to be one of those ladies employed to maintain propriety by acting as companion to any lady choosing to play against a gentleman.

Mrs. Hemming said, "Mrs. Melton, very reliable woman. Well, Lily, if you wish it, I see no harm. I see Lady Edith over there without a whist partner, perhaps I will join her. As long as you do not mind it."

Lily did not mind it at all.

Hours later, she had left with forty pounds. She'd not found Mr. Shine a particularly skilled player—Lily had played against far better in Surrey. She had even suggested they quit after the first play, when he had only lost five pounds. Though she liked to gamble, she did not like to take advantage and he was not a very worthy opponent.

He did not see himself as unworthy, though. He seemed to think himself very skilled and only the victim of terrible luck.

Mrs. Melton watched him like a hawk, and not a very friendly or amused hawk. Aside from what Lily presumed was her general opinion of men, that they must be monitored at all times, she also did not seem to have much faith in this particular man's skill at cards. She *tsk-tsked* at his every loss.

Mr. Shine was only pushed to quit when Mrs. Hemming came to collect Lily, otherwise he might have gone on all night, facing down Mrs. Melton and hoping to be granted a reversal from his terrible luck.

Lily stretched out and pulled the coverlet up to her chin. Lady Carradine's club had been marvelous. She closed her eyes and saw the whole room before her, from the chandeliers with their sparkling crystals to the intricately engraved packs of cards, the backs a charming drawing of a garden gate with pink roses winding round it. Her aunt had promised they would return soon, and it might even be as early as this evening. They were to go to a dinner held by one of Mrs. Hemming's longstanding friends and those dinners did not have a propensity to run late.

THE LORDS ASHWORTH and Cabot had taken a table at Destin's and waited for their coffee.

"How goes the regiment?" Hayes asked.

This was understood by Lord Cabot to be a reference to his current living situation. Since the old dukes had halved their incomes, he and Grayson had found it convenient to move into Dalton's house. Ashworth had not and paid the bill on his own rented house with gambling. He'd gamely pitched in for his friends' upkeep, but he had no intention of living with them. He'd said he'd rather starve than recreate his military career and its inherent lack of privacy. Further, he'd never shared a butler or a footman since he'd reached his majority and would not start now.

"We go on jolly enough," Lord Cabot said. "Dalton has a cracking wine cellar, though he's got some churlish servants. I'll swear they make faces behind one's back when one has announced one will stay in. Dalton says they are used to drinking his wine when the master is not at home and they wish we would all go out and stay out."

"I do not know why Dalton puts up with Bellamy," Hayes said of his friend's butler.

"If you saw some of the company Dalton entertains and Bellamy's lack of raised eyebrows over it, you might not wonder at it," Lord Cabot said drily. "By the by, I heard from Grayson that Lady Catherine's ball was more entertaining than usual. He seems thoroughly set on your lovely nemesis, Miss Farnsworth."

Hayes bristled to hear it spoken of so casually. "Grayson must stop this nonsense. If he wishes for female companionship, he might go to the theater and find himself a mistress. This toying with ladies of the *ton* will be the undoing of him one of these days."

Lord Cabot straightened his cuffs and said, "Perhaps it will be Miss Farnsworth who is his undoing. Though, God knows if another of us fall I do not see how we'll ever convince our fathers to leave us alone for another year or two."

"Miss Farnsworth will hardly find herself mesmerized by Grayson's smarmy advances," Lord Ashworth said stiffly. "She is a deal too clever and she is pretty enough to capture wide attention. He will not be the only gentleman giving chase."

Lord Cabot looked at his friend critically. "And you, Ashworth? Shall you give chase?"

"Certainly not," Lord Ashworth said firmly. "I have no intention of even considering marriage for another two years. At that time, I will consider my options. But even then, I will not tie myself to a lady who is…"

Lord Cabot suppressed his laughter. "Who is what?" he asked. "Certainly, there is nothing against the lady but her skill at cards."

Marty Destin set two coffees in front of them and then disappeared to the back of the house. It was one of his skills to be as unobtrusive as possible and seem as if he'd heard nothing.

Hayes toyed with his spoon. Though he had

come to admire Miss Farnsworth, he found he did not like to admit it. Not to himself or anybody else. "I simply find that the lady is too out of the ordinary," he said. "I do not like to think of a future duchess gambling like a card sharp. After all, how much time must she have spent perfecting the skill? I have to assume that the development of more feminine arts was cast aside in pursuit of it."

Hayes forced himself to stop talking. He sounded ridiculous. Since when had he come up with a list of attributes for a duchess? He was perfectly well aware that he'd run on in such an absurd fashion because he could not precisely explain what his true feelings were in regard to Miss Farnsworth. He could only be certain that he did not look with favor upon Grayson turning his eye toward the lady.

"Ah," Lord Cabot said. "I had not known you were so interested in a lady's skill at sewing, or drawing, or painting fire screens, or whatever else they get up to. Do not allow Miss Darlington to hear of such opinions, I believe she has thrown over all of those pursuits for her horses."

Hayes waved his hand. "Miss Darlington is her own case, she is the daughter of Lord Mendbridge. I do not see how she would be anything other than what she is. You see, that is the difference."

That his friend Cabot failed to see the difference was all too apparent. Hayes focused on his coffee and changed the subject to Cabot's own horses. If there was one thing Cabot could be depended upon to expound on endlessly, it was his horses, other people's horses, horses he'd seen in the park, and horses he intended to breed someday.

LADY CARRADINE WATCHED in some trepidation as Mr. Shine laid in new packs of cards in the parlor. She still had quite a good stock of packs, bought from a reputable printer, and had seen no reason why new packs must be employed. Further, though the design was the same, she did not know the printing house. She'd examined them closely, wishing to be certain they were unmarked, and had been satisfied on that front. That left her to conclude he'd got them on the cheap, and that did not suit. Her club was appreciated for its quiet elegance. She did not think it would do her reputation much good if the new cards turned out to be less than well made. Cheap cards did not hold up well and players noticed when they held something flimsy in their hands.

"I really do not see why you must upend everything you look at," Lady Carradine said.

Mr. Shine turned to her and said, "Nancy, you have been only muddling along. If I am to make my fortune, changes must be made. You spend too much to account for what comes in."

"Do not call me that name!" she said in a heated whisper. "A servant might overhear you."

Mr. Shine chuckled. "But they would not understand what they heard, would they? It is only I that know that you were, and are, a lady's maid. Though you do a creditable job of pretending otherwise."

Lady Carradine's heart sank, as it had so often during these awful weeks.

When Mr. Shine had first arrived with her secret in his pocket, she had thought she might learn to live with her new business partner. After all, what else was she to do and splitting the profits still gave her enough to live on. Over time, though, she'd begun to understand that she was in grave danger.

First, the day she'd been unaccountably ill. She'd risen in good health, but shortly after breakfast a heavy tiredness had stolen over her. She'd gone back to bed and did not awaken until the late afternoon. She'd dressed and fetched her keys from the dresser, suddenly noticing that two seemed a different shade, not as tarnished as they had been. She'd made her way downstairs and looked at the locks around the house. All seemed as it should, until she noticed a small shaving of wood on the floor outside the bank room and felt wet paint around the locks on the front doors. She was certain Mr. Shine had drugged her so he might have the locks changed at his leisure. He had his own keys.

Her senses had been heightened since then and she did all she could to watch his every move. He seemed always to be looking about the house, though she did not know what he was looking for. He seemed always to be staring at her when he thought she would not note it.

One evening, after the last guest had left, she'd found the courage to challenge him. She'd said he might go ahead and carry out his threats to tell the world her secret. She claimed that if it came down to it, she would be believed above some unknown person just arrived from America. He could not prove she was not Lady Carradine.

All he'd said was, "Nancy, do not be daft. I've already dug a hole six feet deep in the basement in case of any unpleasantness."

She'd pretended to laugh it off, but once the house had gone quiet and she could hear his snores down the corridor, she'd crept down to the basement. The kitchen took up one half of it, but beyond a door was a near empty storeroom with an unfinished dirt floor. She'd unlatched the hook and pressed the door open. On the other side of some stacked boxes was a hole the size of a grave.

Whatever was to be the end of this ghastly situation, she would not wait to find herself buried in the basement.

She had searched her mind, high and low, for a way to rid herself of Mr. Shine. She had even got so far as to consider poisoning the man and burying him in his own recently-dug grave, but recoiled as she imagined herself swinging from the gallows.

She could not stay in her current situation, it was untenable. She never knew what he'd do next. Might he not poison *her*, claim she'd returned to America, and forge documents leaving the establishment to himself? *She* might fear swinging from the gallows, but she doubted Mr. Shine would be put off by the idea. All her waking hours felt dangerous just now, she was always on edge. It could not continue for much longer.

The only real idea she'd come upon was to steal away with the bank and leave the house and her business behind. With what she had learned about managing a gambling establishment, might she not start over somewhere? Might she not try New Orleans? She understood the city to be a wild and unregulated sort of place—precisely where she might slip in as Nancy while Lady Carradine would never be heard from again.

Watching Mr. Shine just now with his dirty

hands all over her tables, she decided to do just that. The bank was healthy, Mr. Shine believed her to be in his power, and she thought she had an excellent chance to board a ship. When she had first considered the idea, she had consulted Lloyd's List. She might board the Marie Louise to Charleston if she could reach Portsmouth in time. There was no use in waiting. Her difficulties with Mr. Shine would only continue to worsen until one of them was dead.

She must leave tonight.

LILY HAD FELT in great need of a walk in the afternoon, before their evening engagement at Mrs. Millican's and the hoped-for visit to Lady Carradine's club afterward. In the country, she had been used to long meanderings over the estate, either on foot or on horseback. Now she felt her legs had almost grown weaker from so much sitting and being carried here and there in a carriage.

Mrs. Hemming, never liking to walk when she might sit, had sent Pips and a footman to accompany her niece. While there was not much to see and admire on Cork Street, Berkeley Square was not too far a walk and had the benefit of providing welcome shade from the maples that adorned its park.

They had reached the square as Lily suppressed a smile over Pips' huffs and puffs and quiet mutterings. She thought the lady's maid could do with a bit more exercise than she'd been in the habit of taking.

She slowed her gait to allow Pips to catch her breath. She might have slowed herself in any case. The park was lovely and the shade from the trees welcome. At such a spot, there was no cause to hurry oneself. As she passed number thirty-eight, a young urchin flew down the steps and collided into her. Fast behind him was a starched and irate butler wielding a long wood paddle.

The boy clutched her skirts and said, "Don't ya let him kill me, miss."

Lily looked up sharply at the butler, who had paused himself on the steps. He said sternly, "Unhand that lady this instant, you low devil!"

Lily then looked back down at the boy, whose face was now upturned to her own. He still clutched at her skirts, and she would rather he did not as his hands were exceedingly dirty. In truth, his whole person was exceedingly dirty. In his favor, though, was his youth. This was no hardened lad, he still had the rounded cheeks of babyhood and could not be more than six or seven.

She unclenched his hands from her skirts and said, "Now, nobody is going to harm you."

The boy looked dubious over this idea, especially since the butler still had the club in his hand. And then especially dubious because Pips scolded him in harsh whispers over the marks on Lily's dress.

Lily said to the butler, "Do lower that weapon, sir. Now goodness, what is happening here?"

Pips leaned in close to her ear and whispered, "Let us get on, now. This is none of our affair."

Lily inwardly sighed. It was an attitude that rankled. If one who could did not stand up for one who could not, was not the human race doomed? Her father, despite his straightened circumstances, had always done what he could for those in even worse circumstances. Her mother had not shied away from letting herself into the slovenliest hovel to tend a sick child. Here was a very young boy in some distress. Was Lily Farnsworth to pretend it was none of her concern? She rather thought not.

"Humanity is always our affair, Pips," Lily said sternly. She glanced at her aunt's footman to see if he would dare counter the sentiment. He smiled at her and she thought he understood her sentiments exactly.

"Now sir, do lower that bat," Lily directed the butler, "and tell me what all the fuss is about."

The butler had the good grace to lower his club, though he did not put it down. He said,

"The fuss, as you inquire into it my good lady, is that *this* young ruffian is forever hanging about on *these* steps. It is not the first time I have chased him off. Further, when he is not lounging about he is begging for money. In front of this very residence!"

Lily looked to the boy. "Is that true, young man?" she asked.

The boy shuffled his feet. "I only sit on these steps 'cause they got the best shade from the trees. It gets hot, don't you know."

"And begging for money?" Lily asked. "Is that true as well?"

"Not a lot of money, miss. I only need a tuppence a day. I ain't what's called greedy and I don't steal it, mind."

"Get your tuppence in your own neighbor-hood!" the butler cried.

The boy looked at the butler with a solemn expression. "Not nobody in St. Giles got an extra tuppence."

"Goodness," Lily said, "and do you live with your parents there? Do they know what you get up to?"

"I live with me ma and the tuppence is for our dinner so a'course she knows it. Me dad, whoever he is, went and flown the coop," the boy said matter-of-factly. "I don't mind it, she says he was a rotter from the start."

Lily's heart nearly broke for the boy. While

there were those in Surrey who lived quite poor, there always seemed to be some person or charity who could meet their most basic needs. Here, though, in London, she knew it was not so. There were too many people in need, and the people who could give did not know them. They were the faceless poor and did not garner much sympathy.

"Really, miss," the butler interrupted. "Am I to expect that Lady Jersey is to be forced to step over this rapscallion when she arrives or departs her own house?"

Lily was a bit shaken to hear the name Lady Jersey. She had not, when she'd challenged the butler, considered what sort of great personage he might work for. She should have, she supposed, as it *was* Berkeley Square. No matter, she must not be put off by a quaking in front of rank.

"I would certainly not expect Lady Jersey to countenance such a thing," Lily said, gathering courage for the boy's plight. "Therefore, the matter can be simply rectified. This young man will come at an appointed time, early in the morning, I think, as I doubt your mistress to be up at that hour. He will knock on the servant's entrance, he will be given a cup of water, a roll, and a tuppence. You probably ought to give him a bath once a fortnight. You might even give him the odd job to do, as I'm sure he shouldn't mind some work. Certainly, you can afford such a small sum. Then, he will not bother you further."

"I work like the devil when I can get it," the boy said, with a steely determination not often seen in one so young.

"Don't speak of the devil, boy," Pips said, "lest he come for you."

Though the boy seemed unaffected by the idea of the devil coming for him, the butler was very much affected by everything Lily had proposed. He had sputtered and his face had gone near purple during her speech. Lily thought he was on the verge of apoplexy.

"Am I to understand," he said in a low and controlled fury, "that I am to pay this little blighter to stay off my steps?"

"And give him a roll and water," Lily added. "And the occasional bath."

"But, it is very irregular! What if I am to be besieged by an army of them? What then?"

Lily turned to the boy. "What is your name?"

"Sam," he said. "Samuel for those all fancy-like. Named after me ma's dad what got crushed by a wagon."

Lily chose to ignore the demise of Sam's departed grandfather. "Sam, now, would I be correct in thinking that if you were to find a regular source of income at this house, you'd be very loath to tell anybody else about it?"

"Only a fool would do that!" Sam cried. "I

ain't no fool."

Lily looked up to the butler and smiled. "And there you see, sir. Sam is no fool. In fact, I suspect he would guard this house jealously should some other fellow think to stop by."

"I'd pound him to bits," Sam said resolutely, as if he were a renowned boxer.

Lily did not hold up much hope that the little fellow could pound anything to bits, but she thought it impolitic to say so at this particular moment. "I rather think a tuppence a day is quite cheap to have your own guard on the house."

The butler threw up his hands. "It's robbery, is what it is."

Lily raised her chin defiantly. "It's charity, is what it is. Further, the servants below you will think you very liberal for doing it. I suspect they all know someone in a similar circumstance."

Lily glanced at Mrs. Hemming's footman, who nodded gravely.

"They will think of that person they know and pray that person runs into *your* brand of kindness. While you," she went on, "may satisfy yourself that your problem is at an end."

The butler seemed swayed by the idea that he was to be thought liberal. Lily suspected that butlers in general, while severe in mien, would not mind being thought a hero by their staff.

"May I have your word, sir?" Lily asked. "As a gentleman?"

Being referred to as a gentleman by a finely dressed lady seemed to sway him even more.

"Very well," he said grudgingly. He shook his finger at Sam. "But no shenanigans! No asking for more! No hanging about the place! And a bath only once a month, in cold water, mind. Further, if Lady Jersey ever gets wind of you, that's it! You hear?"

Lily laid a hand on Sam's shoulder. "You'd better run as fast as you can to the servant's entrance, before this fine gentleman changes his mind."

Sam, having spent a childhood grasping at every opportunity that came his way without the slightest pause to think it over, shot off as if he'd been unleashed from an arrow.

HAYES HAD JUST returned to Berkeley Square from his meeting at Destin's with Cabot. He'd thought to attend to some papers in his library before a dinner engagement with his aunt. As he pulled up to number forty, the footman jumped down and opened his door.

Seeing the remarkable scene thirty yards in front of him, Hayes waved the footman off and quietly closed the carriage door. Miss Farnsworth was talking to a wretchedly dirty street urchin, her maid looked on with disapproval, her footman appeared delighted, and Lady Jersey's butler, Riddick, was waving a cudgel on the front steps.

He carefully opened his window so he might hear what was said. He assured himself that he had no particular wish to speak to Miss Farnsworth. On the other hand, if he must intervene as a gentleman, he would like to know what he was getting himself into.

After ten minutes of one of the most remarkable conversations he'd ever overheard, the boy raced to the servant's entrance, Riddick slammed the front doors, and Miss Farnsworth walked on, appearing very pleased with herself.

He closed the curtain as she approached and let her pass by. The last he heard her say was, "You see, Pips, it has all come out well."

After Miss Farnsworth was well away, Hayes motioned to his footman. "Go and ask Riddick, Lady Jersey's butler, if he will be so kind as to wait upon me at his convenience. We have need of a stable boy and I fear Riddick is just now plotting how to rid himself of such a boy."

MRS. HEMMING HAD been alarmed at the state of Lily's dress when she returned to the house, and then even more alarmed to hear the tale of the street urchin and Lady Jersey's butler. She might not have been as alarmed as she was, had not Pips embellished the story to make it out as a battle for the ages ranging across the front steps of number thirty-eight. Lily's aunt had fretted that Lady Jersey might be put out to hear that Miss Farnsworth had done battle with her butler.

Lily had quite rightly pointed out that it was highly unlikely Lady Jersey's butler would ever mention where a tuppence a day was going.

Mrs. Hemming had been soothed by that idea and mused that for all she knew, Ranier had his own urchin coming to the back door. She could not say she was against it, though she wondered if that was what happened to the radishes every year. She'd blamed it on mice; her neighbor Mrs. Makefield blamed it on rats. But they may have both been fooled. Perhaps those radishes had been happily sliced up in St. Giles all along.

By the time they'd set out for Mrs. Millican's dinner, Mrs. Hemming had entirely forgotten Lily's street urchin in favor of her own imagined urchin lurking somewhere in the back garden. Whether or not she was right in that particular prediction, Mrs. Hemming had been quite right when she'd speculated that the dinner they attended would not run long. Their hostess did not favor cards. In truth, she was very much against them. All who knew the lady understood that her late husband had nearly ruined her with the habit and she did not permit one pack in the house—not even in the servant's quarters.

To atone for her lack of entertainment at cards, Mrs. Millican was known to give a very good dinner. Her friends all considered this a fair bargain and were happy to attend her for an early evening.

The dinner had been a small affair and Mrs. Millican had proved herself an amusing wit. She sparred with Mr. Ellsworth so delightfully that Lily wondered if there were not some attachment there. They were widow and widower and seemed well suited to one another.

After dinner, Lily played the pianoforte for a time, but except for that, quiet conversations and tea were what ruled Mrs. Millican's drawing room. It was not more than an hour after they'd retired to the drawing room before guests began to depart.

Mrs. Hemming had seemed tired when they got in their carriage. As much as it felt disappointing, as they had thought to stop by Lady Carradine's club, Lily inquired if it might be best if they went home. Mrs. Hemming brushed off the idea and said they might stop in for an hour and she'd be no worse for it.

Now, Lily and Mrs. Hemming had arrived to the club and made their way to the back room.

It was not overcrowded and Lily instantly noted that Lord Ashworth was in attendance. He faced away from her, but she recognized the height, the tailored coat, and the fair hair easily enough. He played a gentleman she did not know.

Though she had not been introduced to the man Lord Ashworth played, she thought she could guess his circumstances well enough. He was young, and his mode of dress exceedingly dandyish. He would be some young buck just recently set loose upon the town and out to prove his worth. He would be desperate to find his set, and hopeful that some of the loftier-titled gentlemen might take him on. He would think to do something daring to attract notice, and what could be more daring than challenging Lord Ashworth at cards?

The few times that Lord Ashworth actually lost, as Lily was so well aware, it was the talk of every drawing room. There was a distinct cache over playing him and Lily was all but certain that was how Lord Ashworth was able to find a person still willing to bet against him.

This poor fellow would no doubt have a generous allowance at hand to attempt the feat, though his father would have warned him against gambling for high stakes. As many a young man was prone to do, he would cast aside his father's sage advice and be foolhardy enough to believe in his own luck.

From his expression, it appeared that the Goddess Fortuna was disabusing him of the idea that she could be called upon at will.

Lily could not claim to be pleased to see Lord Ashworth. Mrs. Millican's dinner had been remarkably pleasant and she was still silently glorying in securing a tuppence a day for young Sam. She was in a happy frame of mind and had no wish to mar it with any less than genial conversation. It was one thing to enjoy a dance with the gentleman at Lady Catherine's very awkward ball, but extended conversations with the lord generally came with an aggravation. She consoled herself with the idea that she would likely not speak to him as he was thoroughly engaged in relieving the pockets of the young and foolish gentleman.

Mrs. Hemming gazed round the room, looking for one of her usual whist partners. According to her rather doleful sigh, she did not find who she looked for.

Mr. Shine slid up to them and bowed deeply. "The esteemed Mrs. Hemming and her charming niece, Miss Farnsworth," he said.

Mrs. Melton, one of the matrons of the club, was close on his heels. Lily thought the lady did not like to see a gentleman roaming the room and would make it her business to know what he was about.

Lily acknowledged Mrs. Melton. Then she acknowledged Mr. Shine, though she would rather not. There was something about Mr. Shine that she could not like. It was not his obsequious manners, those were common enough. It was something about his expression. She had noticed it when she'd played against him. His mien did not settle into any one attitude, but changed ever so slightly with strange rapidity. It was as if he could not settle upon a particular feeling. There was something that felt false about it.

"You have come at a fortuitous moment," Mr. Shine said. "I have been conversing with Mr. Gentry, a very reputable fellow, and he happened to express a great interest in trying his hand against Miss Farnsworth at piquet. He is intrigued that the lady should have beat Lord Ashworth on two occasions and wishes to try his skill against such a formidable opponent. I was pleased to inform him that you did occasionally come here of an evening. I cannot claim to know his skill, but as dear Mrs. Hemming *did* warn me of Miss Farnsworth's skill…"

"Why does he not play Lord Ashworth if he is wishing to test his skill?" Mrs. Hemming asked.

Mr. Shine rubbed his hands together in an unpleasant fashion and said in a low voice, "As it happens, Lord Ashworth does not favor the fellow. Calls him a blowhard who does too much talking over his cards."

"Oh, Aunt," Lily said. "May I? I am certain he is a great fool who only wishes to brag to his friends that he has defeated me where Lord Ashworth could not. I should very much like to take him down a peg *and* take him down a few guineas."

"I would be pleased to watch over Miss Farnsworth," Mrs. Melton said. Though, to Lily, her tone sounded more along the lines of—*I would be pleased to knock Mr. Gentry about the head if he does the least thing untoward.*

"Quite kind, Mrs. Melton," Mrs. Hemming said, "but I shan't play whist this evening. I will stay by Lily myself."

Mrs. Melton nodded, but looked rather dubious. Lily guessed the lady only thought herself a suitable chaperone.

Lady Carradine swept up to their little group. "Mrs. Hemming, Miss Farnsworth, lovely to see you here tonight."

Mrs. Hemming laid a hand on Lady Carradine's arm. "Can you tell me of Mr. Gentry and what do you think of him?"

"Oh, he is just there, in the blue coat."

Lily looked at the gentleman with interest. He was not in the first bloom of youth, though his clothes might beg to differ. He had stuffed himself into far too tight breeches and his neckcloth sought to do battle in height with every young fop in town. Most amusingly, he scanned the room with an ornate quizzing glass, as if he were Brummel, himself.

Lady Carradine followed Lily's gaze and said, "He's a fine enough fellow, if somewhat silly. Though, Mrs. Hemming, I am afraid I am almost certain he does not favor whist. If he does, I could not vouch for what sort of partner he'd be."

"No, Lady Carradine," Lily said. "I believe he wishes to play against me at piquet, though we have not been introduced. Do you think it should be all right?"

Lady Carradine said, "Certainly. I've known Mr. Gentry for quite some time, though he has been out of town for these past two years. He is a bit puffed up for my taste, but I can say he is in no danger of defaulting on you—he always pays his debts."

Mr. Shine appeared to take this as a ringing endorsement and set out to fetch Mr. Gentry. Mrs. Hemming nodded and said, "I depend upon you, Lady Carradine."

Mr. Gentry, for his part, seemed nearly overcome as he spoke to Mr. Shine. He hurried over in what Lily could only call mincing steps.

After they had been suitably introduced, and Mr. Gentry had several times said it was an honor, he led Lily to an open table while Mrs. Hemming trailed behind.

As Lily sat down, she noted Lord Ashworth note *her*. He quickly averted his eyes, but she smiled to herself. The young gentleman he played picked up the trick and she had a notion that she had momentarily discomposed the great Lord Ashworth.

Mr. Gentry declared he thought they ought to play for fifty pounds. Had Lily not played for such a vast sum at Lady Montague's, she might have quaked at hearing the number. But then, she'd already had the experience of high play and was less alarmed by it. She also thought she had a very good chance of winning. She usually *did* have a good chance of winning, and this gentleman did not look to be much of a challenge. If he *were* a challenge, he played a very deep game indeed.

She nodded in acquiescence.

Mr. Gentry appeared to consider this a victory of sorts and then foolishly claimed the right to deal. Lily dismissed Lord Ashworth from her thoughts and turned her attention to the play.

As the game went on, Lily became more and more certain that Mr. Gentry was a buffoon. He did not seem to have any kind of strategy, at least not that she could discern. His expressions gave him away at every turn, his squint here and bitten lip there and scrunched up nose toward the end of every play telling the tale well enough. He was like a child denying he'd stolen a cake while his face was covered in crumbs. His hands nearly quaked when he held low cards. She suspected piquet was not even his favored game, but he'd held out some sort of hope that the cards would all go his way and he might squeak out a victory against Miss Farnsworth. It was an entirely ridiculous hope.

Lily might have felt sorry for the gentleman, but he was proving himself to be a terrific braggart. Apparently, he wished her to know of any and all gambling experiences he'd had, where he'd come out on the winning side. She supposed she should be grateful that he confined himself to tales of winning, as she suspected his tales of losing would go on a good deal longer.

"I once won five hundred pounds in one evening at faro," he said, watching another of his cards slide away from him.

"Course," he went on, "I am most proud of the night at White's, when Sir Luther and I partnered at whist and defeated Lord Mallon and Lord Edgewater." Mr. Gentry looked over her head at some far-off vista, as if he were recalling to mind the scene of his victory. "*To* the tune of four hundred pounds," he said. "It is recorded. In the book. For posterity."

"That must have been very gratifying, Mr. Gentry," Lily said, hardly attending to her own words. Her attention was on her cards. She was, however, forced to admit that Lord Ashworth's opinion of the gentleman was correct—he was a blowhard who talked far too much. Mrs.

Hemming's rambling speeches had a charm to them. Mr. Gentry's were simply irritating.

"And then of course," Mr. Gentry went on, "you have heard the tale of my extraordinary run of luck at White's hazard table?"

"I am afraid not," Lily said.

Mr. Gentry looked hopefully at Mrs. Hemming. She shrugged.

"Well, I suppose it is only still spoken of amongst gentlemen," Mr. Gentry said. "Of course that would be it. I can tell you, it was *quite* the scene. Unforgettable if you ask me."

Lily laid down her last card. An ace of hearts against Mr. Gentry's nine of clubs. "That is one hundred points, Mr. Gentry," Lily said.

Mr. Gentry seemed entirely nonplussed to see that they had reached the end of the game.

Mrs. Hemming stifled a yawn, though she looked pleased that Lily had dispatched Mr. Gentry so handily.

"I must have a rematch, Miss Farnsworth!" Mr. Gentry said with some feeling. "I see how you play now and am prepared to take myself to victory."

Lily was vastly amused and would not mind at all to relieve Mr. Gentry of another fifty pounds. However, she could see that her aunt was tired.

"I must decline, Mr. Gentry. My aunt will wish to go home by now."

"Indeed, my dear," Mrs. Hemming said. "I am exhausted."

"It cannot be!" Mr. Gentry exclaimed. "Lady Carradine," he called, "do come over."

Lady Carradine, always alarmed when a person called her over with such urgency, hurried to the table.

"There is no problem here?" she said hopefully.

"I am distraught, Lady Carradine," Mr. Gentry said. "Miss Farnsworth refuses a rematch on account of Mrs. Hemming wishing to retire. Surely, there must be a solution. I must have my chance."

Mr. Shine had slid over to their table. He reminded Lily of a garden snake, weaving its way around the shrubbery.

"Certainly, there must be, my dear Mr. Gentry," Mr. Shine said smoothly. "Nothing easier. If Mrs. Hemming were to return to her house in their carriage, the carriage could then be sent back and Miss Farnsworth could return safely at her leisure. Mrs. Melton is here to watch over her."

"I must intervene on that point, Mr. Shine," Lady Carradine said. "Mrs. Melton was looking a bit peaked and I have sent her home."

"You, then," Mr. Shine said smoothly to Lady Carradine. "You could watch over Miss Farnsworth. Nothing more respectable and it would have the further benefit of allowing Miss Farnsworth to view the upcoming game of the evening. Lord Ashworth has agreed to play *me* when he is done with young Medham over there."

Lily could hardly suppress her mirth. Mr. Gentry would insist on his right to lose another fifty pounds and Mr. Shine had somehow the lunacy of playing Lord Ashworth. Mr. Shine, as she well knew, was no expert. While *she* might be able to prevail over Lord Ashworth, *he* had no chance whatsoever.

"You are to know, Miss Farnsworth," Mr. Shine said with a hint of pride in his voice, "that I have become a great student of the game and am vastly improved. I would consent to match with *you*, if you dared. Though, I bet rather high."

"Indeed," Lily said, pressing her lips together to stop her laughter. It seemed now there were *two* gentlemen lined up to throw her their money. She might make a very tidy profit before the night was through. She turned to Mrs. Hemming and said, "Oh, Aunt, might we arrange it?"

Mrs. Hemming squinted her eyes, as she did when she was deep in thought. "Well," she said slowly, "if Lady Carradine were to take charge of you as a chaperone and stay nearby, I might send the carriage back with the addition of two footmen and Pips. You already have two grooms and the coachman—I suppose five men and a lady's maid could not be safer. In truth, I would put Pips up against the five men in both spirit and ferocity, once I apprise her of the scheme. But then, I rarely inconvenience the woman so I dare say she might lump it for once."

Lily had followed her aunt's calculations closely. "Then I shall stay?" she asked hopefully.

"Oh, do say so!" Mr. Gentry cried.

Mrs. Hemming looked to Lady Carradine. Lady Carradine appeared to waver, then she said, "Of course, if you wish it."

Mrs. Hemming said, "It appears all arranged. But mind, do not stay too late. I will have Pips here by two."

"Yes, Aunt," Lily said, enormously pleased.

Mrs. Hemming appeared satisfied and kissed her niece's cheek. She was escorted to the carriage by Lady Carradine, and Lily picked up the pack and dealt the cards.

CHAPTER NINE

ILY AND MR. Gentry had, for the most part,
been left to their game. Lady Carradine
came by from time to time, but she appeared to
deem the gentleman not a particular threat to any
young lady's virtue. Lily thought that wise—it
was not likely his conversation or his person
would conquer anybody, nor did he have the
daring of a rake.

Most others in the room had drifted over to
Lord Ashworth and Mr. Shine's game.

Mr. Gentry had long since given up recount-
ing his various wins at various tables. Lily could
not be certain if that was because he'd run out of
them, or whether he was cognizant that he was
on the verge of losing another fifty pounds.

Whether or not *he* knew it, Lily knew it.
She'd sunk a triplet of kings and was just playing

them as her last cards, well aware that Mr. Gentry could not beat them.

As she took one trick, then two, then the final, the sink seemed to dawn on Mr. Gentry. He laid down his last card, the ten of spades, and sighed deeply. "That's it, then," he said quietly.

"That *is* it, Mr. Gentry." In a kinder tone, she said, "I wonder if I might advise you."

Mr. Gentry seemed to perk. "You will give me some trick to winning? he asked.

"No," Lily said firmly. "I will give you a trick to avoid losing. Do not play—I imagine you are skilled at a great many things, but piquet is not your game."

Mr. Gentry hung his head. "I was foolish, I suppose. I told my friends I could beat both you and Lord Ashworth if I had a mind and they laughed at me. So then, I was determined, you see."

"I do see," Lily said. "Though, if they are really your friends, they will not mind you being foolish on occasion. We have all been guilty of it."

Mr. Gentry nodded sadly and said, "I will settle the debt promptly."

Lily smiled, hoping she had convinced Mr. Gentry to cease throwing away his money. Her attention was drawn to an audible gasp coming from Lord Ashworth's table. Lily presumed the lord was trouncing Mr. Shine.

"Let us remove and watch the play," she said, rising. Lily held out a high hope that Lord Ashworth might dispatch Mr. Shine speedily and there would be time for her to play him. That was, if Mr. Shine had the stomach for it, which he might not after playing the lord and noting how little his scholarship of the game had actually advanced his prospects.

Mr. Gentry nodded resignedly, and they moved to Lord Ashworth and Mr. Shine's table.

As Lily gazed down at the scene, she at first could not quite discern what she was seeing. What she had expected to see on the two men's faces were confidence from Lord Ashworth and chagrin from Mr. Shine. The picture was a deal more muddled than that. Lord Ashworth appeared some combination of irritated and confused. Mr. Shine seemed nervous and elated.

Mr. Medham, the young gentleman who had played Lord Ashworth earlier, stood next to her and said softly, "Extraordinary. That fellow is about to prevail."

Lily did not see what was so extraordinary about Lord Ashworth prevailing. After all, he was a very good player and Mr. Shine was a very bad player. The outcome could not be more predictable.

The gentleman on the other side of Mr. Medham answered him. "His reputation will be made. It is not often that Lord Ashworth loses."

The gentleman colored slightly, seeming to realize that she was nearby. Since Lady Montague's party, she had grown used to being known for her victories over Lord Ashworth. "Not often, anyway," he murmured.

Lily turned back to the game. It was impossible that Lord Ashworth lose to Mr. Shine. She had played the man; she knew precisely how unskilled he was. Something was not right.

Lily moved behind Mr. Shine to see his hand. It was strong.

There was some mystery here. Perhaps Lord Ashworth had been taken ill and fought on despite it, thereby affecting his play. Or more likely, perhaps Mr. Shine had all along been an expert and had concealed that fact—overconfidence could lead to ruin and Lord Ashworth may have fallen for the ruse. If that were the case, Lily must admit she'd fallen for the ruse, too. It was a strategy as old as the hills—lose one gamble with utter incompetence and then come back for a far larger wager and reveal one's true skill. Lily would never lower herself to such tricks, but she did not doubt the oily Mr. Shine would.

Could he actually be that good? And then, Mr. Shine was a cousin to Lady Carradine. Certainly, he would not dare introduce such trickery into her club. So, if it was not that, what was happening? She dearly wished to know the cause of this strange circumstance.

As she had often done, when she looked for an item either about her somewhere or in her mind, Lily pulled back her view. Rather than attend to one thing or the other, she wished to see the scene in its entirety. Often, when she looked at a thing in such a manner, something would leap out at her and call her attention to it.

As if gazing at a painting, Lily saw the tiniest scratch in the wood near the corner of the table—it was new, it had not been there the last time she'd come. There was a faint ink stain on one of Mr. Shine's fat fingers. Lord Ashworth's fingernails were buffed, and there was the smallest droplet on the table near the corner of one of Mr. Shine's cards, as if someone had been careless of a drink. Her eyes roved over the slight fray on one of Mr. Shine's cuffs, the minutest imperfection in the weave of Lord Ashworth's cravat, the cards laid down that had been played...

Suddenly, like a rising flame on a candle just lit, she unlocked the mystery. It was there in Lord Ashworth's hand, it was there laid on the table.

It was the backs of the cards.

Lady Carradine's packs had so far been all alike. It was clear she used a skilled printer to ensure no defects. This pack of cards was similar, but not identical to the cards she'd seen before. Nor were they identical to one another. The changes were subtle indeed, but Lily could throw each version of the card up in her mind and examine them minutely.

Lady Carradine's regular packs and this pack depicted similar scenes on the back—a garden gate enshrined with blooming pink roses. It was a busy pattern with greenery in the background and a gold-leafed border. The pack that was in play between Lord Ashworth and Mr. Shine was similar, but showed the smallest of differences between cards.

The tiny lock on the gate was not uniform. The rose closest to the lock did not contain the same amount of petals.

Lily stared at the cards and let her mind do its work. Searching, searching for a pattern.

It came to her in a moment. There appeared to be four variations in the locks, they must be the suits. The number of petals ran widely—they must indicate the number of the card.

To confirm her idea, she took note of the cards in Mr. Shine's hand. If she were right, when he laid them face down, she would be able to decipher them using the lock shape and number of petals.

As cards were played, Lily watched Mr. Shine lay down a jack of hearts. He took the trick and laid it face down. Yes, just as she'd thought—the lock slightly oblong and the petals numbering eleven. The cards were marked. She was certain Mr. Shine was the author of it, as it thoroughly explained his newfound success.

He'd been clever about it. The shapes of the locks were only minutely different and not at all obvious. The heart was not shown as a heart shape, which might easily have given away the cheat, but rather just a hair more oblong than the spade lock. The diamond had one slightly sharpened corner and the club had the smallest round protrusion.

The same had been done with the petals, they were not boldly shown. In fact, for the higher cards, some petals only peeked out from behind others.

As she finished working out the system, Mr. Shine laid down his last card. He had won the match.

Hushed whispers swirled around her and the observers moved away. As if they were a flock of birds startled to flight, the gentlemen went running for their overcoats. Lily supposed all who had witnessed the game wished to be the first to tell their friends that there was a new gambler in town. She understood that gentlemen often stayed at their clubs until dawn and it was just on half past one—these fellows would race to be the first through the door to tell the tale.

As the room emptied, and Lady Carradine followed her guests to the front of the house to supervise various departures, Lily moved closer to the table.

"I congratulate you, Mr. Shine," Lord Ashworth said stiffly. "It was a well-played game."

Mr. Shine graciously nodded. "I have made piquet my study, my lord, and hope I have grown proficient."

Lily picked up a card and said, "I beg to differ, Mr. Shine."

Both gentlemen looked up, surprised.

"Lord Ashworth," Lily said steadily. "These cards are marked."

"What?" Lord Ashworth exclaimed, picking up some of the discards. He stared hard at them.

Mr. Shine had paled, but he did not falter. "Do not be ridiculous, Miss Farnsworth. As much as we have enjoyed your presence here, I am afraid an insult such as this must lead to an end to your welcome at our club. You may take your foolish notions elsewhere."

Lily did not respond to this spirited defense. She only said, "See here, these small locks on the gates are slightly different shaped, they are the suits. And this rose here, the number of petals changes to match the number of the card."

As Lord Ashworth bent over Lily's hand to look closer, Mr. Shine rose and drew a pistol from his coat. He slowly backed away.

"Mr. Shine!" Lily cried.

Lord Ashworth laid a hand on her arm to caution her.

Mr. Shine had reached the door. Though Lily

fully expected the man would make his escape, he ominously closed it and turned the lock. He advanced back to them in quick steps.

"One word from either of you," Mr. Shine said, "and I'll shoot one of you on the spot. There is a back way out and I can be on my way before anybody gets here with a key. Stand up, Ashworth."

Lily was horrified at the specter of this new Mr. Shine, and she was horrified at herself. Why had she not thought it through? Why had she not realized that to corner a man who was willing to mark cards would be exceedingly dangerous? She should have bided her time and told Lord Ashworth privately, who then could have taken up the matter with Lady Carradine.

Certainly, Lady Carradine could not know of it?

Certainly, when Lady Carradine returned and found the doors locked, she would perceive that something was wrong.

Certainly, someone must come to their aid.

LADY CARRADINE HAD been exceedingly surprised that Lord Ashworth had lost to Mr. Shine, but she did not have time to wonder at it. She had hustled out the last of the guests, but for the lord and

Miss Farnsworth who had stayed behind. She supposed they would get up another game between them and she hoped Mr. Shine would be interested in viewing that game. She could not be certain of it, though, so she must hurry to accomplish her aim before Mr. Shine was upon her. Were he to discover her making off with the bank, she had no doubt she'd find herself buried in the basement.

She had dismissed the servants. They would not think it unusual, she did so on occasion, and they were happy enough to come early on the following day to tidy the place. She then hurried to the bank room. She emptied most of the bank into a satchel, laid bricks in the bank chest and covered the bricks with small notes. She locked it back up and prayed Mr. Shine would have no cause to count it until the morrow. She often retired as soon as the guests departed and she hoped that was exactly what Mr. Shine would think she'd done.

Earlier, when all eyes had been on the play between Lord Ashworth and Mr. Shine, she'd taken her portmanteau from the house. The porter had looked inquiringly but she had only hurried past him, declining his assistance. After the guests departed, she would send him home. He would not be asked whether he'd seen her with luggage until the following morning. Her jewelry had been sewn into her clothes that afternoon.

Lady Carradine, or Nancy Manton as she would go back to calling herself, pulled on a heavy traveling cloak and hurried out the door. She told the porter he might go, and she handed him a series of letters with direction that he was to take them home and then see that they were delivered on the following morning. She wished for those who might wonder where she'd gone to understand that she fled from Mr. Shine. In each of the missives, she claimed Mr. Shine was a cheat. She had no proof of it, but she was all but certain he *would* cheat given the slightest opportunity. In any case, even a whiff of an idea in that direction would shut him down for good. He might have the house, but she would not allow him to carry on with the club.

Nancy pulled her hood low and fled to a hired carriage waiting in the shadows.

Everything she would take with her, including the bank, was gone from the house. All of this must be left behind. She was bound for New Orleans and would never look back.

MR. SHINE HAD forced Hayes and Miss Farnsworth out a door at the far end of the room, toward the back of the house. Hayes had deftly guided Miss Farnsworth in front of him so that he might remain between the lady and Mr. Shine. There was never anybody more dangerous than a man wielding a pistol he'd probably had little practice shooting. For every step they took up the flight of stairs, Hayes expected to hear the loud report of gunfire.

Even if Mr. Shine were not to shoot them on the stairs, what *would* he do? The man was deranged. Anybody finding themselves caught marking cards, and with a pistol in hand and a means of escape, would have taken the rational step of escaping. Instead, Mr. Shine had taken them prisoner.

Why? What was his plan?

They had gone up past the living quarters and were now in the attics. It should have been servant's quarters, but as they passed the open doors, Hayes could see that the rooms were devoid of furniture. Apparently, Lady Carradine did not employ a live-in staff and Mr. Shine had been all too aware of it.

Hayes felt the barrel of the pistol in his back. "To the right," Mr. Shine said.

He and Miss Farnsworth were forced into a small room. It was as empty as all the others and the sort that would have been assigned to two housemaids, had there been any. The floor was bare, unvarnished wood. The walls had been plastered but cracks now ran a riotous pattern across them. There were lighter rectangles visible where some long-ago picture had hung and protected the plaster from the smoke of a fire. The fireplace itself was empty and cold, with only a layer of old ash to say that anybody had ever lived there.

"You will stay here, for the time being," Mr. Shine said. "The house is empty, or will be shortly. Should you be so foolish as to attract attention by making a sound, I will shoot whoever hears you before doing you the same courtesy."

"Mr. Shine," Lily said, "what can you possibly—"

The door slammed shut before Miss Farnsworth could finish her sentence. The lock turned with a resounding clack.

Hayes looked around the room sharply, hoping to see something, anything, that he may not have initially noticed. Something they could use to their advantage. It was entirely empty.

"What does he mean to do?" Lily asked quietly.

"I do not know," Hayes said, "but he has not taken the rational course, which means he is not a rational man."

"He will kill us, then," Lily said. "So that his secret is not discovered."

"He might try," Hayes said. "Though I am not inclined to allow him to succeed."

Miss Farnsworth wrung her hands. "How would he ever be able to explain it? He was the last to see us. Lady Carradine must look for us even now. My aunt will expect me home. He could not possibly believe he could get away with this."

"I imagine he has not thought that far, which is what makes him particularly dangerous," Hayes said.

"He'll think better of it," Lily said. "I am sure he will. He will come to his senses and get himself away."

Hayes was not so certain. Mr. Shine had brought a pistol to the card table. He must have been prepared to use it if things went awry. *That* part, he understood. What he did not understand is why Mr. Shine had not simply fled the scene. A man who'd taken a bizarre and risky step such as this might be counted upon to do anything.

He strode to the windows. It was clear they had been not been opened in some time—the panes were darkened with soot and the hinges were rusted over. He forced them open, the joints grating and creaking for lack of oil.

"Lord Ashworth, we are on the third floor," Lily whispered.

He held up his hand and peered down. It was true they were on the third floor, but ten feet below was a balcony, and then below that a portico whose edge seemed close enough to an old black poplar with sturdy branches. He had spent an entire childhood making escapes such as this. It could be done by him, he was certain of it. The question was—could it be done by Miss Farnsworth?

Hayes turned to her. "I am unarmed. My pistol is in my carriage. We cannot afford to linger and discover what Mr. Shine intends. I am going to lower myself down to a balcony. Then, you must put yourself out the window and trust me to catch you. Can you do it?"

Seeing the look of alarm on Miss Farnsworth's face, Hayes almost hesitated. He feared he would get out and then her nerves would fail her. He would not likely get back in again. He could not leave her to her fate. Hayes had begun to get the idea that Mr. Shine might be one of those individuals who would shoot now and regret later.

He watched Miss Farnsworth take in a deep breath. "I can do it," she said resolutely.

There was no time to wonder. The lady claimed she could do it and they must try. Mr. Shine might return at any moment and Hayes did not think it likely they'd survive many minutes after he did.

MR. SHINE HAD gone halfway down the stairs and then stopped. He must think what to do. He'd panicked, never an ideal situation, and now he must calm himself and think of a way out.

That damned Miss Farnsworth! How had she noted the differences in the cards? It was near impossible, even if one were to examine them minutely. The moment he'd seen the original design on the club's cards he'd known he might easily replicate and mark them. They were a fussy pattern, nothing easier. He'd marked cards all his life, he knew how to find a printer willing to print them for a hefty fee. He'd never been caught except once in those early years when the Duchess of Carlisle had found him out. There had been so many highly-placed people at *that* particular gambit that he'd been forced to decamp to America.

But all that was so long ago. He supposed most of those people were dead by now, or if not dead, then doddering around their country estates. He'd long grown tired of Baltimore, and even more tired of Americans, and it had begun to seem the right time to return to England. Then, he'd *known* it was the right time when he'd discovered Nancy Manton's ruse.

At the time, his run of luck had been very bad and he'd been forced to take a job as a clerk. It had been his duty to record the sales of property and when he examined the sale of the Carradines' property, he knew he looked at a forgery. The signature was too deliberate. It had been written too slowly. The pen had been pressed too hard. There were obvious stops and starts. All amateur mistakes. He had looked into the matter, and after he'd tracked down a servant who had been dismissed, he began to put it all together.

It had taken nearly a year to trace Nancy Manton. He knew from passenger lists that a certain Lady Judith Carradine, now known to him as Nancy, had traveled to England. He'd thought he'd find her retired in the English countryside, living on her ill-gotten gains. He meant to take it all from her by way of blackmail. But then, he discovered she ran a gambling concern. It was all too perfect. It was all too easy.

He'd planned to make a large profit and then slip off somewhere.

Now, he had a lady and a gentleman, not just a gentleman, a *lord*, locked in the attic. And not just any lord—this lord was Dembly's spawn. That particular duke, if he were to ever encounter Mr. Shine after that long-ago card game at that long-ago house party, might very well hold a grudge.

There was only one thing to do. He must collect the bank and be off. He would have to overcome his business partner and dispose of her, which he was fully prepared to do. She would no doubt even now be at the doors to the gaming room, wondering why they were locked and wishing to see about Miss Farnsworth. She would never see the heavy candlestick to the back of her head coming, then it was a haul down to the basement for her. All would assume it had been *she* that had cleared out the bank and been off.

There was still time to save himself, but he must act quickly before Nancy Manton raised an alarm.

HAYES HAD LOWERED himself out the window. He let go of the casement and fell the four remaining feet, landing with a thud. He hoped that thud had not been heard, but there was no time to consider it.

He motioned to Miss Farnsworth, who now peered down at him with wide eyes. He wondered if she'd be able to go through with it. It was one thing to say one could do a thing, and quite another to actually do it.

She suddenly disappeared from view. Hayes held his breath. Was she too frightened? Or worse, had Shine come back?

Just as suddenly, her skirts came into view as she let herself out of the window.

She would do it. The brave girl would do it. Of course she would, only that afternoon had she not saved the young urchin from Lady Jersey's butler?

Hayes forced himself to ignore first one pretty stockinged leg and then the other, hanging above him just now. Miss Farnsworth had lowered herself out and hung onto the casement by her fingers. He reached up and grasped her about the waist.

"Let go," he said quietly.

She hesitated for a moment, though Hayes knew she could not hold on for long. She released the casement and fell upon him.

CHAPTER TEN

M R. SHINE HURRIED through the gaming room, picking up a candlestick as he went, and unlocked the door. He cautiously opened it, prepared with a story about the locked door and the missing Miss Farnsworth and Lord Ashworth. He would say he did not know how the door had become locked, a servant must have inadvertently done it.

Where were Lord Ashworth and Miss Farnsworth? Taking air in the back garden. Perhaps she ought to go see what they were about going out there alone.

She would turn her back to him to make her way there, and he would dispatch her and lock her in the room until he could get rid of the servants.

To his surprise, the corridor was empty. She

was nowhere in sight and the servants were gone too. Perhaps Nancy Manton had forgot all about her little charge and had retired? It had often been her habit to be abed as quick as she could, and a habit to dismiss the servants too. They would have been told to come early on the morrow to clear up the debris from the evening's entertainments.

Mr. Shine smiled. Nothing could be easier than to open the room that held the bank and be off. Weeks ago, he'd dosed Nancy's tea with laudanum and changed the locks as one of his first orders of business upon installing himself in the house. He would collect the money and be on his way. It was, perhaps, unfortunate that Nancy would live to tell the tale and likely send eyes looking for him, but nobody would know a thing about it until the morrow. It was enough time to get well away. He had a notion to try his luck in South America. There was gold there, and diamonds even. He was growing tired of cards—there was no security in it.

He hurried down the hall to the room that held the bank chest. The door to the room had long ago been replaced with a more formidable version—it was solid oak, four inches thick, and swung open silently on well-oiled hinges.

As he unlocked the cabinet that held the chest, he smiled. Poor Nancy would find herself in a fix on the morrow. All her money gone and two customers locked above stairs. She'd be ruined. For that matter, Miss Farnsworth would be ruined too—no lady would be able to explain her way out of an evening alone with a man.

"Serves her right for interfering with me," he said softly.

Mr. Shine pulled out the chest. It was heavier than he expected, which was a very good sign. He placed it on the desk and hurriedly opened the lock. Bank notes were before him, all he need do was transfer them to a more suitable case. A person traveling round with a chest such as this would be robbed within a day.

He jogged out of the room and into the breakfast parlor. There was a case below the sideboard that was meant to hold the silver that would do just fine. It was plain and did not announce itself as anything extraordinary.

Back in the bank room, Mr. Shine swept up the notes. His knuckles grazed something hard.

He slowly moved the notes aside, a feeling of trepidation stealing over him. A set of bricks stared back at him.

In the succeeding seconds, he felt his face turn to fire, as if it would alight on its own. The blocks of stone seemed to look back at him with disdain, as if they mocked him.

The bank was gone. How could that be? Had they been robbed while he'd been otherwise occupied? Had Nancy Manton been so foolish as to forget to secure the room? He would beat her senseless if that was the case.

He grabbed a candle and raced up the stairs to Nancy's room. There was no light coming from under the door. He banged on the door and got no answer. He tried the door handle. It was unlocked.

Throwing it open, he looked about. There was no sign of the woman. The bed was still made, the fire cold. The usual accoutrements of a dressing table had fled. He checked the wardrobe. There were still dresses there, but they were not her best. He knew well enough it was a sign of a hasty packing. A sign of somebody in a hurry, who wished to slip away with what they could carry. He had done it himself enough times to know.

She was gone. Nancy Manton had stolen the bank. She had robbed him. She had fled with the money.

He slowly sat down on a chintz chair. How did he not guess she would do it? He had been convinced she was in his power, that she would not dare an escape. That she was too settled to consider moving on. He had been wrong. What could he do now?

If he would avoid ruin entirely, he must develop a plan. And he must do so quickly.

Where would she go? Was there a chance of catching her? She couldn't have been gone long, no more than an hour. If he caught her, he'd wring her neck and pry the money from her cold, dead hands.

Mr. Shine leapt up from the chair and raced down the stairs. He would find out from the old porter when she had left and which direction she'd traveled. He might be able to catch her yet.

He flung open the foyer. It was empty. The man was gone.

Mr. Shine kicked the wall. He must catch her!

Perhaps he could take Ashworth's horse and just choose a direction out of the city, depending on lady luck to guide him.

No. It would be stupid to even try it. It would only waste time. He suspected she'd head for a port, but he could not fathom which port or where she would set sail to. Back to America? To the Continent? Did she head for a port this moment? Or did she closet herself away in some rented hidey-hole? He could not chase after her on only a guess when that guess was so likely to be wrong. The odds were against him and he never flouted the odds.

What did he have to work with? She had not been able to take the house with her, but how was he to keep it and carry on with the business when he'd got two swells locked in the attic? In fact, those two were currently his only assets. It was not much, it was not at all what he wanted, but it was what he'd got.

As he had so often done in his career, Mr. Shine rubbed his chin, thinking of how to work with what he'd got.

First, he must bind and gag them so there was no chance of escape and no chance of them calling out for help. He would send a ransom note for Lord Ashworth—certainly the duke would let go of a considerable amount to retrieve his eldest son. No need for the old sot to realize that the fellow so genially relieving his purse was the same that had relieved purses at a long-ago house party. It had amused him that Lord Ashworth had known his name, but had not known of *that* circumstance. Father and son could put the whole thing together at their leisure, once he was safely gone from the scene.

The ransom note delivered, he would instruct a drop off of money late tomorrow night. That would give the old duke time to confirm that his son had in fact gone missing and gather the funds necessary. He would move Ashworth's horse to some far away stable so that it would appear that he'd left the gambling establishment and met with disaster on the road somewhere. Then, he would open the doors for gambling on the morrow's evening as if all was as it should be, only claiming that Lady Carradine had gone off to tend to a sick relative.

What of Miss Farnsworth? She was another matter—would there be a hue and cry over her whereabouts when she did not arrive home? Yes, he supposed so. The only thing going for him there was that the girl was under the protection of Mrs. Hemming. He did not think the lady particularly clever or resourceful. He'd invent a mysterious woman, a titled lady, who had taken Miss Farnsworth to the country. Mrs. Hemming might just believe it. That particular ruse would not hold long, but it would hold long enough. In any case, once Miss Farnsworth was located, would Mrs. Hemming really advertise that her niece had been alone for so long with Lord Ashworth? He thought not.

All questions satisfactorily answered, he would proceed to use the marked cards. If all went well, he would win a large amount. Late in the night, he would make his way to the drop off he'd directed to the duke and collect a further large amount for the lord's safe return. In place of the money, he would leave the lord's location, as he would have instructed in the ransom note. Then, he would slip into the shadows and lay low for a few months. He'd establish a new identity and make his way to South America.

He must move quickly and decisively.

He dashed down to the kitchens for rags and then rummaged the house for rope. He'd finally settled on the heavy weaved wool bands that held back the curtains in various bedchambers.

As he prepared to mount the stairs to the

attic, Mr. Shine paused. Like any plan hastily formed, he'd almost forgotten an important detail. Miss Farnsworth's carriage was due to arrive at two o'clock. It was minutes to the appointed hour and would likely be there even now. He must get rid of it.

LILY HAD FOUND herself on the balcony below the window, crashed atop Lord Ashworth. He gently lifted her up, set her on her feet, and whispered in her ear.

"Below is a portico. I will go first and you will come after me, just as you have done. Do not lose courage."

She nodded, willing to follow the lord's direction. He might hope she had courage to lose, but the truth was, Lily was terrified. She was certain Mr. Shine would make himself known at any moment. They might have got out of the attics, but they were still well in range of a pistol shot.

Lord Ashworth climbed over the balcony railing and jumped to the portico. Lily was glad he was so tall—a shorter man might have broken a leg.

She peered over and saw his face upturned to hers, his arms up to catch her. She quickly turned and climbed over, determinedly pushing away the idea that Mr. Shine might suddenly appear at the window above her.

Lily felt the lord's hands on her hips. She let go of the railing.

Lord Ashworth eased her down with strength and she did not collapse upon him as she'd done the first time. He motioned to a sturdy branch that grazed the corner of the portico's roof. She had not climbed a tree since she was a girl, but she would do anything to get away from this place.

They moved quietly and quickly to the edge of the roof.

Below them, a door banged open.

Lord Ashworth grabbed her arm and stopped her progress. He laid his forefinger against her lips.

THE LORD CROUCHED down and pulled her down with him.

"You there," a man called from below.

It was Mr. Shine. Lily felt the blood drain from her face. Could he see her? How could he know that she was just above his head?

"What do you still do here?" Mr. Shine went on. "Miss Farnsworth was taken away by Lady Marchelan over an hour ago."

Her carriage! Lily had forgotten about her

carriage. Her aunt had sent Pips to collect her. The maid would realize that something happened to her. Pips would not be put off.

Lily heard Pips' voice in reply. "Are you certain?" she asked. "We were told to wait here and Lady Carradine was to put me in possession of Miss Farnsworth."

"Lady Marchelan insisted on carrying her off," Mr. Shine said smoothly. "Something about a country party at Lady So and So's. Now, what will you do? Sit there all night when there is no cause for it?"

Pips, her voice ringing with irritation, said, "A trip to the countryside at this hour!"

"Yes, they said they thought to go on the morrow," Mr. Shine said smoothly, "and then decided to set off now. You know how the fancies are—everything is to be at their whim and convenience."

"What a palaver!" Pips cried. "Galloping through the countryside at night with no thought to highwaymen. Really, I think Mrs. Hemming to be too liberal with the girl to allow her to run off so! Well," she said with a huff, "let us go, we might catch a few hours of sleep if we're lucky. Though I suppose *that* won't bother my mistress."

The carriage set off and Lily and Lord Ashworth waited until they heard the door shut behind Mr. Shine.

"Who is Lady Marchelan?" Lily whispered.

"A figment," Lord Ashworth answered. "Come, we must go quickly. The villain will even now be on his way up to the attics."

At the thought of Mr. Shine running up the stairs to the attics, Lily felt frozen to the spot. There was such an enormous horror running through her that she did not think she could move. Somewhere in her clouded thoughts, she thought a terror such as this was why a rabbit suddenly gave up in a fox's jaws. It was too much to fight against.

Lord Ashworth leapt onto the branch and grabbed the one above him to steady himself. He reached his hand out.

Lily stared at him.

"Take my hand!" the lord said urgently.

His words seemed to shake her from her stupor. His outstretched hand gave her courage. She took it.

His strong grasp felt as a link to life. A way to live. A way to escape the fox's jaws. He nodded to her and began to inch them forward. Slowly, footstep by footstep, Lily could feel the rough bark through her slippers. Finally to the trunk. Lord Ashworth climbed down to a branch below them as Lily held on to the trunk. He steadied her, his arms around her waist, as she carefully lowered herself down to him.

Lord Ashworth leapt the last six feet to the

pavement and turned to her. Above them, she heard the sound of the casement window banging against the side of the house. Mr. Shine. He was in the attic.

Lily jumped.

MR. SHINE HAD hurried back into the house after sending Miss Farnsworth's carriage on its way. He gathered up the bindings and rags he had collected, and a second pistol. One could never be too careful—Lord Ashworth was not an inconsiderable opponent. He assumed the gentleman would have come up with some ridiculous plan to overcome him when he opened the door. Perhaps he'd loosened a brick from the fireplace and intended to knock him on the head. It would be well to be able to get off two shots if necessary. After all, if he were forced to kill them, he could still collect the ransom and be off.

He crept down the corridor silently. Reaching the door, he unlocked it and kicked it open, raising his pistols.

The empty room stared back at him. The windows gently swayed with the breeze and the wafting air brushed his face.

He raced to the windows and slammed them open, just in time to see Lord Ashworth running down the avenue with Miss Farnsworth in his arms.

Mr. Shine raised one of his pistols, and then lowered it. He'd never make the shot and even if he'd got lucky, what was he to do with a dead man on the street and a woman screaming about it?

The neighbors would be out in their night-caps before he got out the front door.

Mr. Shine slowly sank to his knees. He was penniless and his quarry had escaped him. He could not ransom Lord Ashworth and he dare not be on the premises a moment longer. He had nothing for his months of trouble and nowhere to turn. Worse, Lord Ashworth would come for him. Once he'd deposited the lady safely at her house, the man would start thinking of a plan. He'd probably send men. A lot of men. Who knows what the lord would say to the magistrate?

He might even say Mr. Shine had murdered Nancy Manton. For, where was she? He might even say Mr. Shine had stolen the bank. For, where was it? They'd never believe Nancy stole it. They'd all known her as the respectable Lady Carradine these past five years. They'd laugh at his story of Nancy Manton taking the identity of the lady. They'd laugh, and then they'd hang him.

Hanging. It was the nightmare that had followed him all his life. The idea that he'd someday be caught at one of his schemes and struggled into a noose.

He briefly considered throwing himself into the Thames. Drowning must surely be better than swinging. Though, when he imagined floating down into the dark water to join the rest of the unfortunate souls who'd gone before, he knew he would not do it. He had too much a care for his own comfort to drown himself. If he were to do a violence to himself, he would procure a sufficient amount of laudanum. It was said to be a pleasant way to drift off and never come back.

Slowly though, his despair began to recede like a Thames tide. In its place, a hunger for life swept over him like a crashing wave. Along with a determination to live, to have more days in front of him, anger came roaring in. Lady Carradine had betrayed him. Miss Farnsworth had been his undoing. Lord Ashworth had upset his plan. They were all guilty.

Somehow, those who could be made to pay must pay. Nancy Manton may have escaped his net, but there were others who had not.

He must only think of a way.

For now, he would pawn the silver and whatever else of value Nancy Manton had left behind. He'd find lodging in some low and out of the way place.

Then, he would think. The hangman's noose and the dark and mysterious Thames could wait. He would purchase a supply of laudanum to have on hand. If he were cornered, he would drink it, rather than be taken.

Just now, though, he had no intention of succumbing to defeat.

LILY HAD IMAGINED the lord would set her down on the pavement, but instead he raced down the street with her in his arms. She did not struggle against it. She was not certain her legs would hold her up and she felt encased in a blanket of safety in his arms.

He turned a corner and put her gently back on her feet.

"There is my carriage, let us go quickly," he said.

Lord Ashworth's coachman appeared expressionless upon viewing this sight, as if his master were in the usual habit of running down the street with a lady in his arms.

Lord Ashbridge waved the footman off and opened the carriage door himself. He helped Lily inside and said, "Cork Street," to the coachman. He then had words with the footman, though Lily could not hear what was said.

Once inside the carriage, Lily felt relief wash over her. They were out of danger. The tingling in her arms and legs, as if they had all fallen asleep, receded.

The carriage set off and Lord Ashworth said, "We must plan quickly. On no account can your servants understand the true nature of what has occurred here."

"Why should they not?" Lily asked, surprised. "Certainly, Mr. Shine will be prosecuted and all will know of his villainy and what we have suffered at his hands."

"Miss Farnsworth," Lord Ashbridge said sternly, "if anybody were to know that you were locked in a room with a gentleman, you would be ruined. Tell your aunt what has happened, I will trust her to keep the secret and she must understand she is never to go near this house again. For the purpose of servant's gossip, you will say Lady Marchelan took you to a late-night rout and then home to account for the missing time. Use Carlton House, the routs go on until dawn. You will say Mr. Shine was mistaken about a country party."

The enormity of what had happened to her seemed to crash upon Lily all at once. Of course, she *would* be ruined if the truth were known. A young lady just out was known to be gambling late into the night, her family member gone home, and then circumstances lead to her being alone with a lord and nobody could say what occurred? Whatever Mr. Shine's crimes, a female could never overcome such talk.

"I do not know what tomorrow will bring," Lord Ashworth said, "or whether Mr. Shine and Lady Carradine work together, I must see how that unfolds. I will make it my business to dissuade people from going there if she dares to remain open. Beyond that, I cannot determine what should be done, except nobody is to know you were ever alone with me. Mr. Shine and Lady Carradine must be dealt with, but they must be dealt with discreetly."

The lord noticed her hands shaking in her lap. He covered them with his own and stilled them.

"You must act the part," he said urgently. "The footman who opens Mrs. Hemming's door to you will not pay the least attention to my coat of arms on the carriage door if you distract him properly. My own footman has been directed to open the door for you as soon as we have stopped and place himself in front of the arms. I will stay back in the shadows. Leap out of the carriage and be gay, as if you have had too much champagne. Say something of Lady Marchelan being so kind to take you to a party. It will cement the talk in the servant's hall—they will only think you inconsiderate for keeping your own carriage out late without cause. Then, see your aunt in the morning."

Lily was not certain if her heart beat so rapidly because of the part she knew she must play, or that the lord had so far not removed his hands from her own.

LILY FOUND HERSELF still shaken as the sun came through her windows. She had played her part on arriving to her aunt's house. She thought she'd played it well, as she was certain there had been a look of irritation on the footman's face. He would think her careless and spoiled, and that was perfectly fine.

She had been enormously grateful that it had not been Ranier who had been standing by to let her in. The butler knew her too well and might see through her playacting. He was also far more observant than the footmen and might have noticed Lord Ashworth's coat of arms, however quickly it had been hidden.

She did not think for a moment that Ranier, if he had known the truth, would ever expose her secret. But it was just as well there was no secret for him to keep.

The house had been nearly dark with only a few candles lit and one handed to her to make her way above stairs. Her aunt had long since retired, having full faith in Lady Carradine as a chaper-one.

It was only upon closing the door to her

bedchamber behind her that Lily felt she was truly safe. That was, until a hundred crowding thoughts came upon her.

Where had Lady Carradine been? Why had she not stopped Mr. Shine from sending her carriage away with a story about a lady who did not exist? Had she known of the marked cards? Had she known that Mr. Shine had taken them prisoner?

Now that Lily had time to think, she thought it must be so. Lady Carradine had been charged to put her in her carriage. It was too unlikely that the lady had simply forgotten about her and gone to bed. Further, when they had made their escape, it seemed as if there were not any servants left in the house. Surely, it had been Lady Carradine who had sent them away.

To think, a lady who had been so trusted by her aunt had engaged in such a scheme!

She must tell her aunt all of it, and she feared the shock would be great.

As she willed the tremors to leave her hands, Lily's thoughts turned to Lord Ashworth. She would be still locked in that attic if it were not for him. No, she would most likely be dead, they both would, if it had not been for his quick actions.

Lily blushed as she thought of all the unjust thoughts she'd had about the man—that he was condescending and could not tolerate being bested by a female. All that rancor over cards—it had all been so petty! She'd bristled over his comment of trickery, though in her heart she knew her peculiar skill *was* some kind of trickery. At least, it would seem so to others.

When her life had hung in the balance, he'd acted bravely and swiftly. *She* might be better at cards, but *he* had been able to decisively plan an escape. He'd got her away, and then he'd told her exactly what she needed to do to protect herself.

While he might have been honor-bound to rescue her, he'd no responsibility to save her reputation. Considering how curt she had often been with him, and considering how she'd got them both into that dangerous circumstance to begin with, she had to admit that she had misjudged him. She'd thought him an arrogant and conceited man, and perhaps he was a bit of both of those things—what eldest son of a duke could escape it after being petted and fawned over all one's life? Yet, he was also of strong character and resolute courage.

It felt both strange and right to revise her opinion of him.

And then, she could not help but think of his strong arms, into which she had landed more than once. The arms that had carried her to safety. The finger that had laid upon her lips to quiet her when Mr. Shine came out of doors to dismiss her carriage. The hands that had laid themselves upon hers in the carriage. The intensity of his eyes as he urged her to act her part.

Pips interrupted her thoughts, unceremoniously charging through the door without a knock, but with a look of murder on her features. She would be tired from her late-night excursion to collect her at Lady Carradine's club. Her murderous expression softened somewhat when she noted that Lily had dressed herself and would not require assistance. Pips turned and left in a huff and Lily thought she could expect many more huffs from the lady's maid before her visit came to an end.

Now, though, it was time to go down and see her aunt.

CHAPTER ELEVEN

Hayes sat in the breakfast room, once more alarming his servants by taking only coffee. His thoughts were too full of the events of the previous evening to attend to the plate in front of him.

Having seen Miss Farnsworth into her house, Hayes had allowed himself to relax, at least for a moment. Somehow, he had gotten them both out.

He'd have to decide what to do—Mr. Shine must be dispensed with, perhaps Lady Carradine too, though at the same time Miss Farnsworth's reputation must be protected.

How brave the lady had been! It had been no easy feat to escape their captor and he'd feared she would lose her nerve, but she had not. She had only hesitated a moment at that first drop, and not once did she cry out. He could think of a dozen ladies who nearly swooned over a bee buzzing their bonnets. Miss Farnsworth had faced a high likelihood of death with nary a whimper. He knew she'd been terrified, but she'd gone forward anyway. Was that not a mark of a good soldier? To cast aside very real fears and carry on?

He pushed away the image of her stockinged legs poised above him, the thought being ungentlemanly. The only man who should see Miss Farnsworth's legs was her husband. Still, it was a picture that did keep drifting back. That, along with the feel of her soft little hands and how light she'd been to carry. Her worried expression and her wonderful hair, disheveled from their adventure. She had always been rather marvelous in appearance and the intensity of their adventure had only made her more so.

As pleasant as it was to consider Miss Farnsworth's charms, he forced himself to put his mind to the situation at hand. There was much he did not know, but as Mr. Shine had been bold enough to wave a pistol at him and lock him up in an attic, he must be careful. Before he'd retired the night before, he'd ordered Cobb to hire men to guard both his house and Mrs. Hemming's house. He'd taken the further step to set a watch on Lady Carradine's house. He wished to know who came and went, and he wished to know if the gambling establishment would dare open its doors again. He also needed to know more about Lady Carradine and if she were in league with Mr. Shine. He suspected she must be, as she had conveniently absented herself from the previous night's activities.

He would wait for a report from the men watching Lady Carradine's establishment. At some point, he would see Dalton and put out the word that the club was now to be avoided. But before that, he would visit Mrs. Hemming's house and speak to the lady. It had always seemed to him that she was a particular friend of Lady Carradine and she might be able to shed light on the lady's relationship to Mr. Shine. He doubted now that they were cousins, but he was undecided on the exact nature of the connection. If he were mistaken in his guesses at her involvement, might she somehow be under his power?

If she were under his power, it would account for her failing to escort Miss Farnsworth to her carriage. If she were under his power, might not she need rescue herself?

There was much to be discovered, principally—would Mr. Shine take flight, or somehow attempt to stand his ground?

The idea that he would soon see Miss Farnsworth again poked at him like a sharp pin and presented various images, some to do with her legs. He dismissed them all.

Of course, he had softened toward the lady. It was only natural after going through such an ordeal. It was only natural after seeing her act so bravely. But it was no more than that.

LILY HAD TAKEN her aunt into the drawing room and waited for Ranier to close the door behind him. She'd taken her aunt's hands in her own and related all of the events of the previous evening.

To say Mrs. Hemming was shocked was an understatement. She'd paled to an alarming degree.

"Dear Lily," she said, "it is my fault. I should never have left you there. What was I thinking? But then, it all seemed so reasonable in the moment. I would have trusted Lady Carradine with my life and so why not my niece? My God, what would I have said to my brother if something had happened to you? It is too awful to think about!"

"But I am well," Lily said. "So, there is no need to tell anybody anything. It is best that way, Aunt. I would be ruined if people knew that I had been alone with Lord Ashworth behind a locked door."

"Oh, yes," Mrs. Hemming said. "Quite ruined. I presume he was a gentleman, under the circumstance?"

"Most circumspect," Lily answered, thinking she need not go into how often she'd found herself in the lord's arms.

"Of course he would be. I know you do not like him, he can have that way about him that the high and mighty often do. For all that, though, he's always struck me as every inch a gentleman."

Lily hardly knew how to explain that her feelings had undergone no little transformation. As her aunt did not look for a response, she gave none.

"But what can have happened to Lady Carradine?" Mrs. Hemming asked. "I cannot understand it at all. I have known the lady these past five years, Lady Edith and I were some of her first members to the club. She is a friend, I cannot conceive that she would do anything to harm you."

"That, I cannot say—"

Before Lily could expound on her ideas regarding Lady Carradine, Ranier entered with a letter on a silver tray. He brought it to Mrs. Hemming. "Just arrived for you, madam. The messenger who delivered it claimed it to be of some importance."

Mrs. Hemming took the letter with a shaking hand. Ranier appeared rather perplexed by it but said not a word and left them alone.

"It is her," Mrs. Hemming said softly. "I

recognize the handwriting."

"Lady Carradine?" Lily asked, surprised.

Mrs. Hemming nodded, all the while staring at the note in her hand. "I suppose she writes to apologize, or to explain. Oh, I cannot imagine what she writes."

"Do open it, Aunt," Lily said. "It is the only sure way to know what she writes."

Mrs. Hemming slowly unfolded the paper and Lily peered over her shoulder to read it.

My dear Amelia,

You will have received this after I am gone. I am sorry I did not put Miss Farnsworth in her carriage, but she was in the company of Lord Ashworth and I remain confident he did the duty. In any case, I have full faith in Pips managing the thing quite well. I could not stay to see to it personally as I have been forced to flee the city.

You will know that Mr. Shine is not my cousin. I cannot go into the details of how it was that he should push his way into my establishment, only that he did. Mr. Shine is a cheat, my dear, and I send you this missive as a caution. Do not bet your money there, as you will likely lose it, he will be discovered eventually, and a shade will fall on all of the members. Please tell your friends.

As for me, I cannot be a part of such a vile operation as Mr. Shine intends it and so must go and make my way elsewhere. Know that I have always considered you a friend and will think of you often, regardless of where the wind takes me.

Judith Carradine.

Mrs. Hemming had just laid down the note when Ranier once more entered.

"I am sorry to disturb, madam," he said. "Lord Ashworth is at the door and quite insistent on seeing you."

"Goodness," Mrs. Hemming said, her voice faltering, "I suppose you'd best show him in."

Ranier nodded, though Lily suspected he was beginning to wonder at the activities of this particular morning. First, she and her aunt closeted themselves in the drawing room, then Mrs. Hemming was visibly struck by a letter he hands her, then a lord arrived at an unseemly hour.

It was only a moment before Lord Ashworth strode through the door. Ranier, never giving over to any strange circumstance, had gathered himself into his usual visage of understated competence. He was prepared to shower down upon the lord all manner of tea things, but Lord Ashworth claimed to want nothing.

Ranier's true feelings on the matter briefly made an appearance. Lily could guess he was deeply disappointed that he was not to show to good effect the skill and readiness in which he kept the kitchens of his household. He shut the door behind him with a decidedly firm hand.

Lily felt a wave of embarrassment upon seeing the lord so soon after their adventure. Perhaps the embarrassment sprung from how often she had found herself in very close proximity to him the evening before, or perhaps it was to do with her altered opinion of him. She could not say, but she clasped her hands together to stop them from fidgeting.

After the lord had suitably greeted Mrs. Hemming, he turned to greet Lily. She had the notion that he was less than comfortable to see her too.

"I have much to tell you both," he said, sitting down next to Mrs. Hemming.

"And we, you," Lily said, handing him the letter from Lady Carradine.

Lord Ashworth scanned it and laid it back down. "This answers some questions, at least," he said. "I had wondered if Lady Carradine might be under Mr. Shine's power and needed rescue, but it seems she's rescued herself."

"I still cannot understand how she involved herself with that person," Mrs. Hemming said.

"I rather think *he* involved himself with *her*," Lord Ashworth said, "though I haven't the slightest idea how he did it. Last night, I set a watch on Lady Carradine's house—too late to catch Mr. Shine in his departure. This morning, I discovered from my man that the house is closed up. The day servants arrived to find the doors locked and a note that said it would be shut for the foreseeable future. They have all been summarily dismissed. Now we know Lady Carradine has flown the coop. I think it's safe to say that Mr. Shine has too. I hope we will not see either again."

"That is a relief!" Mrs. Hemming said.

"But those poor servants!" Lily cried. "To have no notice or reference, what must they suffer?"

"They will not suffer, Miss Farnsworth," Lord Ashworth said. "My man was clever enough to get all of their addresses in case we have a need to ever speak to them about this circumstance. I have made arrangements to pay them all handsomely—two of the younger that were thought promising will be sent to one of my estates to train as grooms. It will be far higher pay, a chance to advance to coachmen, and very comfortable living conditions. I presume they will be well-pleased with the scheme. One, the old porter, will be retired on a pension. The rest have enough to be at their leisure until they secure new employment. I have arranged to write references, as Lady Carradine did not. I will explain their employer was too indisposed to provide one but that I was often a patron and observed their work."

"How good you are, Lord Ashworth," Mrs. Hemming said. "Very generous. Any employer would be gratified to receive a reference from a lord. It must work very much in their favor. And to think—the old porter was such a nice fellow. I like to imagine him comfortably retired."

Lily said nothing, but could only approve of the lord's largesse. She was also surprised by it. She would not have expected one who was so highly placed to concern himself with the various fates of Lady Carradine's servants.

"I take no special credit for that, Mrs. Hemming," he said. "It was not so much generous as it was decent and practical. Very bad form to leave servants in the lurch—a man can hardly be congratulated over remedying such a trifle. Now, I will keep a watch on Lady Carradine's house to be sure Mr. Shine does not return and I have set watches on my own house and this one."

"Do you mean to say, Lord Ashworth," Lily said, "that you believe that the danger has not wholly passed?"

Lord Ashworth momentarily looked away from her, as if considering his answer. "I do not know, and do not like to gamble on it," he said. "My concern with Mr. Shine is that he did not act rational last evening. Even a criminal can be expected to use commonsense and not take undue risks. He threw all caution to the wind and who knows what his actual plan was, as he did not succeed in it. Now, he may be desperate, or he may consider himself lucky to have got away. I cannot guess which. It will simply be a precaution until we feel we can let down our guard."

Mrs. Hemming was even now peering at the nearest window, as if she expected Mr. Shine to present himself there. Lily was deeply touched that the lord should have set a watch on the house.

"We thank you for your consideration," Lily said. She nearly bit her lip in saying so—she sounded over formal and stiff when she'd meant to sound gratified.

"I presume," Lord Ashworth said, "that you have been invited to the Bergrams' ball this evening?"

"Yes, we have," Mrs. Hemming said, "though we will not go. It will do Lily good to have a peaceful evening at home."

"I very much encourage you to go, Mrs. Hemming," Lord Ashworth said. "I believe we have waylaid any untoward gossip that might have sprung up about where Miss Farnsworth might have been while her carriage waited, but you must go on as usual. Nobody must think to examine the thing any more closely than they have, servants included. I suspect they would wonder at you skipping one of the most renowned balls of the season."

"Pips *would* wonder at it," Lily said to her aunt.

"Yes, I suppose she would," Mrs. Hemming said. "I sometimes think she wonders too much."

"You will be safe," Lord Ashworth said. "I will follow you in my own carriage. I will be waiting on the street at eight o'clock. Now, I will be off. I will see my friends and put out the word that Lady Carradine's club is closed and there is some idea that Mr. Shine is not who we believed him to be. That should be enough said."

With that, Lord Ashworth rose and took his leave.

Lily watched him go, his broad shoulders very much reminding her of the arms that had carried her to safety.

After the door closed behind him, Mrs. Hemming said, "It seems Lord Ashworth has things well in hand. I am most thankful for it, I would not have the first idea of what to do next. I rather thought we might hide in the house for some days. To think, he's set a watch on us and will follow us to the Bergram's. I know you do not favor him, but perhaps he was never as bad as you thought."

"Indeed," Lily said softly, "he never was."

HAYES MADE HIS way to Dalton's house. It was still before noon, and as he had fully expected, neither Dalton, Cabot, nor Grayson had yet left the house.

He'd found Dalton and Cabot in the library, engaged in a spirited debate over some horse or other that would run at Newmarket. He'd had to wait for Grayson to descend. As usual, that gentleman took more time with his dress than any thinking man should do.

Finally, Grayson sauntered in, his neckcloth a starched testament to an overworked valet. "What's this?" he said. "Is Ashworth moving in now?"

"Certainly not," Hayes said. "I wished to tell you of a circumstance I would like put about the town."

Hayes had no intention of telling his friends the *real* circumstance. There was too much risk that a slip of the tongue would set other tongues wagging about Miss Farnsworth. He would only tell them what was necessary.

"As long as it is not another rumor about a lady," Lord Cabot said. "I am still getting it on all sides regarding Miss Knightsbridge. I mean, Lady Hampton. My own mother wrote that if I dare turn up before her temper has settled, she may well set the dogs on me. This might be amusing, as her dogs could only attack me at my ankles, but I think I will not try it."

"It's nothing to do with anything like that," Hayes said hurriedly. "It is only this—Lady Carradine's club has closed and it seems her newly-arrived cousin is the cause of it. It appears that Mr. Shine was not all he said he was. They are both gone from London."

"Mr. Shine?" Lord Cabot said.

"Yes, I suppose you met him. An oily and ingratiating individual," Hayes said.

"I did not, I kept thinking I would go to the club and then never got there. Though, certainly, there cannot be another!" Lord Cabot exclaimed.

"Should there be another?" Lord Grayson asked.

"Say what you mean, Cabot," Lord Dalton said. "Are you previously acquainted with this Mr. Shine?"

"Only by a retelling," Lord Cabot said. "Good Lord, Ashworth, I am surprised you do not know of Mr. Shine, your father was on the very scene."

"What scene?" Hayes asked, alarmed that Mr. Shine might have a deeper history than what he'd given him credit for.

"Lockwood told me all about it when he explained to me, though I did not ask, why Lady Sybil's father had such an aversion to his duke," Lord Cabot said. "Ages ago, Gravesley hosted a house party and Mr. Shine was there, exposed as a cheat by Hampton's grandmother. Lord Blanding became convinced that Gravesely and your own father knew all along."

"*That* was the card sharp at Gravesley's house all those years ago?" Hayes asked. He needed to think quickly. Of course, he'd heard the story, as told from his father's perspective, but the villain of the piece had always been called "the sharp." His father had said the sharp had been a fellow he and Gravesley had done some sort of business with and had seemed respectable enough. They'd invited him to a shooting party as he'd claimed a great facility at it.

Now, he was to learn that the sharp was Mr. Shine? My God, the man himself must have been all too aware of the connection. Was there nothing the scoundrel would not dare?

"It was supposed to be a shooting party," Lord Cabot went on, "and then it rained buckets and the gambling commenced. Lockwood said they all assumed he went off to America to avoid paying the price for his cheating. Lady Carradine lived in America too. They must have reconnected as cousins there."

Hayes knew very well they were not cousins, though it was likely they had somehow made a connection in America. He would only wish that his friends would not find the story so interesting. Mr. Shine was appearing more and more troublesome, and the less said about the man, the better.

Thinking to turn their minds, he said, "In any

case, he is gone. I suppose you will attend the Bergrams' ball?"

The men nodded. Dalton said, "But for God's sake, Cabot, do not make a fool of yourself taking Miss Darlington into dinner. You cannot always escort her, it is too marked."

"Nonsense," Lord Cabot said. "She is the only lady willing to spend an entire supper talking of horses. Who else I should take in?"

"I've a mind to set my sights on the charming Miss Farnsworth," Lord Grayson said.

Hayes did not answer, and instead took his leave. Grayson would *not* have the opportunity to secure Miss Farnsworth for supper. His own carriage would follow Mrs. Hemming's carriage and he had a mind that it would be himself that would take Miss Farnsworth in.

It was only a necessity. He did not like to think of Grayson telling the amusing story of Mr. Shine's history, his reemergence as cousin to Lady Carradine, and now his sudden departure. It would only discompose Miss Farnsworth to hear it.

MR. SHINE HAD taken all he could from the house. There was much he left behind that would have fetched a fair price, but he did not have the means or the time to remove furniture and carpets and drapes. He'd packed up the smaller items—the silver, most of the candlesticks, and the crystals from the chandeliers. There were various curios of good quality and slight size. He'd taken a sharp knife and carefully cut away the fine material from the furniture—velvets, embroidered silks, and damasks. He knew what he could carry discreetly, and he knew, from long experience, what he could sell. He'd changed his coat to one he always carried with him—it was decent but not well-fitting, its cut was out of vogue and its cuffs were markedly frayed. It spoke of a middling sort of person who scraped together a living.

Setting off from the house, he'd made his way to the Seven Dials and then chose one of those genially dark streets to follow. It had been no trouble to hunch over and take on the mien of gentle defeat that was so often to be found in that district. He'd grown up in those places and had been in and out of them as his fortunes waxed and waned. He knew how to be of the neighborhood and not arouse undue interest. Though, he was not wholly dependent on blending in, especially at night. Were some desperate fellow to attempt to overcome him, he would find a pistol between the eyes.

It had been no particular trouble to find lodging, even at that late hour. An interesting creature named Meg, she of missing teeth, soiled clothes and reeking of sweat and the blue ruin, had been found lounging in a rickety chair outside of her charming domicile. She had been more than happy to rent him a room, though he must pay for this night, even though it was after three in the morning. Meg, being of generous spirit and wishing to close the deal, had thrown in the inducement of a cup of tea each morning. This allurement faded somewhat when it was explained that he was not to expect it strong on every day. Meg used the same ounce of tea for a week, so by Saturday things were watery, but on Sunday they darkened up again. She then wrung her hands and mentioned that sometimes it was dandelion tea, depending on what was on offer in the black market.

Aside from the ghastly cup he would be delivered of each morning, the room was as he expected. A bare wood floor, a wobbly bedstead that he had no doubt was infested with fleas, a lone candle, and a small fireplace that sat cold. One might think there was no need of a fire in this season, but in these neighborhoods the buildings were so closely packed that precious little sunshine ever penetrated. The roofs and walls were so poorly built that there was an ever-present damp that lingered on a person like fog. Then, there was the smell of the place. Wood smoke went some way to tamping down the odors coming from the various buckets thrown out windows.

He'd paid for a small fire to be built and pulled the lone chair to the small and dirty window. He sat himself down, not pleased with his circumstances but feeling out of immediate danger.

He must think. He must develop a plan. Even after selling all he had taken from the house, he'd need more. What he'd fetched might have been enough to set himself up somewhere, had he been able to stay in England.

That, he could not do. He had the distinct feeling that Ashworth would attempt to seek him out. He could not know it as certain, but he had learned in his life that when the warning bells went off in his mind, he was best served to listen to them.

As had ever been his habit in a long life of uncertainty, he took stock. What did he have that might garner enough to lay low and then slip out, South America bound?

Almost an hour of cogitating went by. A drudge had been in and lit the fire, the room had slowly warmed and dried out. Meg had gamely brought him a cup of tea, though it was Friday so there was not much to it.

Very suddenly, he knew what he would do. It was the only course open to him and it had been lurking in his mind just waiting to be found. He'd always been certain that the overblown ideas of honor the high and mighty congratulated themselves upon could be made to work against them. He would find out if he was right. He must just carefully work out the details.

He was not done with this life yet.

CHAPTER TWELVE

LILY HAD EXPERIENCED a flight of emotions in the past hour. She'd taken considerable care with her dress and had chosen a white silk with embroidered violets along the neckline and hem. Pips had given up her annoyance with her and arranged her hair into charming curls. Lily thought she must feel less embarrassed, less nervous, less whatever she was in contemplating seeing Lord Ashworth again. Their first meeting should have dispelled the discomfort, but instead she felt rather more on edge.

Her carriage had been called for eight o'clock and arrived in good time. Lily had surreptitiously glanced down the street to see if Lord Ashworth would truly follow them to the Bergrams' house. Perhaps he would have rethought and considered it an unnecessary precaution. Perhaps he would have determined that the lady who'd got them both into this circumstance could well enough make her own way there.

He had not thought those things. His carriage had awaited them as he'd promised and had followed them carefully to their destination.

The Bergrams' ball, always well attended, afforded her some time to think as their carriage waited in the line that ran up the drive.

Mostly, her thoughts drifted to the carriage behind her. He was there.

He was so different now. No, that was not it. Her opinions were so different now. As she wended her way through her muddled ideas, she finally came upon the thing that most troubled her. The idea, the question, that had been sending bubbles through her insides all afternoon.

Was *his* opinion of *her* different now?

She did not know. He had followed their carriage. Was that a singular consideration, or only what he thought his duty as a gentleman?

Her aunt had finally pulled her attention away from her roiling thoughts by way of an extensive and winding dissertation on how much of one's life was inevitably spent sitting in a carriage.

Now, they had alighted and made their way in. Lily was conscious of him behind her as she made her curtsy to Lady Bergram. She dared not turn around but followed her aunt inside.

She handed over her cloak and took her card, noticing her aunt looking wistfully in the direction of what could only be the card room.

"Do go on, Aunt," Lily said. "You must hurry to secure yourself a good partner and there is no danger to us here. I see Penny Darlington making her way over, I shall not be left alone."

Mrs. Hemming appeared delighted, patted her hand, and made a determined foray into the crowd.

Just as her aunt had departed, Miss Darlington reached her.

"Dear Lily," she said merrily, "you seem quite recovered from your adventure."

Lily stood stock still. Did Penny know what had occurred at Lady Carradine's? How could she know? If she knew, others must know.

"My adventure?" Lily said softly.

"In my phaeton, you goose."

Lily felt a wave of relief wash over her. She scolded herself for being such a nervous ninny. She smiled and said, "You are to know that I consider it one of the more interesting things I've done and think you fearless to have mastered such a skill."

"Nonsense," Penny said. "Oh, here comes Lord Burke. Do you know him? He is a jolly fellow; I highly recommend him."

"I do not know the gentleman," Lily said. And indeed, she had not yet met with Lord

Burke, though Cassandra had mentioned him as a genial and stalwart gentleman.

The lord in question approached and made a bow.

"Lord Burke, may I present Miss Farnsworth," Penny said.

Lord Burke smiled. "Miss Farnsworth, she of the masterful piquet game?"

"The very one," Penny said, laughing.

"Miss Darlington speaks highly of you, Miss Farnsworth. May I?" Lord Burke said, holding his hand out for her card.

As Lily put her hand out to give it to him, another hand swiftly reached in front of Lord Burke's and took the card from her fingertips.

"Burke," Lord Ashworth said, "I'm sure you do not mind."

"I am sure that I do," Lord Burke said cheerfully, "but if you are in earnest."

As Lord Ashworth filled in his name, Lily felt a thrill. Certainly, this was not to do with protecting her. There was no danger inside the house and no need to dance with her. It must be his wish and not just a sense of duty.

Lord Ashworth did not stay, and Lily had the idea that he was almost embarrassed by what he'd done. After he moved off, she handed Lord Burke the card. Lord Burke said, "Ah, he takes you into supper. I was certain the rumors going round that Ashworth was in a sulk over losing to you at cards could not hold any merit. He is a better man than that."

Lily did not reply, as she was equally certain Lord Ashworth *had* been in a bit of a sulk. But who cared for that now? He had taken supper.

"Do not look so downcast, Lord Burke," Miss Darlington said. "You are engaged to take *me* into supper, in case you have forgotten. I shall be put out if you regret your choice."

"I had not forgotten and would never regret," Lord Burke said, filling in the first on Lily's card. "I am delighted, though I fear Lord Cabot will not be."

Lily looked enquiringly at Penny. Miss Darlington only laughed and said, "Poor Lord Cabot. He will be forced to make civil conversation to some unlucky lady. He only prefers me as I allow him to wax on about his horses."

Lord Grayson, all tightly fitting coat and mile high neckcloth, joined their party. "Miss Farnsworth, charmed to see you again. Miss Darlington, ever your servant. Burke, how do you do?"

Penny looked at Lord Grayson with a small smile and a cool eye. Lord Burke said, "Good Lord, Grayson, if you are anymore starched and polished you will be as frozen as a statue."

Lord Grayson had the good grace to laugh, not appearing at all affected by his friend's comment. He asked for Lily's card and then stared down at it balefully. "Ashworth for supper and Burke for the first," he said smoothly. "I see I am late to the party." He filled in his name for the second.

"Cheer up, Lord Grayson," Penny said. "It is the usual Bergram crush, there will be no end of ladies who would be willing to thrill over your smooth compliments. Now, come Lily, let us go in."

THE REST OF Lily's card had been filled in with alacrity. She did not depend on her looks to have found herself popular. She was well aware that there was still a deal of interest in her as a lady with an unusual skill for piquet. More than one of the gentlemen who led her recounted what he'd heard of Lady Blakeley's dinner and Lady Montague's card party and then wished to have her confirm, or preferably elaborate on, the two engagements.

She did not give them much quarter, but rather turned the conversation to more usual subjects. In truth, she could not think much beyond the usual pleasantries. As each dance unfolded, she grew closer to the dance before supper.

Lord Burke had not been one to press her on her card games with Lord Ashworth. Rather, he had been amusing and kind and Lily thought that was what she could have expected. Both Cassandra and Penny had given him a ringing endorsement. Both ladies could be trusted to form well-considered opinions. Considering her ill-advised condemnation of Lord Ashworth, Lily thought she might learn something from the habit.

Lord Grayson had been charming and exceedingly complimentary. Though, as she had done when she met him last, she could not take him entirely seriously. Her hair, if she were honest about it, was dark and sufficiently curled. It was not the hair of a goddess that Lord Grayson claimed it. Even if she had not thought for herself that his compliments were overblown, she had taken note of Penny's comment to him. She had also taken note that her friend had led her away before Lord Grayson had the opportunity to enter his name on Penny's card. Lily was certain that it was less her effect upon Lord Grayson than his own habit that caused him to run on in such a ridiculous fashion.

Now, Lord Ashworth led her to the floor. She allowed herself to give in to his confident hand, though she found her tongue tied in knots. They could not speak of what had occurred in Lady Carradine's house, there were too many ears about. And yet, what could they say that did not talk of it?

They found themselves talking around it.

"I suppose you will look for a new house for your bets?" Lord Ashworth asked.

"That must be up to my aunt," Lily said.

"There are not so many that would be suitable for a lady," Lord Ashworth said. "I can only think of Almack's and even then, the patronesses would not approve of one so young closeting themselves in the card room. But then, I imagine it is no great matter to give up the amusement. Considering all that has transpired."

Lily chose not to point out that no Almack's invitation had been forthcoming. Her family had not the connections for such a thing. Rather, she said, "I suppose it can be no great matter for you to find the club has closed. I understand there are many such clubs open to gentlemen where you might amuse yourself."

Lord Ashworth's face had grown very serious. "It has never been only an amusement for me. Few are aware, but I count on you to say nothing of it—my family's estates came to the brink of ruin not so long ago and gambling has brought them back to a firmer footing. I have always considered cards a serious business."

Lily was shocked. She had not imagined the lord could have any sort of problems in that direction. Of course, there were those highly placed who seemed always on the brink of ruin, though they would never admit it. Funnily enough, those that teetered on the edge of disaster generally did so as a result of gambling. She had never heard of an instance in which gambling was the *cure* to ruin.

She was further surprised he would own his troubles. She certainly had never thought to admit her own difficulties. Hiding how she'd afforded a season, and hiding her ever present worry over money, had been one of the chief aims of her life.

But the lord *had* just admitted his own circumstances. Perhaps it was the moment in any game when it was time to reveal one's cards.

"I am not unaware of those sorts of difficulties," she said slowly. "My grandfather came within an inch of ruining us forever. My father has spent a lifetime dragging the estate back from the brink."

She noted Lord Ashworth steal a glance at her dress. He said, "I would not have guessed…"

Lily took a deep breath. "This dress, many other dresses, and various accoutrements, were gifted to me by some very kind ladies, one of whom is here tonight. Aside from clothes, you can guess where the funds came to afford a season."

Lord Ashworth did not initially appear to comprehend. Then he said quietly, "Gambling."

"Just so."

Lily did not know what the lord would think of her now, but she could not deny that there was a certain relief in being honest. She had just shown who she was and there was a freedom in it.

"I believe I understand," he said, just as the dance ended.

At dinner, they spoke more about their circumstances. Lord Ashworth was primarily concerned with two estates under his aegis—one in Devon and another in Somerset.

He did not describe the estates, and Lily had no imaginings of the house in Devon, but the estate in Somerset was well known. It went back to medieval times and even bore the markings of a long-filled in moat. She had, in fact, seen sketches of it in a book on the glorious houses of England that had been in her father's library. Dembly Castle was built of grey stone, a behemoth on a hill dominating its countryside as it had for hundreds of years. She suspected it of housing as many as twenty footmen and the stables likely cost more to maintain than her father's entire holding.

It gave her pause to consider what must be required to bring an estate of that magnitude back to a firmer footing.

Lily, now that she had laid down her cards, decided there was nothing left to hide. She spoke of her childhood—the feeling she'd always had of walking on crackling thin ice and waiting for it to give way, of her father's always harried expression, of her mother's care of the kitchen garden lest the rabbits steal the family dinner, or her ever-present worry for her sisters. She spoke of gathering together, pound by pound, the amount for a season. She even revealed that she claimed a sore leg to account for heading to the card room rather than the ballroom. She spoke of the kindness of Cassandra, Lady Lockwood, and Penny Darlington.

"That first evening we spoke," Lily said, "you advised that my father ought to hire a more skilled steward."

"And you rightly hinted that it was not my business to direct another on such matters."

"I was not particularly offended, I only sought to put you off. My father does not have a steward. He is his own steward."

Lord Ashworth nodded gravely. "I had been only speaking what had been much on my mind. I had dismissed my own father's stewards. They were in large part responsible for the estates coming to such danger."

And so they went on, speaking in low tones. Anybody viewing them from afar might have assumed they commiserated over the news of a desperately sick friend, so serious were their expressions. If they *had* spoken of a desperately sick friend, they might have been forgiven for how little attention they gave to anybody else.

The supper passed by surprisingly fast and Lily was sorry to go home. She was gratified, though, that Lord Ashworth made arrangements to follow them to Cork Street. His carriage stopped close behind their own and he descended to the road, scanning it up and down. He'd stayed in that stance until she and her aunt were safely inside the house.

HAYES SAT IN the library with a lone candle and a large glass of brandy. What revelations had been made to him this night!

He'd never have guessed at Miss Farnsworth's straightened circumstances. He had not supposed her to be any great heiress, but she had presented herself as any other well-financed lady just in from the countryside. Now, he knew the truth of those fine clothes. He knew the truth of where whatever money she did have had come from. My God, how had she not trembled when Lady Montague had named the wager at fifty pounds at that blasted card party?

He saw how it had been with her father's estate. Some who did not think deeply about such things would presume that it would be far easier to right a smaller estate with less expense to manage, than it would be to right a larger estate the size of his own. That was not the case, however. His expenses might be higher, but his resources would have far outpaced Mr. Farnsworth's own. His land produced an enormous surplus while a smaller estate could only produce a little surplus. If debts were piled upon the smaller estate it was disastrous. Further, creditors did not dun a lord very often, though they may have felt free to be on Mr. Farnsworth's heels. He suspected Miss Farnsworth's father had made a Herculean effort to keep the thing going.

Hayes had, at times, pitied himself, that his father had brought them to such a pass. What nonsense he thought that now. He had not spent his childhood walking on thin ice and wondering when it might give way. He'd spent his childhood surrounded by everything good. As a boy, he had only to mention a thing and it arrived. He'd been petted and cossetted by an indulgent governess. Even his tutors were likely to give way to his every inclination. Dembly Castle had been rock-solid beneath his feet. He was beginning to think that, while it had been pleasant, it might not have done him much good. Until only recently, the world had felt at his convenience. He might have done better to have experienced some early setbacks.

Miss Farnsworth had no doubt faced setback after setback. It was little wonder the lady maintained such steady nerves at a card table. No wonder she'd done battle with Lady Jersey's butler—the stern and formidable Riddick. No wonder she'd not fainted dead away when Mr. Shine locked them up. She'd been holding her nerves steady all her life.

She was not like any other lady he'd known. She appeared delicate, fragile even, but there was iron under that porcelain skin.

Considering her porcelain skin led to re-membering the smallest curl that had escaped and lay charmingly against her neck all evening. He'd been tempted to touch it, to wrap it around his finger. And then perhaps allow all of her curls to escape.

Contemplating letting down her hair led to thoughts of her stockinged legs as she climbed out Lady Carradine's window.

He downed his brandy and stood up, lest his thoughts take him anywhere else.

LILY SAT IN the drawing room, at a window that let in the morning sunshine, making a great effort to attend to her sewing. She did not particularly care to embroider on a usual day and this day did not feel usual at all. She'd taken a long time to fall asleep the night before, her head full of her conversation with Lord Ashworth over supper.

They had been so direct with one another! There had been no veiling or prevaricating, no social mask hidden behind. She had said all her thoughts, rather than examine them and say only those that might be found acceptable.

It had felt as if she had spoken to a man. Not a tricked-out gentleman at a ball, working to be amusing and showering her with vague and practiced compliments, but a real man.

How much they had in common. How much they had revealed.

Then, he'd followed her home and waited until she was safe in the house. He'd said he'd do the same to Lady Blakeley's half mask this evening.

The night before, as their carriage rumbled through the dark streets, her aunt had once more revisited the idea that Lily's initial dislike for Lord Ashworth might not be quite right. Lily had felt compelled to admit that it was true, her initial impression had been exceedingly revised. Mrs. Hemming had seemed pleased by it and noted the lord's good looks. Fortunately, she did not stay on the subject, as it somehow led her to considering how looks were passed down in families and she did not think the lord's father had ever been that handsome and who really knew how the whole thing worked.

Contemplating the coming evening felt

fraught with excitement and nerves—Lady Blakeley's ball. Lord Ashworth claimed he did not care for such a thing, but he liked Lady Blakeley and would not let her down. His mask the year before had been a gold coin, a comment upon his gambling. He did not know what she would choose this year, but he hoped it was equally good-natured.

That had given Lily some pause. What would Lady Blakeley choose for her? She was very much afraid it would be something to do with cards. That would be unfortunate—she'd begun to get the feeling that her matches with Lord Ashworth were losing ground as the topic of the day. She was still asked about it, but it had ceased to be the sole topic of conversation. After all, there was Miss Darlington's new phaeton to discuss and Lily had heard just the night before that a young lord had flown to France to escape his debts. There would be only so much left to say about a few games of piquet and she hoped her mask would not once again set the subject alight.

She would see him again. Lily felt that the evening must carry some weight. If he were to take the dance before supper once more, it would point to a real inclination.

Yes, they'd had an interesting and intense conversation last evening, but did that say anything? Did she wish that anything be meant by it?

It seemed extraordinary, but she very much thought that she did.

Mrs. Hemming bustled in, Ranier coming behind carrying two large boxes.

"They are here," her aunt said. "The masks."

Lily laid down her sewing, her hands showing the faintest tremble. She would find out now. How was she to walk into Lady Blakeley's ballroom? Who was she to be, for all the world to consider?

Ranier had placed the boxes on the table. He at once looked as if he would depart, and that he had no wish to depart.

"Stay, Ranier," Mrs. Hemming said. "I am sure you will want to know how we are to be cast this evening."

Ranier nodded gravely, as if the reputation of the house hung in the balance. Mrs. Hemming opened the first box. "This is addressed to me and what is it?" she said, pulling away the tissue paper.

Mrs. Hemming unwrapped the mask. It was a gentle face of creamy white and delicate features, with the smallest smile. It looked very like a statue one might find in a book about Rome.

"Oh! I see," Mrs. Hemming said, reading the note that accompanied her mask. "She says it is the Roman goddess Veritas, for my delightful habit of telling truths others leave unspoken.

Well, I suppose I *am* inclined to the habit."

Lily was gratified that Lady Blakeley had been kind to her aunt. She prayed for the same consideration.

"Let us see what she has sent for you now," Mrs. Hemming said, opening the second box. She lifted out a remarkable mask. It was iridescent and comprised of thin ovals of mother of pearl, laid out in a pattern like fish scales. The note read: A young lady bold enough to challenge a consequential lord is as rare as a mermaid."

Lily breathed a sigh of relief. Somehow, Lady Blakeley managed to reference her card games with Lord Ashworth without being direct about it. The mask was lovely.

"Aunt," Lily said, "might we do some shopping this afternoon? I might find a shawl that complements the mask. Or we might even stop into Woods. You know they often have such a selection of slippers on hand and one might be lucky enough to find a pair that fits without waiting for a pair to be made. A certain shade of blue would do nicely."

"I do not see why not," her aunt said. "I know you do not like to be kept indoors overmuch, and perhaps shopping will be the thing. You could always go walking with Pips, but then one wonders how many other butlers are chasing young urchins off their steps just now. Perhaps one altercation in that direction is quite enough."

And so, on account of young Sam and Lady Jersey's butler, they made plans for a shopping excursion.

TWO HOURS LATER, packages had been loaded into the carriage and Lily and her aunt were just coming from Woods. She had been unsuccessful in her idea that she might find a perfect sample of the slipper she had in mind, but had ordered a pair made nonetheless. The slippers would not arrive in time for Lady Blakeley's ball, but they would be charming for Lady Hathaway's ball. In the meantime, Lily had purchased a few novels at Lackington Allen that she would send down to Surrey for her sisters, as well as a lovely sea-green shawl for her mother.

Quite satisfied that they'd ventured into every shop they cared to, and not wishing to tire her aunt, Lily said, "We ought to go home now, so you can rest and have some tea."

Mrs. Hemming had nodded eagerly at the suggestion and they made their way to their waiting carriage.

The footman had just swung open the doors when Lily heard her name called.

"Miss Farnsworth!"

She turned and saw Lord Grayson barreling toward them in a most determined manner. He was as dandified as ever and carried a most ridiculous walking stick as if he meant to clear a path ahead of him.

She inwardly sighed, bracing herself for the ridiculous compliments to come.

"Dear me," Mrs. Hemming said softly.

"Mrs. Hemming, Miss Farnsworth," Lord Grayson said, nearly out of breath, "ever your servant. How fortuitous to encounter you so unexpectedly on this fine day!"

"How so, Lord Grayson?" Mrs. Hemming asked.

Lily suppressed a smile. Never let it be said that Mrs. Hemming did not know how to discomfit a young gentleman bent on pleasantries.

Lord Grayson was not at all slowed down. "This evening is Lady Blakeley's ball. Dear Miss Farnsworth, I must know how you have been cast. Venus? Aphrodite? Or perhaps the queen of all, Hera?"

To be compared to goddesses made not the least impression on Lily. Rather, she said, "I believe Lady Blakeley wishes us all to arrive and reveal ourselves and would not like to hear it spoken of on the street."

"I suppose so," Lord Grayson said. "I must only spend the next hours tortured with wondering."

"That seems a mild bit of torture, if you ask

me," Mrs. Hemming said, to Lily's amusement and delight.

Lord Grayson did seem a bit taken aback that his flattery was not having the desired effect, but swiftly regained his composure. "Ah!" he said. "But I have managed to discover one thing. You will attend. You cannot say you will not reveal your mask without also revealing that you will be there."

"We will be there, my lord. Now, I must get my aunt home before she overtires."

Lily turned to take her leave, but Lord Grayson was not so eager to end the meeting. He said, "May I claim supper then, Miss Farnsworth?"

Lily felt consternation flow through her. He could not claim supper. It was supposed to be Lord Ashworth that claimed supper. She would not agree to it. No, she would not.

"I am afraid I am already claimed," she said hurriedly.

"Is it Ashworth again?" Lord Grayson asked.

Lily did not answer. She could not answer. Good Lord, nobody had claimed her for supper. She might pretend somebody had, but she could not positively name the gentleman. What if she said it was Lord Ashworth and he discovered it before the ball? Or worse, did not ask her?

"You ought to throw him over, Miss Farnsworth. I am certain his mother has set her sights on Miss Blaise. She's worth ten thousand, or so

I'm told."

Lily had climbed into the carriage as quickly as she could and Mrs. Hemming followed. Her aunt gave the footman leave to close the door, thereby ending anything further that Lord Grayson might say. They set off and left him standing on the sidewalk.

Lily was beginning to positively dislike Lord Grayson. And as for Miss Blaise, she could fling herself off a roof for all Lily cared about it.

HAYES STARED AT his mask. He supposed he should not be irritated by it, or even surprised by it. Cards of seven, eight, nine, and ten fanned out—piquet's carte blanche. One would take the points for such a hand, but it was not the sort that would lead to a likely victory. He should have known his matches against Miss Farnsworth would be pointed to, though that all seemed as ancient history. He did not care for himself, he only hoped Miss Farnsworth would not be embarrassed by it.

Cobb came into the library with a letter on a tray. He held it out and said, "A very dirty boy has just delivered this, my lord. As evidenced by the black thumbprints upon it."

Hayes picked up the card, examining the

handwriting. He did not recognize it. "Who would send me a carefully folded letter in such a manner? Very strange," he said.

"As I did think, too," Cobb said. "I questioned the boy to determine from whence he'd come, but he was as saucy as you might expect. If I may quote that charming lad, he said: 'I ain't never tellin' ya, you old blighter.'"

"Very well, Cobb," Hayes said, suppressing a smile. If there were one thing Cobb could not abide, it was a lack of respect for his person and position. Hayes imagined that his butler placed himself rather high in the order of things. Finding himself named an old blighter by a person so far beneath his notice would poke at him for days.

After his butler had closed the door behind him, Hayes tore open the letter. He scanned to the signature and his fingers tightened on the paper. It was from Mr. Shine.

Ashworth,

As you know, I was left in desolation when last we met. However, my natural sunny disposition never eludes me for long. I am particularly sunny at this moment, having considered what means I have about me to add to my future prosperity.

I am certain you have somehow hushed up why Miss Farnsworth did not return home in her own carriage on the fateful night. Of course, I cannot know what was said, but I CAN recall what I said to her servants. I claimed she'd gone off to the country with Lady Marchelan. That lady, naturally, does not exist.

Having such knowledge that could cause you embarrassment and ruin Miss Farnsworth has made me sunny, indeed.

If you would prefer that the news not get about that the illusive Lady Marchelan does not exist, and that you were quite alone for a shameful amount of time with Miss Farnsworth, and that nobody else was in the house as the servants had been dismissed and Mr. Shine and his cousin Lady Carradine had departed, you will do the following:

Hayes read through to the end of Mr. Shine's missive, hardly believing what he was reading. The man was reckless and dangerous.

CHAPTER THIRTEEN

HAYES HAD BEEN afraid that Shine was not rational. The letter he'd just crumpled in his hand was further proof of it. If Shine had any care for his skin, he would have taken what he could from Lady Carradine's house and made for the nearest port. He'd not done that, though. He'd decided to stay and fight.

Hayes could not allow the information to get out. How could he explain it? Those hearing of it would look to what could be proved. What else could be proved than Lady Marchelan did not exist and Mr. Shine and Lady Carradine were gone? Even if the real circumstances were known, what did they prove but that he and Miss Farnsworth had in fact been quite alone for a period of time. If Lady Carradine could somehow have helped, she was long gone. My God, he'd even paid off the servants and taken two of them into his employ. He knew what the truth of *that* was, but it would look as if he'd bought their silence.

Mr. Shine must be stopped at all costs. He must pay him. His feelings upon considering enriching Shine were violent, but there was no choice. The only way to rid London of the man and protect Miss Farnsworth was to enable the reprobate to set up elsewhere. He might murder the fellow; he might even get away with it. But it would be inevitable that there would be some kind of investigation and the story would then come out somehow. Further, if he did not give him the money that would inspire him to decamp, Shine might only go on to more desperate plans.

Shine must be paid, despite Hayes' feelings about it. When he had paid the man, he would threaten his life if he dared turn up again in future. He would mean the threat, too. He would ensure that Shine knew he meant it. It must be strong enough to convince Shine to make no more reappearances. In any case, as a practical matter, he would not find himself the victim of blackmail twice. If Shine returned in future, he *would* kill him and take his chances. He might be blackmailed now, but he would not make a career out of it.

It was fortunate he had enough winnings on

hand to cover it, though it would set him back. He supposed that was what Mr. Shine had counted on. The others of the Dukes' Pact might be in straightened circumstances just now, but he had other means.

He examined the address given by the villain—the place they were to meet to hand over the money. It was in a lonely area of Hyde Park and the meeting was to be at half past midnight. Hayes determined he'd better bring pistols, if not to defend himself against Mr. Shine, then to fight off the footpads that would have an eye out for an opportunity.

Apparently, Mr. Shine had all confidence that he would come to this desolate spot at the appointed hour, as he'd not even had his messenger wait for a reply.

Hayes grabbed a sheet of paper from his desk and composed a note.

"THIS IS RATHER extraordinary," Mrs. Hemming said, bustling into the drawing room, waving a paper. "I cannot say that I am disappointed myself, there never was anything less comfortable than attempting whist behind a mask, but for you dear. Terrible. And then, what can he mean by it? Does he know something? I do wish he had been more clear."

"Aunt," Lily said, feeling a sense of alarm, though Mrs. Hemming was not being particularly clear herself, "what has happened?"

"Lord Ashworth writes that we are not to go to Lady Blakeley's half mask. We are to stay indoors and we will be guarded by some of his men. Something must have happened, though he does not bother to say what. A bit highhanded, if you ask me."

Lily was some combination of frightened and disappointed. She too wished the lord had sent more information. Certainly, he had discovered something. Perhaps he'd discovered that Mr. Shine was still in town. Had he somehow divined that Mr. Shine had not, as they'd all hoped, fled the country?

But even if he were still in London, what could Mr. Shine hope to accomplish? What did Lord Ashworth suspect him of, that they were not to dare venturing out? Lily felt a shiver run down her back. Perhaps the lord thought she might be in danger of a kidnaping? She knew she should not speculate, as speculations were so often wrong. Even so, she would assure herself that every door and window to the house was locked come sunset.

Then, the lord would present himself in the next day or so and tell them all about it. She must think his not very elucidating missive was caused by some hurry on his part. They must just trust him for now.

Though, it was a shame that they were to miss the mask. Worse, they must disappoint Lady Blakeley, who had been so kind to them and taken such care and expense over their masks.

"Aunt," Lily said resolutely, "we must trust in Lord Ashworth and send our excuses to Lady Blakely. We must say we have both been taken ill—claim we ate a bad fish, I think. That would account for both of us indisposed and be vexatious enough to keep us at home, but not a thing that would lay us low for long."

Mrs. Hemming nodded. "Very good idea. I was thinking we say we had colds, but then we would eventually be seen without red noses and people would wonder at it. I never knew of a cold that did not come with a red nose. Goodness, I have not had a bad fish in ages, though I remember it most clearly. After I recovered, I fired my cook as it became known to me that she was in the habit of buying cheap goods and pocketing the extra money. That is how I ended with a turned fish on my plate. Well, I wonder where she is now? Poisoning some poor family in the countryside, probably."

Lily did not follow the travails of her aunt's old cook. She was too busy thinking ahead. It was true, she would not see Lord Ashworth at Lady Blakeley's ball. But he must arrive here, if not today then on the morrow, to explain his note. She glanced down at her simple muslin dress and wondered if she should change to something more flattering.

HAYES HAD SAID he'd meet Grayson at Destin's and he'd decided he better turn up. He did not want anybody to notice anything unusual about his movements on this particular day.

Grayson had arrived before him and acquired one of the better tables. That had been no great effort, as the place was thinly occupied at that moment. As usual, his friend was starched to oblivion. Hayes thought it looked an uncomfortable and silly way to go on.

He sat down as Marty Destin hurried over with a coffee. Hayes had frequented the place so often now that Destin understood his habits—he did not favor wine or other spirits so early in the day. It was well he did not engage in the habit, as he would not for the world drink anything stronger than ale on this day. His mind must remain sharp.

"Any further news of Mr. Shine?" Grayson asked.

Hayes was momentarily startled by the question, until he recalled that Shine had been such a topic of interest at Dalton's house. It was devilish inconvenient that Shine had been the same man who'd attempted a cheat at Gravesley's house party. He hoped there was not anything else about the scoundrel that might come out, thereby keeping him a topic to discuss.

"I have heard nothing," Hayes said.

"Wellburn says he knew the fellow was a sharp as soon as he clapped eyes on him and never went to Lady Carradine's since," Grayson said.

"Wellburn always claims to know everything. After the fact," Hayes said drily.

"True," Grayson admitted. "But then, Banks said he'd heard from somebody that *somebody else* heard that Shine wished to marry Lady Carradine. He was so persistent that she decamped and nobody knows where she's gone."

Hayes inwardly sighed. He should have known the invented stories would begin their rounds. Wellburn always knew it. Banks heard it from somebody who heard it from somebody. He wished they would all stop talking.

"I suppose it is nothing to us what the two of them do," Hayes said.

"I suppose not," Grayson said. "Anyway, guess how I am to arrive to Lady Blakeley's ball?"

"As an over-starched neckcloth?" Hayes asked.

"That might have been better," Lord Grayson said. "As it is, I am to go as a magpie. The note said, *for the collector of hearts.*"

"You might take the hint, friend," Hayes said.

"I might, but not just yet. There is a lovely young lady who will serve to distract me from Lady Blakeley's condemnation. Though, I just saw her with her aunt on the street and she refused to tell me of her mask. I wonder how Lady Blakely has seen fit to cast Miss Farnsworth?"

"Give over chasing Miss Farnsworth," Hayes said abruptly.

"Ah! Do I detect a note of jealousy?" Grayson asked. "I already know you have secured her for supper. She would not positively say it, but I divined it all the same."

Hayes stared at his friend. *Had* Miss Farnsworth hinted such? He could not be certain—Grayson was in the habit of inventing elaborate teases. Whatever the case, he would not encourage his friend to speak further on Miss Farnsworth.

"You know no such thing," he said. "Further, Miss Farnsworth is too intelligent to succumb to your false flattery."

"But perhaps not so clever as to fail to succumb to my jokes," Grayson said with glee. "I hinted that your mother was set on Miss Blaise as the next duchess."

Hayes would have liked, just then, to hit

Grayson on the head with a nearby plate, though he hid the inclination. He was less successful at hiding a shudder over the mention of Miss Blaise and her ever-searching eyes. "You're disgraceful," he said, "I hope you know it."

Lord Grayson shrugged. "And you—how has Lady Blakeley seen fit to describe you this year? What do you come as?"

"Carte blanche," Hayes said stiffly.

He ignored Grayson's laughter and downed his coffee. Had Miss Farnsworth really claimed he would take her into supper? It was impossible to know. Grayson might say anything to amuse himself. But what if she had?

In any case, the joke was shortly to be on Grayson. Neither of them would have the opportunity to divine Miss Farnsworth's intentions this night, as the lady would be safe in her own house.

»»»—«««

THOUGH THE DAYLIGHT hours had not unnerved Lily, when the shadows grew long and the sun began its descent, she felt decidedly unsettled. Her aunt felt it too. They had eaten dinner quietly and attempted to keep to their habits, retiring to the drawing room as they would normally do on an evening in.

They'd had to tell Ranier a terrible fib—the note they had received from Lord Ashworth was purported to be news that Lady Blakeley's kitchens had caught fire, the smoke damage was extensive, and the mask was off. Ranier had seemed disappointed that they would not be able to advertise Lady Blakeley's high opinion of Mrs. Hemming and her niece, but he had not questioned the veracity of the story.

Ranier had lit the candles in their usual places near the windows, but without speaking of it she and Mrs. Hemming had moved them to the far side of the room.

Mrs. Hemming had instructed Ranier to ensure that the house was locked up tight. She told him she'd heard of a recent break-in only two streets away.

Dear Ranier, hearing of the offense, had thrown off his disappointment over Lady Blakeley's kitchens afire and puffed out his chest in the most marvelous fashion. He assured his mistress that no criminal element would make it past the front hall while *he* was the butler. He even took two heavy silver candlesticks to the front doors, ready to clobber the brains out of anybody being so foolish as to test his mettle.

Lily and her aunt, being both assured of Ranier's determination, had picked up their sewing.

The minutes had ticked by slowly. They did

not speak much, and when they did it was in low tones. Lily was certain her aunt listened for some sound out of doors. Though she had not communicated her fear of a kidnaping or some other danger lurking about from Mr. Shine, she was sure her aunt thought just the same. Why else would Lord Ashworth tell them to stay at home? There must be some plot afoot that the lord could not see his way clear to protect them from if they had been on the streets, coming and going from Lady Blakeley's house.

Though both Lily and Mrs. Hemming worked to appear as if all was as it should be, they gave it up before an hour had passed. Mrs. Hemming had suggested that Lily sleep in her bedchamber, the bed being of enormous size. Lily had hastily agreed—she'd no wish to be alone on such a night.

Ranier was convinced that both his mistress and Miss Farnsworth were terrified that the house would be broken into by dangerous low characters. He'd also had to deal with the housekeeper and the maids, who were a deal less calm than himself and frightened of being murdered in their beds. Pips had claimed she would sleep *under* her bed, so that the murderous beasts who were bound to break in would find it empty for their trouble. This had set the housemaids wondering if they too should sleep under their beds.

That idea only lasted a moment, as somebody mentioned what they should do if a mouse were to crawl upon them. As far as anybody could tell, the housemaids regarded hardened housebreakers and adventurous mice as equally perilous. The footmen, at least, maintained some outward stoicism, though their bold claims to be ready to fell the criminals with one blow like any Gentleman Jackson were perhaps more wishing than fact.

Ranier took the further step of pushing a heavy desk across the foyer to block the front doors and he nailed shut the less sturdy wood door that led to the kitchen garden. He and the footman would sleep in the library, ever at the ready to leap out upon the housebreakers.

Lily had been grateful for Ranier's care, and thought he seemed energized over the whole idea of overcoming thieves. Still, she was perhaps more comforted to know that some of Lord Ashworth's men were out of doors somewhere. If Mr. Shine and some associates would dare something, she'd rather some hardened types leap upon him than her dear Ranier.

Now, she lay on one side of the massive four poster, listening to her aunt's gentle snores. The house was quiet and she prayed it stayed that way. She must trust Lord Ashworth to direct them. And protect them.

HAYES HAD MADE an appearance at Lady Blakeley's ball. It would already be remarked that Mrs. Hemming and Miss Farnsworth had begged off. It might be suspicious if he did too. It might be said that their absence had something to do with *his* mask, and *their* card game. He did not wish any circumstance to connect them all together in people's minds.

He'd taken the early dances but was careful not to commit himself any further. He could only hope he would not be missed at supper. He especially hoped that Grayson did not think to joke that his friend had hoped to take in Miss Farnsworth and had left in a sulk over her failure to appear. His pistols and the money were packed in his panniers and one of his own grooms stayed with Horus to guard them.

When it was time, he'd slipped out to the terrace just outside of the ballroom, hopped over the low rail and made his way out, ripping off his mask and glad to be done with it.

As arranged, Freddy watched for him and led Horus and his own horse forward. Aside from the panniers on either side holding the money and the pistols, a great coat and a hat were thrown over his saddle. The weather was too warm for the overcoat, but it would conceal his weapons and have them at the ready. He nodded to the boy, mounted and set off, leaving Freddy to make his way home.

He was certain the groom longed to know the cause of this intrigue, and that there would be much speculation over it. That speculation would circle around the stables and then eventually creep its way into the kitchens before finally ending up on Cobb's lap. When he returned to the house, he fully expected Cobb to greet him with raised eyebrows, though the man would say nothing of the matter. To the servants, Cobb would likely pretend he knew all about it, but could not reveal what he was privy to. While Cobb wasn't looking, they'd debate it and eventually decide it was some sort of romantic assignation, likely with an irate husband lurking somewhere.

The streets were not desolate, there were plenty of people in carriages and horseback, and some on foot, going from here to there. Hayes pulled the brim of his hat low. London might seem a big place, but it was extraordinary how often one encountered an acquaintance. He did not wish to be seen on the way to this particular assignation.

He made his way into the park, vaguely uncomfortable with the quiet of it. It was more usually the scene of sunshine and crowds and the low hum of hundreds of people talking. Now, it was dark, silent, and empty. At least, it appeared he was alone. He could not know what sort of rogues lurked in the shadows. All he could do was make it clear he was not drunk. It was the drunken fool, swaying on his horse, that always presented the most alluring opportunity.

He stopped Horus and took the loaded pistols from his panniers. He carefully placed them in either pocket of his great coat. If there were a rogue lurking nearby, it would be well he noted that his hoped-for prey was not unarmed.

Mounting, he trotted Horus over a wide field, making his way toward the north side of the Serpentine. The meeting was to take place under a tall stand of trees just beyond the Cake House.

The building came into view, and the stand of trees beyond it. Hayes scanned the area for any sign of Shine, or the horse he might have tied up somewhere. He saw nothing. The night was still and not even the leaves moved. It felt more a painting than a living landscape.

Hayes decided to make a wide skirt around the Cake House, careful to be out in the open. He did not trust Mr. Shine and could not know if the man had brought with him some low associates. Open ground would leave him vulnerable to a shot, but too close to trees would leave him vulnerable to an ambush. If he had to guess, he imagined Shine to be more experienced with sneaking up on a person than he'd be with steady aim over long distance.

Through the murky darkness, he saw a lone figure under the stand of trees he'd been directed to. There he stood—Mr. Shine.

Hayes spurred Horus. He'd decided that the only way to deal with a person of Mr. Shine's dark intentions was to be the aggressor. Therefore, he intended to come in fast.

Horus galloped over the remaining ground, and Hayes wheeled him to a halt.

Mr. Shine stepped back to avoid being trampled.

"This meeting need not be long," Hayes said, removing one of the pistols from his coat.

"Hey ho!" Mr. Shine cried. "No need for violence, that I can assure you, my lord."

Hayes thought that was particularly rich, coming from Shine. He said, "There may not be a need for violence at this moment, but I wish you to understand that this is a well you may only dip into once. If you come back for more in future, if you cause any harm to Miss Farnsworth, I will kill you."

"A person might get themselves hanged for such a thing," Mr. Shine said, a subtle tremor in his voice.

Hayes thought the man worked hard to appear confident, though he was not wholly successful.

"It is unlikely that a hew and cry over *your*

murder would ever be made," Hayes said. "One less scoundrel plaguing the town will not concern anybody. You will leave England and go somewhere. Where, I care not."

"Yes, all right," Mr. Shine said in a conciliatory tone. "I was going anyway. Just give me the money."

Hayes unbuckled the panniers and threw them at Shine's feet. "I mean what I say, you rogue. If one whisper of you comes to my attention, I will be murderous. Make your way now to a port and be gone."

Hayes turned Horus. Behind him, he heard Mr. Shine say, "Couldn't be happier to be on my way. I *will* need a horse, though."

A shot rang out and Haye's felt a burning explosion in his right arm. The pistol in his hand fell and the force of the shot toppled him off his horse. He landed on hard packed ground.

He heard Mr. Shine laugh and footsteps approach. The man was deranged, he should have seen it! Shine had been reckless from the first, why had he thought the scoundrel would be rational at the final hour?

Hayes rolled over and grabbed the pistol from his left pocket, all but certain Shine intended to finish him off.

He fired, his aim not as good from his less-favored hand. He hit Shine in the leg, though he feared it was only a graze.

As Shine fell, grasping at his leg and crawling through the dirt toward his pistol, Hayes leapt up and struggled with one hand to mount Horus. That stalwart beast had not spooked at the shots and run off, leaving him to his fate. It was well he was master of such a horse, as Hayes could feel the blood running down his arm. He was bleeding profusely and must get away before he lost consciousness and was at the villain's mercy.

Horus stood stock still as he climbed into the saddle, seemingly aware that they were in a perilous situation. Hayes was seated and his feet in the stirrups as Shine rose, clutching his leg and fumbling with his pistol. He briefly thought of grabbing the panniers and taking them back, but quickly threw off that idea. He knew well enough that would only drive Shine to even more desperate plans. He might decide to kidnap Miss Farnsworth or some other lunatic act. In any case, he could not be sure how much blood he was losing or whether the pistol in Shine's hand needed to be reloaded or was a second already loaded.

"If I see you again, I will not miss," Hayes said. He turned Horus and spurred him across the open field, galloping toward the gate and holding on as best he could.

CHAPTER FOURTEEN

Though Lily had waited all morning for Lord Ashworth to make an appearance and explain his note of the day before, it was Miss Darlington who was led in. She was dressed smartly in a fitted jacket of yellow silk with thin blue stripes over a skirt of the same blue hue. Lily was certain this was a joke upon the Four-in-Hand Club and their blue waistcoats with yellow stripes. The remarkable phaeton and its scowling tiger sat just outside the window.

"Dear Lily," she said, sitting down by her friend. "I thought to come and check on you as Lady Blakeley said you were indisposed last evening. But here you are, blooming roses."

Lily was not surprised her cheeks might have pinked. She never did like to tell a fib, though she reminded herself that it was necessary in this case.

"It was only a temporary illness," Lily said. "A bad fish, we think."

"Oh dear, I cannot claim to have had that particular experience, though once my entire family was sickened and we were certain it was a fricasseed chicken. It had been smothered in a heavy sauce so we did wonder if the cook had rolled the dice on that one and come up short. In any case, I am glad you are well."

"Most recovered," Lily said. "You are very kind to have thought to look in."

"Of course, I would. Such a shame about the timing of it, though! To have missed Lady Blakeley's ball, which is always so amusing. Can you imagine what she made for me? The goddess Epona, protector of horses. I was very pleased, as you might imagine. What had she sent you, Lily?"

Lily rose and crossed the room. She brought her shimmering mask over to Penny.

"It is lovely!" Penny cried.

"I was to be a mermaid," Lily said. "She wrote that a lady bold enough to challenge a consequential lord was as rare as any mermaid."

"Ah, I see," Penny said. "She obliquely references the card games with Lord Ashworth no doubt."

"Yes, but she was kind about it," Lily said. "I should have liked to have gone."

"I do wish you had been able to. We had an

exceedingly merry evening," Penny said. "If you can imagine it, Lady Montague came, I believe for the first time. She has always been invited, but it is said that Lady Blakeley always sends her an insulting mask, knowing she will not wear it. Everybody was surprised to see her."

Lily felt a vague wave of trepidation, as she always did upon hearing the lady spoken of. "Goodness, what was her mask that she dared it this year?"

Between peals of laughter, Penny said, "She was a Yorkshire pudding! It was a particularly unattractive mask and of course referenced her retreat to the north last season. She came in as bold as anything and claimed she was happy to celebrate the famed dish from her county. It seems she is determined to be everywhere this season."

Though Lily had been distressed to miss the half mask, she found herself not at all sorry to have missed Lady Montague. She was a dangerous creature and Lily would not have liked to have been one of the party amused by her discomfort. While the lady would have played it off with confidence, she might have also taken some notes.

"Lord Grayson was a magpie," Penny went on. "It was said to have represented his habit of collecting hearts. He found it very amusing, or so he said. Oh, and you would have laughed at the sight of Lord Ashworth too," Penny said. "A fan of cards totaling piquet carte blanche. A small dig at him for losing to you, we all thought. Though, I will give him credit for appearing good-humored about it."

Lily felt frozen in her seat. Lord Ashworth had gone to the ball? Why on earth would he, and then find it not suitable for herself and Mrs. Hemming? All this while, she had imagined him deep in the mystery of Mr. Shine. Perhaps even prowling around the town with his hired men or having turned his library into a center of command as men came and went with news. But that had not been the case, he'd gone to a ball. He'd just made sure that she did not.

And then, his note had been so vague. He'd not given any reason why they should stay away. She had invented the reasons; they had only been her own imaginings.

Lily had a sinking feeling that she might be able to account for this unanticipated circumstance. He meant to extricate himself from whatever attachment had been formed by their adventure together. She could not know it for certain, but she felt it.

"Oh, goodness," Penny said, "I can see from your expression that I ought not joke about Ashworth. He remains a sore spot. Never mind, shall you like to go on a drive? We might have your carriage follow us, just as your aunt prefers."

"No, I thank you, Penny," Lily said, forcing herself to appear cheerful. "I had better not. I am much recovered, but I think I should stay close to home for today."

Penny patted her hand. "Quite right, I should not like you to have a setback. Lady Hathaway's ball is in a week. It comes early this year as her daughter is close to her confinement. Last year was divine, it was everything Russia. Lord Cabot tells me that this year we will encounter a Tudor court—we will dance the pavane and eat conger eel."

Miss Darlington did not stay much longer, as she became convinced that Lily had begun to look a bit peaked.

Lily stayed by the window, watching Penny easily mount her phaeton while her tiger glared at all passersby who dared to look at his interesting mistress.

The phaeton trotted off and Lily propped her chin on her hands. She could see now that her intimate conversation with Lord Ashworth had caused him discomfort. Though she was deeply stung, she supposed he was attempting a kindness. He wished to put some distance between them. He wished her to know that while they had shared an extraordinary situation, and though they had experienced similar circumstances, there was nothing significant in it.

What a rube she'd been! To have imagined

that because her own opinions had changed, his had as well. He had rescued her. She ought to be grateful for that, and not ever have expected more.

Lily felt her face flush. How important she'd begun to think herself! As if a country girl of her not-at-all considerable stature had any sway over a lord. She'd been so nonsensical. A lord like Ashworth would marry high or he'd marry an heiress. Knowing his circumstances, it would certainly be an heiress. Lord Grayson had as much said so—it was Miss Blaise who was favored. Lily had got the distinct impression at Lady Catherine's ball that Lord Ashworth did not care for the lady, but he would do his duty. Had he not been working all this time to regain his estates' footing? Of course, he would do what was necessary.

But how had she given herself away? He'd somehow sensed that her heart was in danger and moved quickly to disabuse her of her own inclinations. She supposed he'd done it in the gentlest way he could think of. After all, what had been the alternative? That she would go to the ball and he would not put his name on her card? Or he would, and then revert to his earlier aloofness? At least now she could suffer her foolishness in private. Nobody need know of it. Nobody would ever guess at it—it was the general opinion that she did not like him. Nobody need ever discover that her feelings had changed.

But perhaps she was allowing her thoughts to take her in the wrong direction? That idea began to cheer her. Could there not be another reason that it had been necessary for Lord Ashworth to attend the ball, and yet equally necessary that Lily was to stay home?

She could not imagine what such a reason could be and feared she grew over-fanciful. As her practical mother had often said—*the truth is right in front of you, if only you would care to look.*

Lily sighed. It was no use trying to talk herself round. The truth *was* right in front of her.

She straightened her skirts and picked up her sewing. She must not let her ridiculous notions overcome her. Lily Farnsworth was here for one season only. She had a duty to her mother and father, and most of all, her sisters. All that had happened recently was only a mad adventure that must be forgotten.

She must see if she could like some gentleman who would find her dowry sufficient. One not placed as high as Lord Ashworth. It would not be as thrilling to think of, as whoever that gentleman might be, he would not be as dashing. Or courageous.

Thrilling and *courageous* must be cast aside for practicalities. She would not return home with nothing to say but having made a fool of herself.

THE HOUSE AT Forty Berkeley Square went on in hushed tones, all overseen by Cobb, and Hayes' valet, Molton. On the night he'd arrived back from his meeting with Shine, the doctor had been fetched and come quickly. The man had pried and poked and then said, rather merrily if Hayes remembered it right, that the shot had lodged deep near a bone but had not broken it. He had a vague recollection of the surgery—he'd been laid on a table in the kitchens as the housekeeper clucked round, scolding housemaids for staring. He was liberally dosed with laudanum, then would wake and be dosed again in what seemed an endless cycle. He had no memory whatsoever of being transferred from the kitchens to his own bedchamber.

After that, he was tended by a series of old women hired by his housekeeper, overseen by Cobb, and harassed by Molton—the valet failing to be impressed by their skills. Mostly, he remembered the women laying hot compresses on the wound and then covering it with honey and fresh bandages. Two days went by in a haze of being forced to swallow medicines and broths. Finally, he began to feel more in the world. His fever had abated and the danger passed.

As the fever left, memories flowed back.

Shine's betrayal, the explosion in his arm that had knocked him to the ground, his returning shot and struggle to mount his horse. Then, his wild ride through the streets, hanging onto Horus. His ever-stalwart horse had sensed the danger and had stepped lightly but swiftly back to the house. Horus had even whinnied and stamped his feet when they'd arrived to the door.

Freddy had run out, only thinking to relieve him of his horse. Hayes had noted the whiteness of Freddy's face as the boy stared at his drab overcoat soaked in blood as he'd slid off his horse. Cobb and Molton had been out in a trice and they'd carried him into the house. He had a vague recollection of being hauled down the stairs to the kitchens and complaining loudly about it.

Cobb had since told him that he'd lost a fair amount of blood. To quell the servants talk, Cobb had given them a story. Their lord had acted as a second to a friend and then been set upon by highwaymen on the way home. His panniers had been packed with bandages and such, in case his friend was hit. The highwaymen must have thought the panniers carried valuables.

Hayes had grimaced upon hearing the tale. There were vast holes in that story—his pistols had not been dueling pistols and nobody met for a duel in the dark. The only detail that had the ring of truth was the panniers. Cobb had been observant enough to notice that he'd had them when he left and had returned without them. Although, it would be rather foolish to believe a second and not a surgeon had brought bandages. He did not know if they believed half of it, but Cobb had taken the further precaution of warning them all that if the matter was spoken of again, they would be dismissed without reference. The housekeeper had sniffed at the threat; Molton had been equally unimpressed. However, the rest had been cowed to silence. He hoped that silence would hold over time.

As far as Mr. Shine was concerned, Hayes prayed they'd seen the last of him. There was always the danger that an unhinged individual might try something else, but just now Shine would be nursing a wound in his leg. With any luck, it would fester and kill him. If he lived, Shine had got enough money to relocate himself. He hoped the man had some sort of self-preservation instinct and would move on.

Hayes felt stronger now and had been out of bed for a half hour at a time. That was well, as he'd had to beg off on a number of engagements already. He'd claimed a fever—a vague enough complaint that it might be construed as anything. Though, he would have to make a reappearance soon. He would also have to send some sort of communication to Mrs. Hemming. There was still a guard on her house and they were followed from place to place, but it must seem odd that nothing had been heard from him beyond telling them to stay home and not attend Lady Blakeley's half mask. He supposed they might have gone after all, but at that moment he had not known if Mr. Shine had associates who might try to kidnap Miss Farnsworth while he attended his midnight meeting in the park.

He thought it would be best if Miss Farnsworth and her aunt never knew what had actually occurred—it would only serve to frighten them. He must just communicate that the danger had likely passed.

Hayes went to his desk by the window and pulled a sheet of paper from the drawer.

Mrs. Hemming,

Please excuse my absence, I have been much taken up with discovering more about our mutual acquaintance. By the evidence I've gathered, I have hope that we will not be troubled further by that particular gentleman. For now, I will leave my men in place on Cork Street and you will continue to be discreetly followed but I believe the danger has passed.

Hayes bit his lip as the wound began to pulse in his arm. He might wish to write more, but he dared not test the wound before he had to. He might wish to write something that would be a hint to Miss Farnsworth. Though, he was not certain what that hint should be. As he'd laid in bed hour upon hour, she'd been much on his mind.

What a start they'd had! Both with their backs up. She'd claimed a particular skill at piquet. He'd condescended. She'd taught him a lesson. He'd found he was neither used to nor fond of being taught a lesson. They had gone on prickly and uneasy.

His feelings had begun to change in some slight way at Lady Catherine's ball. They had been more affected as he'd watched her rescue young Sam from Riddick's cudgel on Lady Jersey's steps. Sam, who had now become a favorite in the stables, due to his propensity for telling of the horrors of St. Giles. And there was Sam's mother, who was less of a favorite with the housemaids for her propensity for telling of the horrors of St. Giles.

Then, he and Miss Farnsworth had been locked together in a room, under threat, and she'd shown her real worth. Her bravery. Her nerve. And of course, the Bergrams' ball, where he'd stared at the ringlet of a curl against her neck. Where he'd found out her real circumstances. Her dowry would be small. Too small for him to consider.

Hayes paused. He was not considering her dowry! Good lord, the laudanum was playing tricks with him. Why else would he be thinking of dowries?

He was a gentleman of the Dukes' Pact. He would take his time, no hurry to marry. He would have his way, and his way was to avoid the state for a year or two. His way was to have the estates on firm footing before committing himself. Miss Farnsworth would be off the scene before it was his time to declare to any lady. A woman like that did not drift from season to season. In any case, he doubted she could even afford to come back for a second round.

For all he knew, she was being courted as he lay there. Why shouldn't she be? She would make a rational choice for a husband, she would not leave the town without her future secured. She had too much care for her sisters to do otherwise.

Though, why should some worthless fool win the lady? He could imagine the fellow—he was of a suitable estate and would provide adequately. It would all be very adequate. She would accept him as her duty. Or worse, she would like him, though Hayes was certain she should not. *Adequate* did not seem adequate for Miss Farnsworth.

Or, Good God, what if Grayson prevailed? Grayson was intent on making Miss Farnsworth his latest romantic conquest. The lord might think he'd toy with the lady's feelings and then be off to the next. But Grayson played with fire and one of these days he would not escape. Why should he not take his fall at the feet of Miss Farnsworth?

Like a wayward horse, his thoughts went this way and that way as he used all of his strength to steer them back to the right path.

None of it mattered, he did not know what he would write if he could and he could do no more just now than sign his name.

MRS. HEMMING SORTED through her various correspondence. Lily saw her pause at one particular letter. Her aunt's expression was so singular that Lily wondered if it were another communication from Lady Carradine. She'd given up wondering if Lord Ashworth would write something—she'd spent too many days waiting with bated breath for the post to arrive, and then nothing to show for it. She had allowed herself to hope for naught, his silence said everything that needed to be said.

The past days had been spent fulfilling their engagements, always aware that there was a man on horseback who trailed them. Both she and Mrs. Hemming were cognizant of the idea that Lord Ashworth did not yet believe it entirely safe to dispense with the precaution. He would provide a guard for them. Though, he would *not* provide himself, as he had done on the way to the Bergrams.

She had not seen him at the Findlay's dinner, though Lord Findlay was a cousin and she'd been certain she would. Then, she'd heard he had some sort of fever complaint—the flimsiest of excuses one used when one wished to absent oneself. A person claiming such a disease had bought themselves at least a week if they cared to and were in no danger of having visitors. Lily knew in her heart that it was not fever that kept him away. It was she. After all, was not a hopeful female more dangerous than any disease?

She wished they would finally meet again, so that she could show him she had no thought of him. That she *did* was beside the point. She was skilled enough at hiding her feelings that she might convince him of it. She would wear her card player face. Then, they could go back to their old footing.

"Ranier," Mrs. Hemming said, laying down the letter, "I wonder if you might give us a moment alone?"

Lily dropped her napkin. Was the letter her aunt had just read indeed another from Lady Carradine? Or even, finally, from Lord Ashworth? Surely, it was something of importance.

Ranier appeared as surprised as Lily at the request, but shooed the footmen from the room and closed the door behind him.

Mrs. Hemming slid the letter across the table.

Lily instantly recognized the handwriting; it was from him. He had finally written, though as she scanned it she wished he had not. It was the shortest of missives, only to say he believed Mr. Shine gone, though the watch on them would stay for now.

He could not have written any less and she understood him very clearly.

"He is not very voluble, is he?" Mrs. Hemming asked.

Lily laid the letter down. "I think he must be much engaged and only wished us to know the facts."

"I wonder that he does not call on us, considering what has transpired. I should like to know what he knows. How has he concluded that Mr. Shine will trouble us no more? And if he knows it, why does he keep the watch on the house? For that matter, why have we been turned over to some nameless fellow when it was himself that escorted us to the Bergrams?"

"I believe it was said at the Findlays' that he suffers from a fever of some sort," Lily said.

Mrs. Hemming looked critically at her niece. "But my dear, he cannot be both much engaged and abed at the same time."

Lily flushed and twisted her napkin. "Perhaps that is it—he is too ill to write a long letter."

"Even *I* can write a letter when I am sick enough to be abed. In truth, I write rather more in those circumstances, it passes the time."

Mrs. Hemming paused and Lily hoped her thoughts would take her in another direction. Then her aunt said, "There was nothing between you that has somehow gone amiss?"

"No, certainly not!"

"I only ask because of the unusual circumstance that occurred in Lady Carradine's house. I only thought maybe…"

"Maybe what?" Lily asked, alarmed at where her aunt's thoughts seemed to be taking her.

"Oh, I do not know, perhaps an ill-advised kiss that both of you would prefer to forget."

"There has been nothing like that," Lily said hurriedly. "Nothing at all, I can assure you."

"Very well," Mrs. Hemming said, seeming satisfied. "I suppose Lord Ashworth will illuminate the matter further at his leisure. Now, we'd best open the door or else Ranier will think we are scheming."

THE GRACE KELTER had set sail two days ago. On the night of his encounter with Lord Ashworth, Shine had bound his leg, stowed the money from the panniers in various pockets, limped his way back to the road, and hired a carriage. He'd been forced to leave the park without the horse he'd intended to take from the lord. It had been a good plan—take possession of a fine horse that would carry him to the port and then be sold for a good price. He'd planned on taking the money, the horse, and whatever valuables Ashworth had on his person. He'd even take his clothes, at least the ones not bloodied. They would not fit him but would be of sufficient quality to fetch a promising amount. He'd not worried that he'd be connected to the murder. Ashworth would not have told anyone of the meeting. To tell of the meeting was to tell the tale of Miss Farnsworth and he was certain Ashworth would keep that close.

As for a gentleman murdered in Hyde Park in the dead of night? That it was a lord would cause a stir, that could not be avoided. But it would be assumed the lord had been very drunk and beset by footpads. Why else would a lord enter the park at such an hour?

He'd debated if it were strictly necessary, but he knew that rumors of him being a cheat might follow him across the globe and resurface at any time. Ashworth would be the source of those rumors. He had only to hope Miss Farnsworth would be so frightened to hear of the lord's demise that her lips would remain shut forevermore. He thought she would stay silent, to say anything about it must reveal her part in it. As much as these fine ladies pretended at swooning and being over-delicate, he had the idea that they could hold up well enough when their own safety and comfort were at issue.

Of course, there was Meg to worry over. He'd meant to be off that very night, but he'd been hit and must tend to it. He'd got out of the carriage a distance from Meg's crumbling abode, he must be seen to come on foot to support his story. He'd known he would not have been able to hide his wound, he'd bled too much. So, he'd told Meg of being attacked and barely escaping with his life. After all, they were in the neighborhood of the Seven Dials. Nothing more usual than that. In any case, he did not think Meg bright or likely to be solving mysteries. She was too wed to the blue ruin to do much beyond rent her rooms, buy tea on the black market, and purchase bottles of gin. He suspected she'd often forgone dinner in pursuit of her liquid lover.

For a few coins, she'd dressed the wound. He'd have wished to have a nurse with cleaner hands and better breath, but he'd had no choice. He was intent on not involving anybody beyond what was necessary. In any case, it was only a deep graze and would heal soon enough. He'd left Meg's genial household on the following morning in order to make the ship for Venezuela.

It had been a mistake. As he traveled, the wound had festered. He'd taken care of it as best he could with hot water and clean bandages at the inns he stopped at. He purchased yarrow, and when that had no effect, he'd tried comfrey. And yet, every day it grew deeper. It suppurated through the layers of bandages and on the last day of his journey to the port, he had begun to smell it and covered it in honey. He wrapped extra layers of bandages around it before he boarded the ship so that it would not be noticed. Short of bad weather or a leak, there was little a captain liked less than a sick or injured passenger.

He had laid low in his cabin for two days, hoping if he kept his leg still the infection would begin a retreat. He'd liberally dosed himself with the laudanum he'd purchased on the off chance he was caught and kept himself quiet that way. The infection only grew worse and the pain had finally driven him to the ship's surgeon.

Mr. Hennesey had poked around in the wound for what seemed ages, sending waves of pain through him such that he had never experienced.

Finally, the doctor had straightened himself and cleaned his hands with a rag. "The leg will have to come off."

In the coming years, Mr. Shine would work to forget the next hours and days, so filled with horror were they. That he lived was all he could say for himself. That he would arrive to Venezuela missing a vital appendage, that particular appendage drifting down in the ocean deep somewhere, was too grim to contemplate. He rued the day he'd become suspicious of a signature and chased after Nancy Manton.

He had played a game of hazard and the dice had come up against him.

CHAPTER FIFTEEN

L ILY DID NOT know if Lord Ashworth would avoid Lady Hathaway's ball or not. If he did, she could not hope for a firmer answer. If he did not, she might also receive a firm answer, told to her by his attitude. Though her logical mind knew she had already received her answer, her less than logical mind had fretted for hours before they had set off.

It was a brief reprieve that the entry into Lady Hathaway's house was such that Lily had never experienced or imagined. Penny had been right—the theme of the ball was the Tudor court. Lily had not had any idea how far Lady Hathaway was prone to take a notion, but it blessedly captured all her thoughts in that moment.

Rather than enter by the front door, they were led by a footman dressed in the Tudors' favored green livery down a lit path to the back of the house. Whatever Lady Hathaway's gardens had been, they were transformed to such that Henry VIII might have looked upon them with favor. First, a charming knot garden filled with hyssop, sweet briar, rose campion, and peonies, all cleverly made of colored papers. Then, hedges smartly trimmed and laid out in perfect order to guide one to a bridge fashioned as a barge, with running water flowing beneath it representing the Thames. It seemed they had arrived to Hampton Court.

Entering the back of the house, they were led down a series of corridors to the cloak room to deposit their coats and Lily was handed her dance card. Then it was on to the great hall. The space had been transformed into a scene from the 1500's—wood beams had been installed on the ceiling and silk flags embroidered with the Tudor rose hung over their heads.

Lily was almost breathless with wonder by the time she made her curtsy to Lady Hathaway. Their hostess was dressed as a court lady, her ornate wide sleeves embroidered with pearls and gold thread. Her stiff headdress framed her face and was embedded with multi-colored stones.

Lily moved away and stood with her aunt, looking about for acquaintances. She would not admit who it was she looked for, but while she was at it, she could not help but notice a petite lady standing by a powerfully built gentleman. The lady was looking at her in the most determined manner. Now, the lady was making her way over.

Lily glanced behind her with the thought that perhaps she was mistaken. Perhaps it was not herself that lady sought.

She had not been mistaken. The lady said, "A friend pointed you out, though I feel I know you through your letter to me. Miss Farnsworth, I am Sybil—Cassandra's friend."

"Lady Lockwood!" Lily said, curtsying deeply.

"I am so pleased to find you here, may I know your friend?" Sybil asked.

"Of course," Lily said, in a fluster. "This is my aunt, Mrs. Amelia Hemming."

The ladies smiled at each other. Mrs. Hemming said, "Goodness, you're a pretty little thing."

Sybil's amusement at the comment was evident, for which Lily was relieved. Sybil said, "You sound very like my husband, Mrs. Hemming."

"I cannot thank you enough for your kindness to me," Lily said. "All of you—Cassandra, Penny and yourself. I wear one of the gowns from your own modiste."

Sybil examined the deep green silk with a pearl studded net overlay with an approving eye.

"Very close to Tudor green, most fetching, I wish I'd had the notion. Now, I am very glad to see you, as my husband and I have only come down for Lady Hathaway's evening. We are at sixes and sevens with redecorating at the moment, but I could not stay away from a Tudor ball. My father claims a winding descent from Margaret Beaufort, so family honor you see."

"I am very glad you've come and we've had the chance to meet," Lily said. In fact, she was delighted with Lady Lockwood and could see how Cassandra had so easily fallen into friendship with her.

"Mrs. Hemming," Sybil said, "if you do not mind it, I will steal Miss Farnsworth away. The ball will open with a pavane and Lord Lockwood and I will be showing the steps to those bold enough to try it. We have been practicing for weeks and my lord will even now be gathering us all in the ballroom."

"I do not mind a bit," Mrs. Hemming said. "I've a mind to seek out the card room. A few games of whist will suit me."

"You will find my father already there," Sybil said, "Lord Blanding does enjoy his cards."

"Lord Blanding is your father?" Mrs. Hemming said. "Oh yes. I know him. Very good player. I wonder if he's matched up yet?" With that, Mrs. Hemming hurried off, set on seeking out a skilled partner.

Sybil grasped Lily's hand and led her into the ballroom.

As had the great hall, the ballroom had been transformed from what it must usually be. It was all dark-paneled wood and overarching beams. The musicians were in Tudor court dress. While most of them had charge of the usual instruments for an orchestra, there were a few standing to one side that held lutes, while an enormous harpsichord stood in a corner.

A crowd of people of an age to dance were gathered at the far end of the ballroom. As Lily approached, she noted Penny there, with Lord Cabot by her side. Lord Grayson was there too, as well as some other acquaintances.

Lily had been so distracted, first by the unique entry to the house, then all its wonders and her introduction to Lady Lockwood, that she'd hardly had time to think. Now, her thoughts reverted back to Lord Ashworth. Those thoughts followed the same pattern they had all the day long. Certainly, he would not miss Lady Hathaway's ball. Though, if he did choose to stay away, it must speak to his horror of having led her to believe in any sort of attachment. She had even heard of gentlemen thinking themselves gained of the unwanted affection of a lady hastily retreating to the countryside to allow things to cool off.

She put on her card player face and looked about.

He was not there.

THOUGH BOTH COBB and Molton had expressed how very much against the idea they were, Hayes had been determined to go out. The wound was nearly healed and only a small spot bled from time to time—something that could be easily managed with the right bandaging under his coat. It still ached, that could not be helped, but the danger of infection was long past and he did not think it would fully open under stress. He must make an appearance in public soon to avoid talk of his dying, or worse, rousing speculation that it was something other than a passing illness that kept him away.

Much longer in hiding and he would be accused of meeting another for a duel and becoming injured. Were that idea to go round, the speculation over who exactly he'd met would prove inconvenient. Why should he not go to Lady Hathaway's ball? It was always amusing and he would put a stop to rumors before they started.

He had, at least, given in to his butler and

valet regarding the means of his conveyance to the evening. It would be more usual that he rode his horse to such a crush—it was far simpler and very much quicker to get in and then back out again when it was only he and Horus. Cobb had outlined all the advantages of a carriage, including the idea that the grooms would be remarkably slow to saddle his horse, though remarkably fast to hitch up his carriage. Molton had only stood with crossed arms and nodded vigorously.

His whole house was in revolt over a horse. It was tedious, but he knew they were right. Into his carriage he went.

Sitting in the vehicle behind a long line of other carriages gave him time to think with no distractions. He could not claim the time was particularly welcome—he had found recently that his thoughts had got in the habit of going in only one direction. He had found it convenient to blame it on laudanum, but he took so little of the stuff now that it was less convincing.

He was certain Miss Farnsworth would attend the ball. He was also certain, as his thoughts had gone round and round on the subject, that he did not wish Miss Farnsworth to marry another. Especially not Grayson. He was not worthy of the lady.

He had tried to avoid the truth—that he minded what Miss Farnsworth did. However, he *did* mind. He minded very much.

But what did that mean in real terms? Was he to throw over all his ideas and pursue the lady?

He was very glad Dalton could not read his thoughts at this moment. His friend would jail him, just as he'd attempted to do with Lockwood.

And then, he'd been so disparaging of both Hampton and Lockwood for marrying. They'd both let their friends down. They had all sworn they would take at least two more years as bachelors. They would come and go as they pleased with nobody inquiring when they might be expected back. They could set off for Salt Hill with only a moment's notice. They could go to a play, find it tedious, and leave for a gambling hell with no thought of transporting wives back to houses.

Over the years, all of them had kept a keen eye on their parents. All of them had seen what power a wife really yielded. The idea that the man was to go unquestioned was nonsense. Wives generally had nothing but questions. In the country, his father spent half his time hiding from his duchess. It was only bachelors who went on unquestioned. They had been agreed—they would be free for now, though not forever. The six of them were meant to stand united against their fathers—was he to be the third traitor to their cause?

As if a veil lifted from his eyes, Hayes suddenly saw the truth of it. What business had he to join in this foolish game they all played? Was he really to throw over any future happiness for the satisfaction of a few of his spoiled friends? Or, more stupidly, for a run to Salt Hill?

And *would* he be throwing over his future happiness?

Yes, he knew he would. There would not be another Miss Farnsworth. There would be an endless parade of pleasant females happy enough to become a duchess. There would not, however, be another Miss Farnsworth.

His friends would rail against him once his attitude was known. Dalton might go so far as to beat him about the head.

Hayes began to laugh. It occurred to him that he had very much decided that they could rail themselves to hell and back for all he cared about it. As for Grayson, he could rail himself to hell and stay there.

His carriage had finally reached the front of the house. He leapt down before Freddy could open the door. He had a lady to see and a future to plan.

LILY SOMETIMES THOUGHT it was unfair that a female must wait to be chosen, rather than make the choice herself. Had she been able to make her choice, she might have passed over Lord Grayson. She had not had the luxury though and was just now attempting to pay attention to the demonstration of the pavane by Lord and Lady Lockwood, while trying to ignore the overblown compliments Lord Grayson saw fit to whisper. *Eyes like the night sky*, indeed.

Suddenly, she felt Lord Grayson's fingers remove themselves from her own. Behind her, Lord Ashworth said, "Shove off, Grayson."

Lord Grayson said, "My good fellow, do not be cross because you were delayed. I had the good fortune of arriving first and securing Miss Farnsworth for the pavane."

"The pavane is a Tudor dance in which the lady chooses the partner," Lord Ashworth said, as Lily slowly turned toward him.

"Is that so, Lord Scholar?" Lord Grayson said, with faint irritation in his voice. Lily got the idea that the lord had never heard such a thing, and neither had she.

"Yes. It is so," Lord Ashworth said.

"Well, Miss Farnsworth," Lord Grayson said smoothly, "it seems you must choose between a gentleman who admires you greatly, or the sullen figure just arrived."

Lily felt her cheeks burn. What should she do? She had vowed she would convince Lord Ashworth that she held him in no particular regard. But why would he put himself forward in such a manner? Why push in when he might have asked another lady?

She did not know, but she was inclined to follow her heart and find out.

"Sullen and just arrived will suit, I think," Lily said gaily, attempting to pass it all off as a joke.

Now, it was Lord Grayson who took on the mien of sullenness. He stepped aside, though not with particular good grace.

Lord Ashworth gently took her fingers and they turned to Lord and Lady Lockwood.

As they attempted to copy the steps, Lord Ashworth said, "I highly doubt ladies chose their partners in the Tudor court. Though, perhaps they did—I wouldn't know."

Lily could feel her heart beat a little faster. The lord had completely invented the idea.

"Lord Grayson," Lord Ashworth went on, "is a friend to me, such as he is. But I do not view him a friend to any innocent lady."

Lily's heart clutched in her chest. Did he mean to say that he only stepped in because he thought Lord Grayson a bit of a villain? Was it only his perceived duty to shield her?

Boldly, she said, "The gentleman's compliments are absurd and do not affect me in the slightest. A moment ago, I was to know my eyes were as the night sky."

"Ridiculous," Lord Ashworth said. "They are

far more like a lake at midnight."

Lily momentarily froze her steps. The lord's fingers tightened on her own and they began the steps again.

The ballroom had filled and the musicians were tuning. Lord and Lady Lockwood led them through the pavane one more time. Cassandra had told Lily some of Sybil's history with the gentleman who was now her husband. It seemed extraordinary that they'd faced any difficulties at all. Just now, they seemed a perfect pair. Certainly, the lord doted on his wife—at least it would seem so. She scolded him mercilessly for missing a step and he seemed delighted with it.

As they came to the end of their practice, Lord and Lady Hathaway formed the head of the column. The music struck up, the tempo much more sedate than a modern dance. Lily could almost imagine Henry the VIII leading the procession. It was a pleasant thought, until her mind drifted to which queen might be found on the king's arm. Where would that queen be in her history? At a glorious beginning or a fatal end?

Lily and Lord Ashworth had been silent since the remarkable comment upon her eyes. Lily attempted to put all her concentration on the steps of the dance. It was a blessing that it was a slow-moving processional without an endless array of changes. Even so, Lily had not paid enough attention to Lady Lockwood's instruction—she had been too distracted by Lord Grayson and too engrossed with Lord Ashworth. Then, there was the further complication of finding her thoughts racing. Why would he compliment her eyes? Surely, he'd meant to drive her off, not lure her in. Had he changed his mind?

She must know the truth of it. As they stepped lightly to the side and then back again, she said, "My aunt and I were sorry to hear that you were indisposed."

Lord Ashworth did not respond but only nodded slightly. Mrs. Hemming was right, he was *not* a very voluble person.

"Of course," she went on, "my aunt has been anxious to know the details of the circumstance of our mutual acquaintance."

"Are *you* anxious?"

"Yes," Lily said, "I will admit that I am."

"Then I will tell you the whole of it. Someday."

Lily was baffled. The lord was being very mysterious. And then, was it her own wishful thinking to read too much into the word *someday*? Was she foolish to think that meant there was to be some sort of ongoing connection between them?

Whatever had happened since his disappearance and rather curt note, he seemed to have changed his stance. Certainly, he did not run from her as she had expected. But, what *was* he doing? She could not make it out but wished desperately to discover it.

If she did not know the truth, if she was left in this limbo, her heart would always hang in the balance. She would inevitably allow herself all sorts of fantasies that might collapse into a heap of ash at any moment. She might be having a pleasant conversation at a dinner, and then someone would suddenly mention his engagement to another. Miss Blaise, perhaps. Or maybe she'd hear of it by letter when she was back in Surrey. She must know where she stood.

Lily was so distracted by her roiling thoughts that she missed their time to turn. She stumbled and clutched at Lord Ashworth's arm to keep herself upright.

He winced, and her hand came away with a wetness. A trace of wetness had seeped through his dark coat. "My Lord!" she whispered close to him. "I believe you may be bleeding!"

Lord Ashworth glanced down at his coat. "It is nothing, only an annoying scratch that has taken it's time to heal."

Lily searched his face for the truth. She had looked on that face often enough and thought she saw a flicker of prevarication.

"I do not believe you," she said, as they made their way down the final procession.

Lord Ashworth revealed a moment of surprise that was just as quickly hidden. "In any event, it might be prudent that I leave off dancing for the rest of the evening," he said. "I might play cards."

Lily was a mix of worry and disappointment. What had happened to him? Did it have anything to do with why he had been missing for over a week? Did it have anything to do with Mr. Shine?

"If *you* would think to play cards," Lord Ashworth went on, "you might claim a twisted ankle from your stumble. You have told me yourself that you are no stranger to claiming a sore leg when cards might be had."

He wished to play her again. Why? Why would he when he generally found it irritating? Did he suppose she would allow him to win?

Though, wouldn't she?

The pavane came to an end. As the audience that had gathered round them clapped, Lily said, "I *do* feel my stumble has strained my ankle. I suppose it would not be sensible to stress it more."

Lord Ashworth nodded and led her toward the doors of the ballroom. Mr. Gentry, he of the disastrous piquet skills, halted their progress. "Miss Farnsworth," he said, eyeing her dance card dangling from her wrist, "might I prevail upon you?"

Lily had no intention of being prevailed upon by anybody save Lord Ashworth. She said, "I am sorry, Mr. Gentry. I have strained my ankle and retreat to the card room."

After she'd said it, she wished she had not. As she passed by the gentleman, she heard the whispers. Miss Farnsworth and Lord Ashworth would play. She had almost forgotten that it was of such interest to the *ton*.

Quietly, she said, "I suggest we play whist. It will not be nearly as interesting to any onlookers."

"Yes," Lord Ashworth said.

THE CARD ROOM was lively—tables had been set up, each to accommodate four players, and a small adjoining room contained a sideboard with refreshments. Let it never be said that those who viewed themselves too old for dancing were without spirit. Lily's aunt was surprised to see her there, but happy just the same. She had partnered with Lord Blanding and handily trounced Mr. and Mrs. Beltemham, who declined another round. Lily and Lord Ashworth would take the couple's place.

Their table had the advantage of being at the far end of the room, with a wall behind. They might have some onlookers peering at their game, but they would not be surrounded.

Lily was introduced to Lord Blanding, though it appeared that Lord Ashworth was already known to him. Lord Blanding was rather stiff on the greeting and she supposed he maintained certain attitudes of the young bucks in town. Lily thought him friendly enough to herself, especially when her aunt pointed out the connection between Lily, his own daughter Sybil, and Cassandra.

That there were a few that came to view their game had seemed inevitable to Lily. Lord Blanding seemed to take it as a compliment to himself. When he took a trick he issued vague mutterings along the lines of "As you see, that is how it is played."

Lily had no great wish to win the hands. She was quite content sitting across from Lord Ashworth. Though, they seemed to be in sync and did win often. It seemed they both instinctively played the same strategy and though she doubted the lord's memory as good as her own, it was superior to most.

When Lord Blanding began to seem annoyed at his losses, she exchanged glances with Lord Ashworth and they altered their play. The wager was only a pound and so it was nothing to lose the hands, but it seemed a great deal to Lord Blanding. And to Mrs. Hemming, for that matter.

Sooner than she expected, Lord Blanding quit. He claimed he wished to see his daughter dancing, as he missed having her by his side ever since she'd married. Though Lily did not doubt he missed his daughter, she also was certain that

Lord Blanding liked to spend most of his time winning. It seemed he would quit while the cards still went his way.

Lord Blanding offered to escort Mrs. Hemming to the refreshments. The lady had hesitated and looked at Lily.

"I am quite all right, Aunt," Lily said, not wishing for her aunt's care to force her from the table. Or from Lord Ashworth. "I am surrounded by matrons, you see."

In truth, Lily was chaperoned well enough. There could not be a safer place for a young lady than a card room at a ball. Every older lady of consequence was there to ensure nothing untoward went on.

Mrs. Hemming had seen the sense of it. Though, she may also have been swayed by Lord Blanding's description of the cakes on offer. It seemed there was a particular cake with raspberry preserve that was exceptional. Mrs. Hemming had a fondness for raspberry preserve, as long as it was well-sugared. Lord Blanding had assured her that he would hardly recommend a preserve that was not. He put his arm out as they went in search of that marvelous confection.

Lily and Lord Ashworth were alone. Of course, there were many other tables set up and filled with card players. They were not alone as they had been in Lady Carradine's attic. But at least none were left at their own table.

Lord Ashworth took the cards and began removing the lower. "Piquet?" he asked.

Lily smiled. "If you wish it," she said. "Though I would not like to play for high stakes."

"But we have all along been playing for paltry stakes," Lord Ashworth said.

Good Lord, they had played for fifty pounds at Lady Montague's card party. Did he wish to play for some even more enormous sum? That would present a quandary. She could not afford to lose such an extravagant amount. And yet, she did not wish to go back to their relations after his previous defeats. What was she to do?

"I am afraid not, my lord," she said. "You are aware of my financial situation. I dare not attempt it."

Lord Ashworth waved his hand, as if to dismiss what she'd said. "You speak of money. Perhaps we could play for more important stakes? Name anything you like."

Lily considered it. There were questions she would like answered regarding his feelings, though she did not dare ask them. There was also the question of what had happened to his arm, and that she thought she *could* dare ask.

"If I win, you will tell me what really happened to your arm," she said.

"Done," Lord Ashworth said.

Two young gentlemen had drifted toward their table, intrigued to see Miss Farnsworth and

Lord Ashworth once again at play.

"And you?" Lily asked. "If you were to pre-vail, and I am very sorry to say that I do not think you will, what would you claim as your prize?"

Lord Ashworth smiled. "I admit, my chances are slim, and yet I will try it. I will make a desperate pledge for the hand of Miss Farns-worth."

CHAPTER SIXTEEN

L ILY FELT SHE had gone white as a sheet. She was almost afraid she had misheard, until one of the young gentlemen repeated the idea and made off toward the ballroom with the news. The other stood behind Lord Ashworth, rapt.

"You see," Lord Ashworth said, "I have finally come to admit your skill to be superior to my own. Therefore, it will be you who chooses who will win and who will lose. If *you* lose, I will be made the happiest of men. If *I* lose, I will know your mind and not burden you with repeating the sentiment."

Lord Ashworth began to deal.

Lily sat stock still. He wished to marry! Yes, he did, he'd said it. And not privately either. Everybody was to know he wished for the hand of Miss Farnsworth. A *desperate pledge* for her hand. All she had to do was lose to him.

She picked up her cards as the room became more and more crowded. Her heart sank as she looked at them. It was a good hand. Too good! She must rid herself of all these face cards!

She discarded them and picked up from the stock. Excellent. They were dreadful. They were so dreadful that she waited for Lord Ashworth to discard, and then she said happily, "Oh dear, carte blanche."

Lord Ashworth's hands tightened ever so gently on his cards. As she had noted when last they played, his lips pressed ever so slightly together—a sure sign he was happy with his hand. He knew she would work to lose the game. He knew her mind.

So they went on, Lily making every mistake she knew how to avoid. She sunk nothing and was rather gleeful over the fact that she'd nothing valuable enough *to* sink.

She played one bad hand after the next. She must get Lord Ashworth to one hundred points as soon as possible.

Lily did her best to ignore the talk swirling around their table. She could not help hearing some of it, though.

"I do not see why everybody has claimed she is so good," one young gentleman said.

His friend nudged him in the ribs and said, "The wager is will she have him, you numbskull.

If she loses, she will have him. What do you think she means to do?"

Lord Ashworth laid down a final trick. "To one hundred, Miss Farnsworth. Do you admit defeat?"

"Oh, yes," Lily said, laughing. "And you had better call me Lily."

Lord Ashworth reached across the table and took her hand. "I will ride for Surrey on the morrow to see your father. In the meantime, I believe I have the right to escort my fiancée to the gardens for air?"

THE NIGHT AIR was fresh and cool after the heat of the crowded card room. The paper flowers waved gently in the breeze, their colors showing in the moonlight. Lord Ashworth led her through the garden paths.

Lily was deliriously happy, though she said not a thing. What did one say at such a moment?

"I fear you must have been shocked at my declaration," Lord Ashworth said. "I have not represented myself in a particularly favorable light. I certainly have not gone about a courting in the usual way."

"We have not gone about much in the usual way," Lily said, glad he'd broken the silence. She had more to say, things she wished to know, she only did not know how to begin.

"I did think," she said slowly, "that you avoided me this past week."

"I did not," Lord Ashworth said. "I was truly indisposed, just not with a fever."

"Your arm?" she asked.

"Yes."

"Tell me what happened."

The lord seemed to hesitate, as if he were not certain he would tell her. Then he said, "Mr. Shine thought to blackmail me. To blackmail us. He threatened to put it about that we had been alone for a period of time in an empty house. I met him in Hyde Park the night of Lady Blakeley's half mask."

"But you attended the mask," Lily said. "And told us to stay away, so I thought—"

"I made an early appearance and then slipped away. I did not wish to cause talk by not appearing and I did not want you and your aunt to be out on the town. I could not be everywhere at once and I could not be sure if Mr. Shine worked with any associates that might attempt a kidnaping as a further means of funds. The men I employ are experienced, but I would not have risked it."

"And then he shot you in the park?"

Lord Ashworth nodded. "And I shot him too, but I think only a graze."

"Though yours was more than a graze."

"Yes, well, he took me by surprise. He shot

when my back was turned."

"You might have been killed!" Lily said. "It would have been my fault. I was so foolish to get us into that situation to begin. Why I did not hold my tongue when I realized the cards were marked, I will never know."

Lord Ashworth's hand had been slowly traveling from Lily's hand to around her waist. Lily had been very accommodating in pretending not to notice.

He pulled her close and lifted her chin. "Come, my little piquet genius, no regrets now."

He softly touched her lips with his own. It was a gentle kiss and over too soon. Lily surprised him by kissing him back not quite so gentle, though it appeared to be a not unwelcome surprise. She thought it well that he was to know how to steal a kiss or two, as she hoped that he stole them often.

A sudden thought broke into her happiness. "Your estates," she cried. "My dowry is not… Oh! Miss Blaise!"

Lord Ashworth kissed her again to put a stop to her words. He pulled away and whispered, "Do cease being a ninny about money and, good God, never mention Miss Blaise again. We will find a way forward and I will provide for your sisters, too. My holdings are on their way to profit and I will see that they stay that way."

Lily felt relief flood through her. There was

no need to consider Miss Blaise or any other heiress.

"You shall have everything you wish for," Lord Ashworth said. "I have always vowed my wife shall not be pinched. Now, tell me—what would you prefer as a wedding present?

Lily had not grown up swimming in fripperies and did not much care. She had what she wanted. Though, the smallest idea presented itself to her.

"I wonder," she said, "if you would ever have a need to employ a young man. A very young man with no particular skills."

"Would this be a young man once seen lurking on Lady Jersey's steps?" Lord Ashworth asked.

"Indeed, Sam," Lily said, surprised. "How can you know him?"

"Because I was in my carriage listening to that rather remarkable exchange. I am certain I fell in love with you when you demanded water, a roll, a tuppence, and a bath for that scamp. I employed him that very day, and his mother too—you could not really expect that Riddick would continue to pay him a tuppence forevermore?"

"I did hope he would…"

"He certainly would not have. Now *you* must tell *me* when you fell violently in love with me," Lord Ashworth said, playing with a curl at her neck.

"So you are violently in love with me?"

"Terribly."

"Violently, well… I suppose there were the two times I fell into your arms and then the interesting trip to your carriage."

"Hah, had I known, I might have carried you round Berkeley Square days ago."

"Riddick would have been appalled," Lily said, laughing.

"And what care we? In any case, my darling," he said, "I thought we might take a wedding trip to the Continent. I imagine there are no end of players who would challenge us. Then, we can return at our leisure and scandalize a hundred Riddicks if we like."

Lily felt a lightness about her that she had not yet known in her life of worry. She erupted in peals of laughter. "Do we dare it? We may become notorious."

"Of course we dare it. No lady has the steady nerves of my Lily," Lord Ashworth said, "Further, after we have built up our fortune, I propose we keep ten thousand in a bank between us. We might bet one another for years to come."

"Are you certain you could ever prevail?" Lily asked playfully.

"Perhaps," he said. "If I can ever figure out your secret."

"Oh, it is no secret really," Lily said. "I see

details where others do not, and I remember them."

"I shudder to think what you have seen in me," Lord Ashworth said.

"Perhaps different things at different moments," Lily said. "Though all seems remarkably clear and settled now."

"I will work to remain the man you see now, then. You will never have to question me again."

Lily touched his cheek and said, "Do not become too staid, though. Even when I disliked you, I found you rather dashing."

"Then I'd best sweep you off your feet and take you in," Lord Ashworth said, "just as I carried you to my carriage."

"But your arm," Lily said.

"My arms will always be able to carry you."

And so Lord Ashworth swept her up, as he had on the fateful night he'd rescued them both from the clutches of Mr. Shine. They weaved through the garden and the hedges and crossed over the bridge and into Hampton Court once more. Though, far different than when they had left it.

There may have been some who stared at Lord Ashworth carrying Miss Farnsworth down the corridor. Only some, though, as news of their latest bet had run through the ball like a housefire.

Miss Farnsworth had finally been defeated by

Lord Ashworth. Unlike Lord Ashworth's earlier experiences, she seemed to take the loss with all good humor.

WHILE IT WAS true that Mrs. Hemming had encouraged Lily to think better of Lord Ashworth, she was rather staggered to hear that her niece had engaged herself to the man.

Lord Ashworth's wound did open again, and his butler and valet could not imagine what had gone on at a ball to cause it. He'd only ordered it bound up and rode for Surrey hours later. He'd gone on Horus, which was the height of carelessness. However, being young and strong, the wound healed up in less than a fortnight, despite his egregious lack of care.

Permission to wed was easily granted once Mr. Farnsworth was assured of Ashworth's circumstances, as well as Lily's own intentions by a letter from her that he'd carried with him. Not only would Ashworth make his daughter a duchess someday, but on further acquaintance it was discovered he was a man who understood the business of an estate. There was nothing else more important to Mr. Farnsworth, save his family. The estate had been the driving force of his life and it pleased him to discuss various strategies with another likeminded gentleman.

The contract was easily done, though there had been some wrangling over the inclusion of dowries for Mr. Farnsworth's two youngest daughters. He did not like to discuss the idea that those dowries did not yet exist. Lord Ashworth pressed hard on the subject, pointing out that if the girls were to come to him and Lily when they were of age, they must be suitably situated. He eventually won the debate, as Mr. Farnsworth had always been a man of good sense.

Letters went out to both the duke and the duchess. Hayes knew his father would be delighted, as he could crow about it to his friends. He'd written his mother's letter more carefully and in stronger language. It was his mother who might take issue with the idea that Lily Farnsworth was neither titled nor an heiress. He wished to convey the finality of his decision.

The duchess had not answered his letter. On the one hand, that might be viewed positive   she had not written against it. On the other, he could not be certain she was not silently fuming. No matter, whether she was for or against, it would be done. The duchess was sure to come round eventually. Or, if she did not, she could hold her peace.

A FORTNIGHT LATER, Lord Dalton raged in his

library. Lord Cabot came into the room and found a letter thrown at him. "They'll never give it up now," Dalton said. "We're as good as defeated. Resign yourself to poverty, my friend. There has been another traitor in our midst."

Lord Cabot picked up the letter and smoothed it out.

Dalton, Cabot and Grayson—

I address you all together as you are living under the same roof and I am too busy to write you separately. I have married Miss Farnsworth under special license this fine morning in Surrey. Burke acted as my best man, as of course none of you could be trusted to do it. It was a small affair as that was what we both preferred. As well, I had no wish of you discovering it before the deed was done. I have not forgotten that Lockwood was once jailed in that house.

I am fairly certain Dalton is gone through the roof just now and you other two are in a sulk. Especially you, Grayson— though, really, your compliments never had the slightest chance with my wife. I will see you when I return from my wedding trip. One hopes you might have regained your equanimity by then.

Though you will not wish to hear my advice, I give it anyway. You will all marry, whether there is a pact between your fathers or not. When you meet the lady you are destined for, no amount of struggle will free you from the net. You ought to resign yourselves to it. It is a very pleasant defeat.

Ashworth

"It is a jest, certainly," Lord Cabot said. "Ashworth positively dislikes the lady."

Lord Dalton's fingers wrapped themselves around a marble paperweight. "Do you really think Ashworth would joke on this subject? With me?"

In fact, Lord Cabot did not, and slowly backed from the room before something heavier than a letter was flung at him.

As THINGS WENT along happily in England, so they did in New Orleans too. Nancy Manton had decided to cloak herself in another name once more so that there could be no danger of encountering someone who knew her past. Especially Mr. Shine. She could not know what had happened when he'd discovered she'd made off with the bank, but she shuddered to think of it.

She had refashioned herself as Rose Mendeby—spinster daughter of Viscount Kelberston.

Her parents had both perished long ago and left her little. She'd been forced to make her way in the world. Her American friends approved of her accent and her refined manners and thought her brave to open a gambling establishment. They had been under the impression that ladies like herself, in such a situation, would resort to becoming a governess or companion.

Rose Mendeby would go on happily enough in that swampy town. The only circumstance that would ever disturb her peace was the tale told her by Mr. Jarvis, a gentleman returning from Venezuela. The man owned a mine of some sort and spoke of the eccentric exiles one might encounter in that country.

He told of a particularly gruesome circumstance involving a one-legged fellow who had dogged him for a job. It was ludicrous, of course—the man used a crutch and could barely get around. One day, the fellow actually turned up at the mine. As he hobbled along after Mr. Jarvis, hurling both pleadings and insults, his crutch slipped at the edge of an old and deep shaft. He tumbled in and his shouts could be heard for some seconds before he hit the bottom. Naturally, it was silence after that.

Nancy had listened with complacence to the story, well used to Mr. Jarvis' habit of telling tales that no lady wished to hear.

Then he'd said, "We couldn't get him out,

you see. We had to leave him there. I suppose he was dead in any case. He was English, somebody told me. Lost his leg on the way over, rotten luck. Reginald Shine was his name."

Nancy never knew if her expression had given her away. That she'd gone white was evident, as Mr. Jarvis said he supposed that he ought not tell a lady such a fright.

Her horror did not stay with her long, though. After all, Mr. Shine was dead.

LILY AND HER lord stayed on at Farnsworth House for a week. It was a merry week. They both enjoyed her family's hospitality. Her husband and her father appreciated one another's company and spent a deal of time talking in the library. Lord Burke stayed on for a few days and became a favorite with Lily's sisters. In truth, they were both in love with him and hoped he would not marry before they had their seasons. Lily called them both gooses but allowed them to dream of having a season in which money was not a care. It would be unlike her own and she was glad of it.

In the evening, they had lively dinners. Cards were attempted one night in the drawing room, but were quickly cast aside as nobody would consent to play against Lily and her husband. The days passed by in a dream of happiness, though in the back of Lily's mind was always the inevitable trip to Somerset to meet her husband's parents. Despite his assurances, she could not be certain of her reception. They were a duke and duchess after all, and may have had much higher aspirations for their son.

They had finally set off, with a happy good-bye from her parents and a tearful one from her sisters. It would be an easy journey in five stages, and it had at first seemed as if their arrival was a long time away. Until, that was, they came to the very gates.

Though Lily had known what the house looked like from a sketch, there was nothing that might have prepared her for the enormity of the estate. They passed through a gatehouse of grey stone, a man tipping his hat, and a boy jumping on a horse and setting off ahead to announce their arrival.

Then, they traveled some miles on a lane bordered by old oaks. Beyond the oaks, they passed apple orchards, sheep and cows grazing, and broad fields of wheat just coming up. As the road dipped and turned, Lily caught glimpses of the stone behemoth ahead.

They'd come around a final bend and the carriage trotted through another gatehouse and into a vast courtyard. Dembly Castle loomed over her, its towers reaching for the sky and topped with arrow slits. Lily swallowed as she saw the occupants of the house lined up on the drive. She could not count the number of footmen and maids, there were too many and, in any case, her eyes were riveted on the duke and duchess. *He* was all smiles, though *she* appeared decidedly austere.

As the carriage rolled to a stop, Lily's husband whispered, "To the breach, my love."

THE INTRODUCTION TO the duke and duchess had been formal, as if she were being presented at court. Lily had thought they would be given time to change and then proceed to the drawing room, but the duchess had other plans. She'd sent her son off with her husband to look at a new horse, though neither seemed the least interested in it. Then she'd assured Lily that she must want tea before being shown to her room.

Now, Lily sat alone with the duchess in a drawing room that might have comfortably sat a hundred as her grace poured tea. Though those elusive hundred might have sat comfortably, Lily did not. The duchess had not smiled since her arrival.

"I must say," her grace said, handing Lily her cup, "I was surprised to hear that my son had engaged himself. And then, to marry so hastily with no pomp and ceremony? One would have thought of St. George's at least."

Lily had been afraid the duchess would not be pleased. Still, her grace could not undo what had been done and Lily refused to be unhappy over another's opinion. Even if it was her husband's own mother's.

"Surprise aside," her grace went on, "my son wrote a compelling letter on the subject. He believes you are well-suited. Therefore, I think I may happily resign myself to the union if a few conditions are met."

Conditions? How could there be conditions now? They were already married.

"Foremost," her grace said, "I would wish you to promise that you will exert every effort to make my son happy."

Lily smiled, vastly relieved to hear of *that* condition. "That is easily promised, your grace."

"And two, whenever you are in this house, you must commit to being my whist partner. I hear you are very good at cards and I have the notion of trouncing those two gentlemen who wander the stables just now. We might even play for significant stakes."

Lily suppressed her laughter. Whatever further conditions she had thought the duchess might demand, being a whist partner had not been among them.

"I should be happy to oblige, Your Grace,"

Lily said.

The duchess waved her hands in a dismissive fashion. "You are in the family now, you had better call me Delilah."

As it would turn out, the duchess was not particularly good at whist. That mattered not, however, as the duke showed himself to be a thousand times worse. No matter how hard his son attempted to prop him up with hints and looks, the duke would make terrible judgments and ghastly moves. It eventually became a tradition that they would have a tournament at Christmas time, with the winnings going to a local charity. That charity thought the duchess and Lady Ashworth very generous.

DEPARTING DEMBLY CASTLE after a fortnight, Lord and Lady Ashworth made their way to the Continent for their wedding trip. They perfected their game of whist on the journey. Piquet was all well and good for those who played alone, but they were husband and wife now and it no longer suited.

That they would cut a swath through Europe, from the Alps to Italy, collecting wagers as they went, was a rather foregone conclusion. They left a trail of disconcerted players in their wake and came back a deal richer. Lily's sisters' dowries had been secured.

In the hours that they did not play, there were long and luxurious mornings in one sunny bedchamber after the next, as no gambler worth anything rose too early. Those mornings often ran into the afternoon, as there might be a debate about going to a museum and then somehow never getting out the door. There were sumptuous dinners, as no gambler began a night hungry—it would only serve to distract.

At a card table, they would look at each other once their hands had been dealt, Lily understanding her husband's every expression. He still gave away those subtle signs that nobody but Lily would note. It might have worked to his detriment in piquet, but it was very much an advantage in whist.

Their pockets were filled, and then overflowing. As far as Lily and Hayes were concerned, though, they had become richer in far more than money.

The End

About the Author

By the time I was eleven, my Irish Nana and I had formed a book club of sorts. On a timetable only known to herself, Nana would grab her black-thorn walking stick and steam down to the local Woolworth's. There, she would buy the latest Barbara Cartland romance, hurry home to read it accompanied by viciously strong wine, (Wild Irish Rose, if you're wondering) and then pass the book on to me. Though I was not particularly interested in real boys yet, I was *very* interested in the gentlemen in those stories—daring, bold, and often enraging and unaccountable. After my Barbara Cartland phase, I went on to Georgette Heyer, Jane Austen and so many other gifted authors blessed with the ability to bring the Georgian and Regency eras to life.

I would like nothing more than to time travel back to the Regency (and time travel back to my twenties as long as we're going somewhere) to take my chances at a ball. Who would take the first? Who would escort me into supper? What sort of meaningful looks would be exchanged? I would hope, having made the trip, to encounter a gentleman who would give me a very hard time. He ought to be vexatious in the extreme, and *worth* every vexation, to make the journey worthwhile.

I most likely won't be able to work out the time travel gambit, so I will content myself with writing stories of adventure and romance in my beloved time period. There are lives to be created, marvelous gowns to wear, jewels to don, instant attractions that inevitably come with a difficulty, and hearts to break before putting them back together again. In traditional Regency fashion, my stories are clean—the action happens in a drawing room, rather than a bedroom.

As I muse over what will happen next to my H and h, and wish I were there with them, I will occasionally remind myself that it's also nice to have a microwave, Netflix, cheese popcorn, and steaming hot showers.

Come see me on Facebook!
@KateArcherAuthor

9 781953 455321